Evergreen Legacy

BY
HEATHER SCHNEIDER

Evergreen Legacy

Copyright © 2026 Heather Schneider.

All rights reserved. Except for brief quotations or reviews, no part of this book may be reproduced without prior written permission from the publisher.

This is a work of fiction. All names, characters, and events are the work of the author's imagination. Any resemblance to real people or events is entirely coincidental.

Summary: A magical botanist works with her secret society to help save her magical college.

Editor: Red Adept Editing Services

Cover Design: Krafigs Design

Paperback ISBN: 978-1-971391-00-7

Evergreen Legacy

BY
HEATHER SCHNEIDER

For those who make wishes on dandelions.
May they all come true.

Chapter One

It's just one tree. The thought should have calmed me, but I was squeezing my fingers into my palms through my knit gloves. *We can plant another one in its place.*

I walked along Wildflower Trail with Callan Rhodes, tree affinity botanist, founder's descendant, and one of two lead members of the Root and Vine Society, the secret club at Evergreen Academy that I'd joined. For the society's first mission a week ago, some of us had traveled to the tree conservatory in Washington State and recovered a centuries-old quill.

We had taken the quill because we thought it could point us in the direction of the *Vanished Compendium*, a book of Floracantus that hasn't been seen for at least one hundred years. While we were successful in recovering the quill, something was blocking its locating features. Instead of acting like a compass that pointed to the book, the quill spun erratically in a circle any time we tried to use it.

And that brought us to our current plan—killing Frank, the oldest tree in Weed, California.

My eyes went straight to Callan's hand, which held the poison that could take down such a majestic oak. I let out a sharp exhalation and stumbled over a loose branch on the trail.

Callan slowed and turned to me, his thick eyelashes sweeping as he scanned my face. "Are you okay, Briar?"

We were almost at Frank. I could just make out the large tree and the letterbox attached to him in the dark. My stomach rolled.

I shook my head. "I'm feeling a little sick."

"The tissue necrotizer we've developed is painless. It will spread through the veins of the tree and destroy any cells—and associated magical spells that it holds—without the tree ever feeling anything." Callan's voice was gentle.

I knew he was trying to console me, but it wasn't working. I ran through the reason we were here in my head, looking away from the poison. Callan had realized that Frank, the oldest tree in town, was the source of the blocking spell on the quill that should point us to the *Vanished Compendium*.

He'd felt magic around the tree on Halloween, then a painting in Professor East's office of a tree that looked just like Frank had tipped him off even further. According to Evergreen Academy records, the painting had been installed roughly one hundred years ago, the same time that the *Vanished Compendium* was rumored to have last been seen.

"Are you sure you felt the blocking spell when you examined Frank yesterday?" I asked, wanting another confirmation that harming Frank wouldn't be for nothing.

Callan nodded solemnly. "The blocking spell is attached to Frank. I ran through several methods to remove it, but the spell wouldn't budge."

If Callan was right, and I was sure he was, a magical botanist had attached a blocking spell to Frank's cells to keep the *Vanished Compendium* hidden. Which meant that as long as Frank lived, the blocking spell embedded in the oak's DNA would interfere with the quill's locating features.

I chewed my lower lip. It was perhaps the worst dilemma I had been in since learning I was a magical botanist. The Board of Regents had been making changes at Evergreen Academy, the magical college Callan and I attended, and we needed to shift the balance of power back in our favor.

Finding the long-lost *Vanished Compendium* was the clearest way to do that, and we were closer than any botanist had been in a long time. To get us over this last hurdle to finding the book, we needed to remove the blocking spell that was running from Frank to the quill. There was no other way. Tears filled my eyes.

"Do you want me to do it without you?" Callan offered, breaking into my thoughts with a gentle voice. He stepped closer and took one of my gloved hands firmly in his. A raindrop landed on my cheek. "If it makes any difference, I don't feel good about this either. For tree affinities, poisoning a great oak doesn't feel right. But botanists also know to look at the bigger picture when it comes to how we interact with and use plants as resources."

I nodded. Logically, I knew all of that. Finding the *Vanished Compendium* might be the only way to save Evergreen Academy from a takeover by the Board of Regents. It could be the key to putting power back in the hands of all magical botanists, not just the founders' descendants.

Despite knowing that, I could barely think of Frank without dread filling me. If we were going to poison the tree, I needed to take responsibility and be part of it. "Let's just get it over with," I said then gently dropped Callan's hand and approached the giant oak tree.

"Will we see anything... happen after we administer the poison?" I asked, reaching out to rest a hand on Frank's bark.

"It will spread through the cells, and the tree will begin to show signs of distress within a few days. I imagine someone will report it to the local foresters, but there won't be anything they can do. By the end of this week, the tree will have deteriorated to the point that it will need to be removed for the safety of those walking along the trail."

I noticed Callan was carefully referring to Frank as "the tree" and "it," likely trying to depersonalize the experience for me. But I had grown up with Frank. I was the local, and I had more of a connection to the tree than Callan, despite his more developed tree affinity.

"And when Frank dies, what will happen to all the cuttings of him around town?" I thought of our annual fall tradition, where people throughout the town of Weed came to the Wildflower Trail and were given cuttings of Frank to plant in their yards. According to Callan's theory, each cutting amplified the blocking spell's effect, and the tradition of giving new cuttings to the residents of Weed every Halloween was a clever way to keep the blocking Floracantus fresh. *But who put the Floracantus on the quill to begin with?*

"I can't be sure, but since they're just serving as boosters, I think they'll stay alive, and the blocking spell in them will dissipate when the one in Frank is gone," Callan replied.

I swallowed, buying time. Rain continued to fall in infrequent droplets, seeming to imitate my uncertain mood.

"Are you ready?" Callan asked quietly. We had put up signs about a mudslide on either end of the trail, and it was rare for people to be in the area at night, but we still needed to hurry in case we were disturbed.

I nodded, and Callan knelt by the base of the tree. With a tenderness that he rarely displayed in public, he placed a hand on the bark and murmured something, and I got the impression he was apologizing for what he was about to do.

He uncorked the vial of poison.

Blood rushed to my head, and my fists knotted once more.

"Wait." I put up my hands, and Callan looked over his shoulder at me. "We can't do this."

Callan paused, waiting for my next words.

"Frank is practically a sacred tree to the city of Weed. Causing his death, even in the dignified way you have so carefully planned, is just... wrong." My stomach relaxed slightly as I voiced what I had been feeling.

Callan stood and put the cork back in the vial. "I trust your instincts. If you don't want to do this, we'll find another way."

"That's the problem, isn't it? There is no other way. It's sacrifice Frank or never find the *Vanished Compendium*."

"Maybe there's some avenue we haven't explored."

But even as Callan said the words, I knew they weren't true. The quill was the most promising lead to the book that the Root and Vine Society had ever had, and since they had me, a magical botanist with every affinity power, just like the Renaissance-era botanists who had written the book with the quill, we had a shot at using it.

"I just wish we knew who had put the blocking spell on the quill and why. Maybe there's a reason they didn't want the book to be found."

"I'm certain there was a reason. But that was a long time ago. Circumstances change," Callan said. He nestled my hands in his, squeezing warmth into them. His eyes found mine again, his long dark lashes sweeping across my face once more. "What do you want to do, local?"

Local. There was that nickname he had given me on our very first meeting. But it wasn't just a nickname. In Weed, California, I *was* the local, and therefore, Frank was my responsibility. No one else in the Root and Vine Society could understand what the tree meant to the community.

No, I couldn't participate in killing the majestic oak, and I couldn't let my friends go through with it either.

"We can't do it," I breathed.

Callan's shoulders fell, but he nodded and gave my hands a squeeze. "Okay. Plan's off. We need to find another way to locate the book."

Even though I was the one who suggested the change, I was full of questions. "What will we do about Wyatt? Once he has an expert examine the fake quill I gave him, he might be back for that one." I nodded toward Callan's backpack, where the real quill resided.

Callan straightened at the mention of his brother but didn't hesitate to respond. "It doesn't matter. The quill can't be used while the blocking spell is in place. As long as Wyatt doesn't know about the Frank connection, he'll never be able to unblock it either. And you are the only one with all the affinities who can use the quill, so he wouldn't get far, regardless."

The little relief in the tightening of my stomach vanished. I was putting Evergreen Academy and the Root and Vine Society at risk by not taking the final step to find the *Vanished Compendium*. But killing Frank was a step too far, even in dire circumstances.

"I'm sorry," I said, barely able to meet Callan's eyes. "I really thought I could do this, but now that we're here, I know it's not right."

"Well, I'm glad to see you two made the correct decision. I'm pretty fond of Frank here."

We jumped at the sound of an unexpected deep voice, and I spun to see a man who had appeared out of nowhere. There was something vaguely familiar about his tanned skin and pine-green ball cap, which were slightly illuminated by the lantern he was holding.

Callan's eyes shot up to the trees, and I realized that was where the man had come from.

How much had this stranger overheard?

"By the looks on your faces, I can tell you weren't expecting me. But if you two are magical botanists and you're doing what I think you're doing, I've been waiting for you for a long time."

Chapter Two

Shock coursed through me. The man who had appeared out of nowhere on the Wildflower Trail had just mentioned magical botanists. Humans didn't know about magical botanists, which left one option. This man was one of us.

Callan stepped forward, positioning me slightly behind him. "Care to introduce yourself?" he asked, and I once again marveled at his ability to sound completely calm in tense situations.

"My name's Oren Cesalpin, and I'm a forester here in Siskiyou County."

My eyes widened. So that was why I recognized him. I had probably seen him at the tree cuttings each Halloween. I stepped forward, coming side by side with Callan. "And you're a magical botanist?"

He nodded. "Tree affinity. Members of my family have been taking care of the trees in this stretch of woods for a hundred years. Before Wildflower Trail even existed, in fact."

Callan and I exchanged a look.

"Want to tell me what you are doing here?" Oren asked. His gaze flicked to Frank.

I glanced at Callan and was relieved to see no trace of the

poison bottle. "You said you've been waiting for us a long time," I said, avoiding his question. "What did you mean?"

Oren cast a look around the trail. "I think this conversation is best done somewhere more private and out of the drizzle. Can you both treewalk?"

"Yes," Callan said.

"All right then. Let's go."

We didn't bother to deliberate before climbing into a tree and following him. We needed to know what Oren had to say. We fell in line in the canopy, with Callan a few paces behind Oren, and me in the back. The branches of the trees formed a narrow path for us, and we worked our way up the steep hill that made up the forest on one side of the Wildflower Trail. The rain began to fall in earnest, and I focused on the branches beneath my feet.

When we neared the top, Oren veered right, and soon, we approached a perfectly camouflaged tree house. It was like the ones at Evergreen Academy, though it blended into the forest even more seamlessly.

Oren invited us inside, and I could immediately see that the tree house served as a kind of office for him. Lit by hanging lights, the room contained scientific materials, papers, books, teacups, a kettle on a camp stove, and other little signs of life scattered around the built-in shelves.

"Have a seat." Oren gestured to some wooden stools then got the kettle warming.

While the water heated, he turned back to us. "I have scouting vines along this trail. They're quite well hidden." He nodded to Callan, who had fallen into the habit of scanning for scouting vines wherever we went. We had never expected to find them along the Wildflower Trail, though. "I knew you were from the academy because I've seen you collecting the letterbox notes. But we aren't due for a collection, so I thought something else might be afoot."

I shifted on the stool.

"Was that vial in your pocket intended for Frank?" Oren asked, again nodding toward Callan.

Abandoning any stealth, as it was obvious we were busted, Callan removed the vial from his pocket and held it flat on his palm. "Yes. It's a necrotizing agent and wouldn't have caused any pain."

"But you changed your minds." Oren looked between us, his eyes finally resting on me.

"It... It didn't seem right," I said. "I'm from here, and we have cuttings of Frank at our house. I think the community would mourn his loss."

"I think you're right," Oren said, tilting his head slightly. "I thought I recognized you from around town. What's your name?"

"Briar Whelan."

"Ahh. Tessa's daughter."

I stilled at my mother's name. Most people referred to me as Vera's niece lately. "You knew my mom?"

"We were a few years apart in high school, but the Belrose twins were pretty unforgettable. I was very sorry to hear about the accident."

I swallowed and nodded my thanks before clearing my throat. As much as I loved hearing memories of my mom from others, we needed to use our time with Oren strategically. "Do you know why Frank is... special?"

"You mean the blocking Floracantus that runs through him?" Oren asked, and I sat upright.

"Exactly that," I said. "Who put it on him? Did you?"

Oren shook his head. "Not me, but my great-grandfather did."

The teakettle whistled, and Oren poured steaming water into three white porcelain cups then handed them to us, and a crisp bergamot jasmine aroma filled the tree house.

"Your great-grandfather did?" Callan pressed.

Oren took a sip of his tea and nodded. "I don't know all the details, but the story within our family goes that he was asked to do so by a very powerful person in the magical botanist community. He never shared more than that it was to protect a book. We all guessed which one but never had any sort of confirmation. My family has been maintaining the Floracantus ever since. Frank links to a network of great trees all over the country."

"That's why the blocking spell was active in Washington too?" Callan asked.

"Yes. Frank was the original tree, likely because whoever tasked my great-grandfather with guarding him was involved with Evergreen Academy. But our family was told that the magic would be placed on other trees as well, especially around the magical botanical conservatories, sort of like power boosters."

"You're the one I sensed using magic when we were here for the Halloween event," Callan said.

Oren nodded. "I amplify Frank's blocking Floracantus every fall so that the cuttings will contain a bit of the blocking magic too."

"So I'm guessing you came to stop us from harming Frank," I said.

"From harming Frank, yes. But not from undoing the spell."

My eyes widened, a dash of hope invigorating me as much as the warm tea. "You know how to undo it?"

"Oh yes. That was built into the blocking Floracantus. Our family always said that when the time was right, we could break the magic on Frank with the help of a botanist with every affinity power." Oren's attention locked on me. "I'm guessing that's you."

My mind swirled as I tried to process what Oren was saying. How did his family know that I would show up one day? Or maybe it wasn't me specifically, but the undoing of the spell could happen at any point, so long as someone with every affinity power emerged.

"Have you got your hands on the quill, then?" Oren continued, not waiting for confirmation of my powers.

I exchanged glances with Callan. It seemed we had no choice but to trust Oren.

"Perhaps," Callan said evasively.

"Good. I try to stay well away from the rest of the society, as I'm comfortable in my little world, but rumors of discontent have reached even me. If it's time to get this book back and fulfill the duties of my family, I'm ready to do it."

"You say you need to work with Briar to break the spell on Frank," Callan said, a hint of caution in his voice. "What do you mean by that?"

"It means I'll be teaching her a new Floracantus. Ready to head back out? Briar and I have work to do."

Chapter Three

I sipped my mug of bergamot jasmine tea while Oren explained what I needed to know to undo the blocking Floracantus woven into Frank's cells. I used my fern and tree affinities to hover protective fronds over myself and Oren, which sent the rain droplets dripping around us in a dazzling curtain of water.

Callan sat on a tree limb about fifteen feet away, his legs dangling. Though he wasn't standing next to me, a slight breeze to the back of my neck told me he was there if I needed him.

"The trick is to connect with as many parts of the tree as possible, since the blocking Floracantus is spread throughout it. Try to hold your attention on the roots, bark, and leaves at the same time," Oren explained.

I closed my eyes and practiced, reaching out to Frank and connecting with as much of the majestic oak as possible.

Once I had successfully connected to the gargantuan tree a few times, Oren nodded. "Very good. Now, say the Floracantus I shared. I'll join you. Make sure to hold on to each cell as you say it."

"*Solve venas*," I said, reciting a Floracantus I had never known until a few minutes earlier. I strained with all my might to hold on to my mental connection with every part of Frank's mass.

"*Solve venas,*" Oren said, adding his power to mine.

As the words flowed out of me, a snapping sensation rippled through my body. I gasped as the tension broke, and I turned to Oren with my eyes wide.

He smiled. "Take a look." He nodded toward Frank.

I returned my focus to the tree, and for a few seconds, the branches flashed a brilliant green before returning to their dull winter brown.

"The blocking spell is gone," Oren said. "And since we removed it here, the magic in the other trees in the network, including the cuttings around town, should rapidly diminish."

"Just like that?" I asked, a smile spreading over my face. *Frank was still alive.*

"Just like that," Oren said, mirroring my smile.

An instant later, Callan was on the ground, standing at my side. He reached out a hand and placed it on Frank's bark. "I can sense that the Floracantus is gone. And Frank looks none the worse for it."

I swallowed a lump in my throat, overwhelmingly glad that the stately tree remained alive and well.

"What was that Floracantus?" Callan asked Oren.

"One my family's been holding on to for a very long time. That and the one we used to boost the blocking spell each year are the only ones we know that aren't in the *Compendium Floracantus.*"

"Think they came from the *Vanished Compendium*?" Callan asked, referencing the very book we were after.

"I've always suspected so," Oren replied. "Where else would they have come from?"

"Should we try the quill now?" I asked the group, suddenly eager to see if our efforts had truly worked.

Callan glanced at Oren, and the man shook his head. "My

involvement here is done. Wherever your next adventure takes you, I wish you good luck." Before he climbed into the tree to return to his tree house, he spoke softly to me. "Your mom would have been proud of you, kiddo."

A tingle of warmth filled me at his words. "Thanks for your help, Oren. I'll see you around?"

"These trees aren't going to tend themselves." Oren winked, then he climbed the tree and was gone.

Callan shrugged off his backpack, removed the quill, and handed it to me.

"Are we ready for this?" I asked, placing my hand on the shaft of the quill.

In answer, Callan used his wind manipulating powers to draw the fern frond rain cover closer around us.

Barely daring to breathe, I knelt and removed the quill from the cloth underneath the protective ferns. It seemed to tremble in my hand, as if ready to be used. I took that as a good sign. With a deep breath, I drew on all nine plant affinities and said in a low, clear voice, *"Simul simus."*

The quill began to rotate slowly in my palm. It made three full circles, and my heart sank. Nonstop spinning was a hallmark of the quill being blocked. We had witnessed it on the occasions we had tested it.

But then the spinning slowed, and the quill came to a quivering stop, pointing southeast.

I forgot how to breathe.

Callan took a step back, and I could see that the gears were already turning in his brain. "Southeast. That could be a lot of places. I wonder how far—"

My gasp cut him off. The quill was vibrating gently, and scratches formed on its shaft. "Something's happening," I said.

Callan leaned in.

As we watched the quill, *3200 miles* materialized, engraved in tiny indentations along the shaft.

"It's in English. This part of the magic must have been added later. Maybe one hundred years ago, by whoever last hid the book," Callan said. "Thirty-two hundred miles."

"This means the book is thirty-two hundred miles from here?" I asked, flipping the quill over and searching for signs of more guidance.

But Callan smiled. "I know something that is almost exactly thirty-two hundred miles from here."

"What?" I asked, meeting his eyes.

Callan's grin split his face. "The aquatics conservatory."

Chapter Four

The plants in Vera's Café seemed to spring to life as the little coffee shop and bakery filled with magical botanists.

The fern hanging from the corner shimmied in acknowledgement of Hollis, a fern founders' descendant. The flowers that filled vases on each table stretched forward, as if wanting to get a better glimpse of Heath, the lead floral affinity in our group. And the tea that Laurus, an herbs affinity student, had brewed for us from a unique combination of loose-leaf canisters on Vera's counter had a divine fragrance filling the room.

"This place is charming," Nalin, the aquatics affinity student, said as his eyes scanned the café. "You said this is your aunt's shop?"

"Yes." I smiled. "We close at four, and I asked her if we could use it for a 'study session' this evening." My eyes drifted to the front door as I double-checked that it was locked and that the Closed sign faced outward. Vera's Café was sure to be clear of scouting vines and a safe place for us to talk. We typically met at the Evergreen Conservatory just off campus, but the freezing temperatures meant an indoor meeting was welcomed by all.

Hollis was standing by the wall, his hands clasped behind his back, studying the two paintings that hung there, their frames perfectly matched. My heart skittered every time I looked at the frame Callan had painstakingly tracked down, all to find one that matched my mom's for my art.

"Are we ready to get this party started?" The dry comment came from Meadow, the moss founders' descendant, who hadn't carpooled with the other magical botanists into town. I glanced outside for another car but didn't see one. Knowing Meadow, I figured she had casually treewalked into town, even though she only had a trailing affinity for trees and the practice was dangerous for her.

Callan turned from where he had been filling his teacup at the counter, and his eyes found mine.

I tried to remain focused, but when he looked at me like that... full of trust, pride, and a touch of something else... let's just say there was a lot to make my mind wander.

I cleared my throat. "Thank you all for coming. We've had a recent development in the Root and Vine Society's mission, and we want to fill you all in. Everyone knows about the trip Callan, Meadow, Hollis, and I took to the tree and moss conservatories last week?"

Nods came from around the room.

"We were told it was a bust. The quill doesn't work?" Nalin asked.

"Yes and no," I said carefully. "The quill didn't work when we first acquired it, but now it does."

Murmurs and intakes of air came from my fellow coalition members. One of the bubbles Nalin had been forming above his water cup gave a soft *pop*.

Once the place was quiet once more, I continued to explain. "There was a blocking Floracantus on the quill. Callan determined the spell was tied to a local tree here in Weed. When we went to the tree, we encountered a botanist who was responsible for maintaining the blocking Floracantus, and he helped me undo it."

"What do you mean, you 'encountered a botanist'?" Meadow arched an eyebrow.

I took the next few minutes to fill them in on the entire story about Frank and the family of magical botanists who had been serving as foresters in the town of Weed for decades. When there were no more questions, I brandished the quill. "It's pointing southeast, and it has a distance meter. If the locating magic in this quill still works, the *Vanished Compendium* is approximately thirty-two hundred miles away."

The room was as silent as a snake plant.

Callan spoke up then. "We don't know for sure if we have the correct location, but the aquatics conservatory is thirty-two hundred miles away in that direction. That doesn't feel like a coincidence."

Nalin sat up straighter. "I've been there a handful of times. It's in the Florida Everglades. You think the book could be there?"

"It's worth investigating," Callan said.

"How precise is that quill's measurement?" Meadow asked. "What if you can't find the book once you get there?"

Kaito, Callan's co-lead in the Root and Vine Society, answered her. "I've been thinking about that very question. Based on how the distance number appeared, maybe the scale changes as you get closer."

"That's the hope," Callan said. "The rest will have to be figured out on the fly."

"So, who's going, and when?" Meadow asked.

"Like with our trip to the moss and tree conservatories, we think we should go as a smaller group to keep suspicion about our movements to a minimum," Callan replied. "Briar obviously needs to go, since she's the only one who can use the quill."

"So that means you're going," Meadow said, a ghost of a smile touching her lips.

Callan nodded. "That's the plan. The rest, we waited to discuss with all of you." He nodded toward Nalin, the aquatics affinity. "Do you think you could drum up a reason to escort us there?"

"Sure, but when? Evergreen Academy is back in session tomorrow."

"This can't wait long. The DBI has our fake quill, and we don't expect the enchantments on it to hold them off forever. If the expert who was at the tree conservatory sees it, it's over. They discovered our first one was a fake pretty quickly."

What Callan didn't tell the others was that the DBI, the Department of Botanical Intelligence, included his brother, Wyatt. So far, only the two of us plus Kaito, Hollis, and Meadow knew about Wyatt's involvement.

"Then we go this weekend," Nalin said. He rubbed his hands together, and a bit of water splashed out from his glass and formed a ball in his hands. He floated it between his palms automatically as he spoke. "But two days isn't enough to get to Florida and back plus search for the book."

I straightened, an idea coming to me. "We know someone who works at the aquatics conservatory. If she were to invite you out for a field studies-related project for a week, do you think it would get approved?"

Nalin smiled. "Dr. Lemna would never say no to that."

"What about you and Callan?" Meadow asked.

"I'll think of something," Callan said. "We'll firm up the arrangements for Nalin to leave this weekend and spend a week at the aquatics conservatory under the guise of research. He'll have some access to searching the conservatory that way. Anyone else have questions or ideas?"

When no one said anything, Hollis rose and clapped once. "Well, we've got our marching orders. I have plans tonight, so I'll just take a few of these lavender scones to go." He reached for one of the paper takeout containers on the counter.

I smiled, knowing my aunt Vera would be offended if any of the scones remained when she returned. "They're all yours."

As I watched Hollis pick up a scone, I mentally ran through the events of the meeting, a tendril of hope wrapping around the nerves that lived in my chest. The Root and Vine Society officially had a plan, or at least the beginnings of one.

We were going to the aquatics conservatory. We had a solid lead on the *Vanished Compendium*. And if we found it, we would have leverage to use with the forces that were trying to change Evergreen Academy, my home away from home.

Chapter Five

After the rest of the Root and Vine Society had stuffed their pockets with lavender scones and filled to-go cups with hot tea, the bells on the door handle of Vera's Café tinged softly as the door closed behind them.

When I turned back around, I realized only Callan and I remained. He was going from table to table, lifting the dishes into the dish caddy with a touch of wind so invisible I wouldn't have noticed the tiny hover below the dishes if I hadn't come to know the look on his face when he was using his powers.

"I can take care of those," I said, motioning to the dishes.

"No way, local. I suggested having the meeting here. I'm not going to stick you with cleanup."

"You know, for a kid who grew up as a founders' descendant, you sure don't act spoiled." I went around the counter and began to fill the sink with warm, sudsy water.

"Youngest of two brothers, remember? Wyatt was good at getting me to do his chores for him."

I didn't turn from the sink, not wanting to spook Callan from talking about his brother. It had only been a few days since Wyatt showed up at the academy and departed with what he thought was the quill we had just used to point us to the aquatics conservatory.

Each night since, I'd gone to bed nervous that the next day would be the one in which Wyatt—or someone he worked with at the Department of Botanical Intelligence—would realize the quill was a fake and come after the real one again. I had put a few extra defensive Floracantus on it in an attempt to camouflage it more thoroughly, but I had no idea how that would hold up under expert scrutiny.

The dish tray appeared at my side, and I could smell the sandalwood and peach fragrance of the cologne Callan had designed with me in mind. I wasn't sure how to feel about the fact that he was still wearing it, even after we'd had an epic kiss that we had to swear off having again for the time being.

We both knew our focus had to stay on finding the book and saving the academy as well as not putting an extra target on our backs with his family and other members of the Board of Regents, but I couldn't help daydreaming about a day when Callan might let his protectiveness of me down a notch, and we could finally be together.

I took a deep inhalation of the lemony smell of the soapy water, trying and failing to mask the enticing scent of the man next to me.

Callan dipped a plate into the water and began to scrub. I reached across, grabbing a mug. Apparently, we were *both* going to do the dishes.

I forced my mind back to the conversation about Callan's childhood. "Someone actually managed to boss Callan Rhodes around? Color me skeptical," I said, hoping to keep my voice light. Callan's family had always been a touchy subject.

"Believe it or not, I wasn't quite this confident as a kid." He used a controlled rush of wind to send a dollop of bubbly soap out of the water, and it landed on my cheek in a delicate kiss of warmth.

Nope. Do not *think the word* kiss, *Briar.* Doing so with Callan so close was dangerous. I tried to focus on his words and *only* his words.

"That's probably a good thing. I'm trying to imagine *the* Callan Rhodes in elementary school, sensing powers and controlling wind. You were either popular or terrifying in the lunchroom."

Callan let out a soft laugh, and I watched his muscles flex under the tattoos on his forearms as he scrubbed a dish then reached across me to put it on the drying rack. "What's a lunchroom?"

I let out a startled laugh. "I meant the tearoom."

"I'm just teasing. I have seen a few movies, you know."

"Let me guess. They were all nature documentaries?"

I could practically hear Callan's smile, and I couldn't resist glancing over to see it.

"Those were good for critique exercises. We'd watch the video and make detailed lists of all the things they didn't mention or can't explain about the plants."

"*Leaves.* Was that your idea of a fun Friday night? We're going to have to get your movie knowledge up to par."

My hand slipped into the water then and I let out a sharp gasp as pain sliced my palm.

Callan's hands were on me immediately, gently removing my hand from the water, which was turning slightly pink.

I winced as his fingers touched the side of my palm. "I must have cut it on one of those deli knives. They're notoriously sharp."

Before I could say another word, Callan placed a clean cloth against my hand. "Wait here."

Seconds later, he was back with a chair and his backpack. He helped me to sit, a completely unnecessary action, as I was steady, but I appreciated the gesture. Then he pulled a compact green kit from his backpack and unzipped it. I craned my neck to see small vials filled with herbs and liquids.

"What's that?" I asked.

"Apothecary bag," Callan said, deftly opening a jar. He removed the cloth from my hand and dabbed salve on the wound. I inhaled a potent mixture of eucalyptus, calendula, pomegranate, and other herbs as the cool salve sank into my skin.

My eyes widened as, within seconds, the slice on my palm sealed. By the time all the ointment had sunk into my skin, my palm was smooth and pain free, as if the cut had never been there.

"How did you... What is that?" I asked, eying the glass vial with new awe.

"It's a wound-healing concoction I've been working on for a while. I test it whenever I get minor cuts rock climbing. It hasn't failed me yet."

"But that's like... a miracle medicine. You could make a fortune selling that."

Callan shook his head, a soft smile touching his lips as he ran a finger over my healed palm. "I don't want to make money from it. I want it to help people. But the human medical market isn't ready for this yet. Maybe it'll be a project I 'complete' when I'm working on my PhD. If my mom hasn't forced me into a senator seat by then."

I studied Callan's face as he gently released my hand and repacked his apothecary bag. He was a treasure. *Does he know it? Do his parents know it? His brother? How can they not be shouting from the rooftops how proud they are of him?*

I was so full of emotion I couldn't express that all I could do was squeeze my hands together and take a deep breath.

Finally, I settled on the only words that felt right, even though I knew they weren't nearly enough. "The world is lucky to have you, Callan Rhodes."

He turned back to me, looking so startled that it made my chest hurt. With a note of forced levity in his voice, he said, "Right back at you, local."

Chapter Six

Aunt Vera arrived at the café shortly after Callan departed. She breezed into the room in a blur of scarlet coat, thick gray scarf, large vegan-leather bag, and a sweet perfume I'd made her for Christmas.

"How did your study session go?" she asked and kissed me on the cheek.

"Good. Thanks for letting us use the space. And for the scones. Everyone was raving about them."

"Of course they were." Aunt Vera nodded then hung her coat on a rack in the back room. "Are you on your way out? I came in to experiment with a few recipes. You're welcome to join me."

I glanced at my watch and was relieved to see that I had some time to spare. I hadn't had any time with my aunt since her New Year's trip to visit the family of her husband, Bryce.

"I'd love to," I said, moving to the sink to wash up. As I scrubbed my hands with the crisp lemon soap, I again marveled at the complete lack of evidence that I had cut myself only a few minutes ago.

"Are you ready for spring classes to start? You're still taking one class at SCC, right?" Aunt Vera asked.

"Yes, prop design is a year-long class. We're making the decorations for *A Midsummer Night's Dream*, which the drama classes will perform later in the semester. I'm excited to see everything come together."

"I can't wait to see it. Speaking of spring, I was thinking about trying something different that we can launch once it warms up. What do you think of flower-flavored cookies?"

"Flower-flavored?" I scrunched up my nose. "Which flavors?"

"Well, we're already famous for our lavender scones. Maybe we branch out to hibiscus, jasmine, honeysuckle."

"Where are you going to source those?" We had an abundance of each of those at Evergreen Academy, but I couldn't share that information.

"I thought I could get a garden growing out at our house. Get it certified then do a farm-to-table kind of thing."

She opened her purse and pulled out a paper-wrapped package. As she unfolded it, I spotted the bright pink of camellia. "Options are limited in the winter, but I'm going to experiment with these."

"What are you going to do? Grind up the flowers?"

"I'm not sure yet," my aunt admitted.

"I talked to Bryce while you were visiting his family," I began, deciding it was as good a time as any to broach the subject. "He said you were talking about flowers a lot and putting bouquets all over his relative's home."

"Who doesn't love flowers? They were all into it. Did he tell you I arranged the bouquets myself?"

"Is this a new hobby? You should have told me, and I would have had you help with the flower arrangements for your wedding." I was still trying to keep my voice light.

"The hobby is a recent development. Come to think of it, I started getting interested in it after the wedding. Maybe it was the arrangements you made that triggered my interest."

I frowned. My aunt had gone full steam ahead with projects

before. The bakery was a clear example of that. I had shrugged off Bryce's concerns, but the new suggestion about making flower-flavored pastries *was* strange. It seemed to have come out of nowhere, and the recipes she was proposing weren't likely to have a large market. As creative as she was, my aunt understood business.

"This interest started after the wedding? You're not having any sort of post-wedding letdown, are you?" I echoed the concerns Bryce had expressed. They had been married for three months. Was my aunt having a hard time adjusting?

"Oh no! Nothing like that." Aunt Vera waved a hand in a subtle motion, brushing off the idea. "It's just that suddenly, I'm noticing every flower I see. I can't pass them in a store without purchasing some. It's like they're speaking to me. I swear they lean in my direction as if asking me to take them home." She let out a little laugh. "You probably think your aunt is going crazy."

A nagging sensation tugged at my chest, and I inhaled sharply as something clicked. "I don't think you're crazy," I said, calling the words back over my shoulder as I went to retrieve one of the bouquets from the tables in the front room. I had a preposterous theory, and there was one way to test it. The blooms in the vase immediately leaned toward me as I gathered them.

When I returned to the back room, I set the bouquet on the table then stepped as far out of its range as I possibly could while monitoring them, my heart racing. Once I was farther away from the flowers than my aunt was, I watched in astonishment as the blooms slowly reversed course, straightening then shifting so that every single bloom stretched directly toward my aunt Vera.

"See?" Aunt Vera said, glancing up at the blossoms. "Aren't they beautiful? It's like they're displaying themselves just for me."

Holy blossoms.

The flowers were drawn to my aunt. She had a floral affinity.

Aunt Vera was a magical botanist. And something had activated her powers.

Chapter Seven

My head was spinning as I tried to casually keep up with the small talk my aunt initiated as we prepared a batch of camellia-infused cookies. The flowers in the vase on the bakery counter were split into two bunches, half stretching toward her and half fanning toward me.

I attempted to piece through the timeline of when my aunt's magic had been activated. If her powers worked the way mine did, they would have had to be unlocked by touching one of Leonardo da Vinci's books. It wasn't like those were just casually sitting around.

I sifted through everything Aunt Vera had said as we prepared the new and unusual recipe. The interest had seemed to start after the wedding, which made me wonder if it could be tied to the wedding somehow.

I continued to rack my brain, scavenging through the memories of that day and night. I had used my powers to put together the floral displays for the wedding. Could that have had some kind of downstream effect on my aunt? Did the massive bouquet she carried activate her powers?

I shook my head as I aggressively rolled a cookie into a ball. The camellia fragrance was so strong that I almost wanted to leave the room. No, the bouquet theory didn't track with what I knew about my magic. Professor Tenella had explained that some magical botanists of the Renaissance period had tied their power to their journals. There was no evidence that the magic could have filtered through me and into the flowers. Plus, I had given my aunt magically enhanced plants before, like the poinsettia at Christmas a year earlier.

The wedding... The beautiful ceremony ran through my mind. I'd been surrounded by the friends and family of Bryce and Aunt Vera. Then there was dinner, speeches, and cake. I had taken the elixir of bliss with Callan, and we had danced the night away. Even the presence of Alex as Maci's date hadn't put me off as much as I thought it would.

Wait... Alex had been there.

Alex, who I saw at the tree conservatory last week. Alex, who had never given so much as a hint that he was a magical botanist until I saw him among the other tree affinities.

Could he have... no. I slapped the cookie ball onto the sheet.

"Whoa there. What's going on with you, Briar Rose? You've been distracted this whole time. And now you're attacking the poor innocent dough."

I tensed then immediately softened at the teasing look on her face, not quite masking a hint of concern behind her brown irises. "I just have a lot going on," I said.

"Things with Evergreen Academy? Or with that handsome man I saw leaving the shop as I pulled up? That was Callan, right? The one with the scary parents?"

I couldn't help it—I let out a sharp laugh, and my shoulders relaxed. "It might be a little about him," I admitted, unable to explain that my primary concern had become about *her*. Callan and I had told Professor East about Alex, and he promised to do some digging, but it had only been a few days since the discovery, and I hadn't seen Professor East at all in that time.

The only thing keeping me sane was hearing from Maci, his kind-of girlfriend and my best friend since childhood, that Alex was still out of town. Figuring out what to tell Maci about Alex was a problem of its own.

I wondered if Alex planned to be back to start the new semester at Siskiyous Community College. Was it possible he knew we were onto him?

My aunt took the cookie tray and slid it into the commercial oven. "All right. Time to spill."

I took a deep breath. If I couldn't share anything else, I could at least share this. "We kissed," I said, the words coming out as a squeak.

Aunt Vera nodded and smiled knowingly. "When did this happen?"

"Just recently. Over the winter break."

"And that's why you're pounding cookies into oblivion? Was the kiss that bad?"

I laughed again. "The kiss was that *good*."

"Ahh. So, I take it you two aren't dating, or else my dough might be less beat up."

"He's concerned about those scary parents you mentioned. He feels like he needs to protect me from them."

"Umm, has he even met you? No one scares off my Briar Rose."

"That's what I've been saying!" The relief at discussing this important piece of my life with my aunt was so great that the words poured out of me. "His parents are... powerful people in his community. They're part of a board that oversees Evergreen Academy. Callan thinks they might try to dictate my future, so he's keeping me at arm's length."

Aunt Vera's smooth forehead wrinkled a little. "Dictate your future? What is that supposed to mean?"

I measured my words carefully, determining what I could safely tell her without breaking my agreement with Professor East.

Though if my aunt was a magical botanist, that rule about not telling her might not apply. "Evergreen Academy has a field studies program. Historically, these were assigned by the school. This year, though, the Board of Regents took over the assignments."

"Why does that make you a target specifically?"

I chewed my lower lip, unable to tell her that representatives from each of the affinity groups were trying to court me as the only known living botanist with all the affinity powers. Was that still true if my aunt's powers had been activated? Could she have all the affinity powers too? "They think I could be... useful in certain fields."

My aunt Vera was quiet, digesting the revelations. This was possibly more than I had ever told her about Evergreen Academy, and for a moment, I wondered if I had gone too far.

Finally, she said, "Well, trust your instincts. Is there anything I can do to help?"

I considered her words. That would have been an easy *no* only a day ago, but since she was exhibiting a floral affinity, maybe things were different.

"Not at the moment," I said. "Except for tasting this recipe before me. I'm not sold on camellia-flavored cookies."

Aunt Vera tossed her long, dark ponytail over her shoulder and laughed. "Back to the brunette heartthrob. If he's the one responsible for the look I've been seeing on your face for months, I hope you two will be able to find balance with boundaries with his parents. Because if I had found a guy that made me glow like that when I was your age"—she flipped a dish rag across her shoulder—"let's just say I would have had to kiss fewer frogs before finding Bryce."

Chapter Eight

When I left Vera's Café, I found a tree that still held a few leaves in the winter. I complimented it to dispel some of its leaves and activate the leaf messaging magic then prepped a brief note for Callan.

We need to talk. Tree house in 30?

I sent the message then hurried to my car and raced—just a hair or two over the speed limit—to Evergreen Academy. The winter leaves were like smears of brown, gray, and dark-green paint on a canvas as I navigated through the forest road.

When I got to the tree house, Callan was already there. He must have noticed the shellshocked look on my face, because he rose and stepped forward. "What's wrong?"

A touch of the anxiety and confusion I was feeling dissipated at his proximity. "My aunt's a magical botanist," I said, barely believing the words as I spoke them.

"Well, we knew it probably came from your mom's side of the

family," Callan said, pulling back and assessing my face for what he was missing.

"Yes, but what I mean is her powers are active. I tested it with some flowers, and they were drawn to her like bees at a picnic."

Callan's eyes widened, his chestnut-brown eyebrows rising just a smidge. "Are you sure?"

I nodded. "Something's been off about her, but there was no denying the flower test."

Callan crossed his arms. "Do you know when this started? She's never shown signs before?"

"According to her, she started taking more notice of flowers after the wedding."

"The wedding?" A muscle in his neck flexed. "You think Alex had something to do with this?" Callan had reached that conclusion more quickly than I had.

"I don't see how, but it can't be a coincidence. That was the only time those two have ever been near each other."

"But how would he have activated her powers?"

"I don't know. It's not like she said anything about receiving a journal of Leonardo da Vinci for a wedding gift. Wait..." I stood up straight, trying to recall the details of the memory that was nagging at me. "Maci and Alex were late to the wedding, remember? She said she couldn't find the wedding gift she had prepared."

"Alex could have taken the gift and swapped it out or added a da Vinci book to it," Callan said, puzzling it out. He let out a breath. "That seems bold. And what would be the purpose? Why would he want to activate your aunt's powers?"

I realized I was shaking, and I crossed my arms, hoping Callan wouldn't notice. If what we were speculating about was true, my aunt's wedding—one of the most special nights of her life—had been infiltrated by a secretive magical botanist who had changed her life forever, without her knowledge or consent.

"Maybe for the same reason we went after the quill," I said, the words coming out on autopilot as numbness took over my limbs.

"If my aunt has all the affinities like I do, she could use the quill as a compass too."

"Leading Alex to the *Vanished Compendium*."

I nodded. "That must mean that he and whoever he is working with didn't know that there was a blocking spell on it that would impede us anyway."

Callan stepped closer once more and slipped his arms around me. "It's going to be okay."

He touched a finger to the bottom of my chin, tilting my head so that our eyes were a perfect path to each other's souls. "I'm not going to let anything happen to you—or to anyone you care about. I need you to understand that."

The tornado in my stomach lessened so that it felt more like a winter storm. "There's just so much we don't know. And the other players in this game are always one step ahead. Maybe more."

Callan's face took on a focused look I had seen many times. He was in problem-solving mode. When he spoke, his words were measured. "You're right. We've been playing this like a game. But that ends now. This is a war. If they want a fight, they'll get it."

I swallowed. "A fight?"

"Not all battles require swords, local. And we're going to prove it. We'll start by going to your aunt's house and seeing if we can confirm this theory about the wedding gift."

I nodded, comforted by the idea of action. And Callan had said *we*. As uncertain as things felt, I didn't have to face this situation alone.

Chapter Nine

When we arrived at Aunt Vera's house, I was relieved to find the driveway empty. She and Bryce were on their scheduled Sunday-night date. I used my key and entered then gasped as I looked around. Vases of flowers covered nearly every surface—lilacs and bluebells, asters and zinnias. When my aunt had run out of vases, she turned to more creative flower holders, and daisies and poppies were bursting out of teacups, mason jars, and soup cans.

"Let's get started," I said, going straight to the two small bookshelves in the living room. I scanned the titles while Callan thumbed through the books on the adjacent shelf, but there was nothing unusual. It was a mix of my aunt's cooking and baking books, entrepreneurial self-help titles, a few romance novels, and some other nonfiction books that I assumed belonged to Bryce.

"Any luck?" I asked.

Callan shook his head and scanned the room.

With a little sigh of consternation, I considered where else in the house they might keep books. "Let's check the office."

We went down the hall, and as soon as we entered the office, I zeroed in on a pile of wedding leftovers in the corner. My aunt had stashed wedding décor and gifts that she still needed to deal with into a few bins.

"This is all wedding stuff," I said. "Maybe we'll find something here."

I knelt on the carpet and began to sift. In the second bin, after I'd moved aside a brand-new set of sheets, my fingers skimmed an old leather-bound book, and a familiar warmth passed through me. My heart racing, I picked it up and nearly jumped as warmth continued to pool in my hands.

I tipped open the cover and found that the book was filled with botanical illustrations. "Callan," I breathed.

"I see it," he said, abandoning the bin he had been searching.

My pulse was so high that I had trouble hearing my thoughts. We had suspected Alex, but confirmation that my aunt had a book belonging to da Vinci hit me like a sack of potatoes to the gut.

Automatically, I moved to the notebook on the desk. "My aunt kept a list of the gifts she received and who they were from."

I anxiously skimmed down the paper—still holding out a tiny sliver of hope—until I saw an item titled *Vintage coffee table art book*. With bated breath, I checked the other side of the column, where the names were scrawled. The name jumped out at me as if its font were larger than the others. I had seen it written hundreds of times and knew it nearly as well as my own.

Maci Phouthavong.

My breath released from my chest in one big whoosh. I'd known it was coming, but this was confirmation. Alex had slipped the book into the gift from Maci, like a devious little weed.

I went back to the wedding bins, where the cards for my aunt and Bryce were preserved on a large metal loop, and carefully sorted through them until I found the one I was looking for.

Congratulations, Aunt Vera and Bryce!

I hope you enjoy this book. My mom swears it brings good luck in a marriage.

Love,
Maci and the Phouthavongs

MY HEART CONSTRICTED IN A WAVE OF FONDNESS AND regret. Maci had always called my aunt "Aunt Vera," just like I did. An ache formed at the back of my head as I questioned how Alex could have used my friend in such a way.

Feeling unsteady, I put the cards away then pulled out my cell phone, still sitting on the floor of the office, and texted Maci.

> Hey, Maci! I'm helping my aunt sort some things from her wedding. What did you gift her?

I sent it without letting myself overthink it, hoping she wouldn't read much into it other than our trying to remember who each gift was from.

Maci responded quickly.

> Hey, girl! I gave her a cookbook called Soups for Soulmates. Silly, I know, but my mom swears by it. Apparently, it brings good luck to a marriage.

Still feeling as if someone else were in charge of my body, I sent a quick text back to Maci then tucked the book into my coat. "Confirmed," I said, not able to meet Callan's eyes.

"I know this is discouraging to see, but this is good intel. We may be able to use this whenever we confront Alex."

"I don't know if we'll ever get the chance. Maci said he isn't back from visiting his family yet, and she hasn't heard from him in a few weeks."

"Maybe that's for the best, where Maci is concerned, at least. If Alex's goal was to activate your aunt's powers to use the quill, he no longer needs Maci."

That thought made my chest ache again, but I was glad that Maci and Alex had never been serious. In fact, a few days ago, when I had casually asked her about Alex, she mentioned that she was talking to her ex again.

When we got to Callan's truck, he got the heater running, and I gratefully held my fingers in front of the warm vent to give myself something to do with my hands.

"Did you mean what you said?" I turned to him and was oddly comforted to see the same righteous outrage on his face that I felt in my whole body. "That we're going on the offensive?"

Callan took my hand in his, squeezing it. "Alex doesn't know we know about your aunt. We still have the quill, and now we have a direction and a plan to search for the *Vanished Compendium*. He and whoever he's working with are no longer a step ahead. We may not know their endgame, but they don't know that we have successfully used the quill. We're going to the aquatics conservatory, and if the book is there, we'll get to it first. I've always known you could do this, Briar." He tucked a wavy lock behind my ear. "We're in this together, okay?"

I nodded. How could I not feel confident with a man like Callan by my side? "Together."

"Now, let's get back to the academy and see if Professor East has found any information on Alex."

Chapter Ten

When we got back to the academy, the grounds were oddly quiet. Normally, on the day before a new term started, students would roam all around, hanging on to their last few hours of unstructured time.

But not a soul was in sight as we passed through the flower gardens and entrance atrium and into the central vein.

"Where is everybody?" I asked, disoriented.

Voices came from the teahouse, and Callan nodded in that direction. "Something's up."

We entered the teahouse to find it full, from the entrance to the tall glass walls in the back. My eyes immediately sought my friends. With a murmured goodbye to Callan—we were trying not to be seen together too much in public—I slipped through the crowd of botanists to stand with Coral, Aurielle, and Yasmin.

"What's going on?" I whispered.

"Professor Tenella just called us in here for an announcement."

A few more students trickled in from the patio connected to the teahouse, then Professor Tenella stepped onto the raised area where Professor East typically spoke from.

"Hello, everyone. I'm sure you're all wondering why I'm

addressing you instead of Professor East. There has been a change at the academy for the rest of this school year. Professor East has temporarily gone on leave—"

The room burst into gasps and murmurs.

"Oh no," I said sharply, my heart sinking.

When Wyatt had come for the quill, I was prepared to offer it up myself. But Professor East had taken responsibility for the missing quill. Callan had said that he thought Professor East might have just fallen on his sword for us. Was he forced out?

It felt as if there were a stone in my stomach. If Professor East had been fired because of me, I was seriously going to be sick. I searched for Callan's eyes across the room. He was already looking at me, and he shook his head slightly before turning back to Professor Tenella.

"Are we all going to settle down, or do I need to pull out the Wisteria Windchimes?" Professor Tenella asked.

The crowd quieted, but Coral whispered, "No, but I could really go for some of Professor Sage's calming pies right now."

"I'm sure you all have many questions, but I do not have many answers. I am here to introduce our temporary new director."

The crowd went completely silent then, and I wondered which of our instructors had been tapped for the job.

When a white man with wavy brown hair and a trim beard entered the room, I frowned. I had never seen him before. But from the surrounding murmurs, I could tell a few students recognized him.

"Scholars, this is Frederick Feathergrass. He is a grasses founders' descendant and the longest-serving member of the Board of Regents for Evergreen Academy. Please give him a warm welcome." She clapped, and there was an unenthusiastic response of gentle hand claps in return.

"Thank you, Professor Tenella," Frederick Feathergrass said. "It's an honor to be serving in this position for the remainder of the year. The board hopes that, under my leadership, Evergreen

Academy will thrive like never before, and each of you will realize your fullest potential as you embark into the society of magical botanists. I will be conducting personal interviews with a random sample of students to get your opinions on your experiences at school, and I would appreciate your honest feedback. Now, I'm sure you all have much to do to prepare for the start of the semester. Enjoy your evening, and I look forward to meeting you all in the coming weeks."

Feathergrass waved a hand, and the ornamental grasses around the room and outside the patio swayed, as if doing a celebration dance.

"What the spores?" Coral said as the crowd began to disperse. "What happened to Professor East? And why did they bring in someone who isn't even a teacher to run the academy?"

"I think I know what happened to Professor East," I whispered, my stomach still twisting with guilt. There was no way I could eat at the moment, not even Professor Sage's food.

"You do?" Aurielle asked.

"Not here," I whispered. "There's somewhere we can talk privately tonight. I just need to find Callan to let us in."

All three friends looked at me strangely, but Yasmin wore a knowing expression. My roommate had sensed I had been hiding some things recently, and I felt guilty about that.

It was finally time to tell my friends everything. With any luck, the Root and Vine Society coalition was about to grow by three.

Chapter Eleven

After night had fallen and most of the academy students were tucked away in their rooms, Callan led me and my friends to a discreet place along the wall at the top of the stairs. Upon my request, he was taking us to the secret attic room he had shown me just a week before. It was an old hideaway of the tree founders, and Callan had shown me the room after our unexpected visit from his brother, when we had needed somewhere private to talk.

We confirmed no one was around, then Callan touched his peridot gemstone to the recess below the wall lantern. The hidden door swung inward—to gasps from Yasmin, Aurielle, and Coral—then Callan led us up the narrow staircase. Hollis and Meadow both sat in the room, casually snacking on roasted chestnuts that filled a beautiful acacia wood bowl.

"Is this the new meeting spot?" Meadow asked, eyeing my friends. "I figured it was only a matter of time before she read you three in."

"Meeting spot for... what exactly?" Yasmin asked, clearly mystified about everything that was happening.

"We've decided to fill them in. On everything," Callan said pointedly. "We need allies, and these three will have Briar's back."

Hollis shrugged. "They're all ferns. They get my vote."

Next to me, Coral raised her eyebrows, but she didn't have a chance to respond before Callan said, "Glad you're both on board. We'll introduce them to the rest of the group as the opportunity presents itself. With Feathergrass here, we're going to have to tread more carefully."

"That name," Hollis said with a snort. "Won't be forgetting which affinity he has anytime soon."

Coral stifled a laugh, and Hollis shot her a rueful smile.

"He and my mom are old friends," Callan said. "He owns more plant-related patents than any person alive. His involvement here means the changes the board wants to make are about to accelerate."

"Which means our countermeasures are going to have to accelerate," Meadow said.

"Countermeasures? I'm sorry. Can someone fill us in?" Aurielle asked.

So I did. I told my friends about the Root and Vine Society, about the quill and our mission to the tree conservatory to retrieve it, about where the quill had pointed, and about my plans to visit the aquatics conservatory. Finally, I told them about how Professor East had covered for Callan and me with the DBI. He was the reason we weren't in trouble for stealing the quill. The only thing I left out was Alex. That secret was between Callan, me, and Professor East, at least for the moment.

"Spores and rhizomes, B. You've been busy this year," Coral said then took a handful of nuts and popped them into her mouth one by one, as if the saltiness would calm her down.

"This actually explains a lot," Yasmin said slowly. "So, how can we help?"

"You already have, in some ways," I replied. "Especially you, Aurielle. Your cartography club found us two new petal portals.

Those could be useful if we ever need to get on or off campus without detection. Do you think you could continue to search to see if there are any more?" The petal portals allowed us to cross over the wall at designated areas of the invisible verdant shield if we were wearing a Shasta lily pendant.

"Of course." Aurielle's words came without hesitation. "We'll prioritize mapping along the wall. I haven't heard whether our club was approved to continue by the board yet, but we'll press forward either way."

I smiled and nodded, unsurprised that my friends were willing to help us so readily.

"So, Professor East is really gone. Do we think it's permanent?" Meadow asked.

"I hope not," Yasmin said. "Do we think he's still teaching at SCC this spring?"

"Good question. We'll have to check once classes start. I'd really like to talk to him." *And apologize.*

"Do you think they fired him? Did he go voluntarily? I have so many questions," Aurielle said. She was repeatedly tucking her blond curls behind her ears, a nervous habit I had noticed when she was working on a particularly tough botany problem.

I turned to Callan. "You said Feathergrass is friends with your mom. They're both on the Board of Regents. Do you think the board voted him out?"

"Those two have always had an outsize influence on the board. If there was a vote, I'm sure they swayed it," Callan said, his voice sour.

"Professor East will be reinstated eventually, right?" Aurielle asked.

"Not without the status quo changing," Hollis answered.

"It's all the more reason we need to get our hands on the *Vanished Compendium*. Whoever has it has power," Meadow said.

Yasmin, Coral, and Aurielle looked like they were all still

processing the idea that the long-lost book actually existed and that we had a quill compass leading us toward it.

"In the meantime, I have something I need a few of us to do tonight," Callan said, switching gears.

"What's that?" I asked.

"The scouting vine seedlings I've been keeping have grown enough to be of use. I think we should plant some in Feathergrass's office. Now that we're one step ahead when it comes to the book, I'd like to make sure it stays that way."

All eyes whipped to Callan.

"You have scouting vines?" Coral asked, clearly shocked. "Those need congressional approval. I thought they were only used at certain conservatories."

"These aren't sanctioned," Hollis said, smirking at her.

Coral pursed her lips, but there was a little twist of mirth in them.

"Count me in. You know I already have experience sneaking into that office," Meadow said.

"Good, because I'm going to need your moss skills," Callan replied.

We all bent our heads together and got to work.

Chapter Twelve

"Hollis, your ferns are shielding us, right?" Meadow asked.

She, Hollis, Callan, and I were pressed against the exterior wall of the academy. Even though it was dark, the ferns would provide an extra layer of protection in case someone approached with a lantern.

"Yes, ma'am," Hollis said.

I held the nursery pots of scouting vines, and Meadow attached a piece of moss to them. With a few murmured Floracantus from the moss founders' descendant, the spongy substance crept onto the scouting vines and wrapped itself around them. Meadow then moved her concentration to the glass wall of the academy, and the moss—carrying the scouting vines—began to slide up the surface.

"Let me know when you reach the windowsill," Callan said.

Meadow nodded, her eyes never leaving the creeping moss. Finally, she said, "Okay, I'm there. Your turn."

Callan raised his hands, and I knew that up above, on the second level, wind was powerfully and deliberately shoving Feathergrass's office window open.

Inside the building, Yasmin, Coral, and Aurielle were making sure Feathergrass was busy observing the late-night studying happening in the teahouse. We had a signal worked out in case he left, but we all hoped we wouldn't need it.

"Window's open," Callan said.

Meadow murmured something again, and I assumed the moss was creeping in to find a discreet place in the office, as discussed. Unless Feathergrass had done a complete overhaul of the room in the few days since Professor East had departed, there would be plenty of potted plants and hanging vines to settle in with.

"There," Meadow said, her posture relaxing. "They're mixed in with the variegated pothos. I don't think he'll notice, unless he has a scouting vine capability we don't know about."

Callan shook his head. "I asked around. He doesn't have any trailing affinity for trees, harvesters, or florals, the affinities that can operate scouting plants."

"Are we all set, then?" Hollis asked.

I had nearly forgotten he was behind us, making a curtain with fern fronds.

"Yes," Callan said. "I've got the sisters to those plants in the hidden tree founders' attic. We'll check in periodically to see if there's anything to report."

"Go, team," Meadow said dryly before turning on her booted foot and heading back for the academy.

Hollis dropped the fern fronds, gave us a little salute, and followed her.

"Okay. I think everything's in place for our trip to the aquatics conservatory this weekend. We just need to work on the getaway plan for the two of us," Callan said.

"About that..." I switched my weight on my feet. I had been thinking about it all day but had been avoiding it. Since we were finalizing plans, it was time to get it over with. "I don't think you should come."

Callan froze. "What do you mean?"

"Think about it. With Feathergrass here and what you said about his being an old friend of your mom's, surely they're in communication. She's probably told him we're friends and to keep an eye on us. If we both suddenly find excuses to be out of school for a week, it's going to raise some red flags."

Callan shook his head. "I'm not leaving you to go alone across the country to a location we're not even sure of yet. Especially when you don't have access to your powers at the conservatory."

I pursed my lips. The lack of access to my powers on campus and in the conservatories was continuing to be a problem. We'd worked on a solution in my field studies assignment the previous term, but we hadn't been successful in countering the poisoning of my powers yet. I wondered when I would hear from my field studies advisor, Petra.

With a shake of my head, I refocused. "I won't be alone. Nalin is coming with me, and Nevah will escort us once we get there. I'll be fine."

Callan was silent, and I knew he was finding it difficult to counter my point about us both leaving campus at the same time. Seconds passed until he finally said, "Are you sure about this?"

I nodded. "Both of us being absent would draw too much attention. You know it would."

Callan nodded, resigned. "Fine. But I'll be asking Nevah and Kai to keep an eye on you."

"Kai?" I asked.

"You'll meet him when you get there. Promise to stick with them?"

"Deal," I said quickly.

"To be clear, I'm not happy about this," Callan said, rubbing the toe of his boot against the soil.

"I'm not, either, but this is our one shot, remember? We don't want anyone chasing at our heels. Maybe you can keep Feathergrass so busy here he'll hardly notice I'm gone."

I caught a ghost of a smile on Callan's lips under the glow of starlight. "Oh, I'll keep him busy, all right. He may soon come to regret taking Professor East's position."

I smiled. There was the Callan I knew—always willing to fight for others, even if it involved a few underhanded tactics fit for a member of the Root and Vine Society.

Chapter Thirteen

"I wonder how these weather conditions are going to affect my field studies," Aurielle said as the four of us sat down in the teahouse for dinner two days later. "The whole northern half of the state has been having an abnormally wet winter."

I swirled the spoon in my bowl, trying not to let my eyes wander to Feathergrass. Unlike Professor East, who had a relaxed mentoring style of leadership, Feathergrass was proving to be a micromanager. It was only the first week of the new term, and already, he was traipsing from class to class, assessing the curriculum.

"When will your field study start back up, B? Didn't you say your mentor went to Italy for winter break?" Yasmin asked, redrawing my attention.

"That's a good question," I said. Petra hadn't given me a firm date on when she would return from Italy. With the replacement of Professor East, I was more eager than ever to regain access to my powers. The sooner my studies with her resumed, the better.

"Probably classified, like the rest of your assignment," Yasmin said playfully.

"Speaking of field study assignments," Coral said, "I got word that my project is going to be expanding. We're joining forces with another group and broadening our focus."

"Does that mean the location will change?" I asked.

"Not sure. But it will be nice to absorb another person. My advisor is an excellent scientist, but they're not the best conversationalist to be stuck in the woods with all day."

"Do you know who is joining you yet?" Yasmin asked.

"I should find out tomorrow," Coral said brightly.

"So, B, is everything in order for... you know?" Aurielle raised her eyebrows.

It was a huge weight off my shoulders to bring my friends into the loop on the Root and Vine Society's work, but they weren't as used to keeping things quiet as I was.

I lowered my voice to barely above a mumbled breath. "Callan reached out to Nevah yesterday. She's working on a formal invite for Nalin to do some research next week. I'll be a bit of a stowaway." I had planned to go under the premise of research as well, but since Feathergrass was here and the board was keeping such a close eye on the school—and me in particular—it would be suspicious for me to go there openly.

If anyone was tracking my movements, then leading them right to the aquatics conservatory, where we thought the *Vanished Compendium* was stored, would be a disastrous outcome.

"How are you going to manage that?" Aurielle asked.

"I'm going to poison myself."

Coral laughed then frowned when she saw the look on my face. "Wait. You're not serious, are you?"

I nodded. Callan and I had concocted the plan the previous day. "I need to be legitimately sick to call out of classes for a few days. Which means we need something Professor Sage can't easily cure."

"But, B, how can you go on the mission if you're in a sickbed?" Yasmin asked, her face full of concern.

"Once I get off campus, I'll have access to my defensive powers and can dispel the poison." No one knew how far my powers had advanced in that affinity because of my classified field studies assignment, and I was banking on Feathergrass assuming my defensive skills were still quite weak. "We'll make it seem like I'm going to my aunt's house to recover, then I'll meet up with Nalin and travel to... you-know-where." I still didn't want to say the words *Florida* or *aquatics conservatory* out loud, just in case. Callan's regular sweeps for scouting vines were still in place, but perhaps Feathergrass had some botanical magic up his sleeve that none of us knew about.

"I don't know, B. That seems unnecessarily risky," Yasmin said, worrying her lip.

"I'll be fine. I've built up a bit of a tolerance in my field studies." I didn't say more, and my friends nodded tightly.

"Ahoy, fellow ferns."

A deep voice caught all our attention, and we looked up to see Hollis appearing behind Coral, who barely hid her scowl.

"Looks like you and I are about to be partners," Hollis said, settling his gaze on Coral.

"*You?*" she asked, the shock evident on her face. "You're my new field studies partner?"

"You seem thrilled," Hollis said, a touch of amusement oozing through his confident tone.

"You'd better be ready to go by eight sharp. And no antics when we're traveling. Or when we're researching. Just no antics generally. Got it?"

Hollis put up his hands. "I'll be on my best behavior. Any other requests?"

Coral scowled. "Pack your own equipment. I won't be carrying supplies for both of us."

Hollis saluted. "Yes, ma'am." Then he winked at the rest of us and walked away.

Coral's shoulders slumped forward. "So much for promising.

Could my luck be any worse? I doubt founders' descendants have ever had to carry their own packs."

I let out a soft laugh. "He's not as bad as you think, Coral. Give him a chance. And Callan always carries his weight on projects."

"Rhodes and Hollis cannot be compared. One has proven himself, and the other... Well, you all had better be prepared for lots of complaining when I get back."

"Sorry, Coral," Yasmin said sympathetically. "I'll brew you a tea for good temper tomorrow to help you put up with him." She turned to me. "And apparently, we're going to brew *you* some poison."

Chapter Fourteen

"Are you ready?" Aurielle asked.

We stood in the Perilous Grove, and I held a concoction Callan had brewed for us. Defensives weren't his specialty, but with a trailing affinity for them, he was able to pull off a basic poisonous-but-not-deadly recipe.

"I doused it with honey," Yasmin said. "So hopefully it won't taste too bad going down."

"I'm surprised Rhodes didn't insist on being here to keep an eye on you," Coral quipped.

Callan wasn't standing in the Perilous Grove with us, but I knew he wished he could be.

"My sudden ailment is less likely to raise suspicion if one of the few people on campus who could have created an oral poison has been seen in the teahouse all morning. Okay, let's get this over with."

I uncorked the vial Callan had provided and tried to imagine I was with Petra in one of our field studies sessions in the cabin on Mt. Shasta. While my own defensive powers wouldn't be able to kick in against the poison on campus, I hoped perhaps I had built up some nonmagical tolerances.

With a shaky smile to my friends, I swallowed the entire contents in one gulp. The effect was instantaneous. I clutched my chest as a sharp pain pooled there, and nausea filled my stomach.

"Safe to say it worked," Coral murmured before I felt arms slipping under my shoulders. Just as we had planned, my friends were going to assist me back to campus.

"Don't forget the second vial!" I heard Aurielle's voice—it sounded too distant—then felt something cool against my lips. "Drink this, B."

Right. Callan had made something that would help with the brain fog effects while allowing me to maintain the physical symptoms that we needed for a convincing ploy. Since it was his own creation, the instructors should have no reason to suspect its use.

I struggled to swallow the cool liquid and, once it hit my stomach, my brain began to clear, and my friend's voices came into focus once more.

"We should have brought a wheelbarrow or something," Coral said.

"Because *that* wouldn't raise any suspicions," Aurielle quipped back. "No one brings a wheelbarrow to the Perilous Grove."

"Just a little bit farther, B," Yasmin said, her soothing voice coming from my left. "Did the second drink help?"

I nodded but didn't speak. The pain in my stomach was drawing most of my focus.

"I'll run ahead and alert Professor Sage," Aurielle said. "You two got her?" Footsteps crunched in the distance as she ran off.

Finally, we made it back to the school building, and my friends rushed me into the apothecary room.

"What happened?" Professor Sage's wheelchair rolled into the room.

I caught a glimmer of wings and realized the butterfly that sometimes followed him around was present. I focused my sight on it, trying not to think about the pain.

Yasmin spoke up quickly, reciting the planned story. "She was collecting castor beans for a batch of eyelash serum, plus a few other things, in the Perilous Grove. She must have mixed the castor bean concoction with another substance, then something must have gone wrong, because she dropped to her knees and started moaning and clutching her stomach."

"Did she ingest something out there? That doesn't seem like a mistake Briar would make," Professor Sage asked, examining my skin.

"I don't know. It all happened so fast," Coral replied, and I was impressed by the very real-sounding note of concern in her voice.

"Go see if any of you can find Callan Rhodes. I think I saw him in the teahouse a little while ago. Ask him to run out to the Grove and see if he can figure out what she might have gotten into. Without Professor East, he's our only botanist with a trailing defensive affinity."

I heard the shuffling of feet as my friends left the room. Professor Sage approached me and brought a strongly scented cloth near my face. "This should help take the edge off, Briar. I'll see you when you wake up."

I caught one last glimpse of the butterfly's delicate wings before everything went dark.

Chapter Fifteen

"How is she?"

"She's tough, but it's going to take a few days for her to recover. Maybe as long as a week. Her friends think she'd like to convalesce at her aunt's home in town," Professor Sage said.

"Don't you think we should monitor her here? She's a valuable asset to the school," Feathergrass said.

I tried not to roll my eyes as I came out of my stupor. Of course that was what Feathergrass cared about, not the well-being of one of his students who had just been poisoned.

"She may be more relaxed in a comfortable environment, away from all the commotion of the school," Professor Sage insisted gently.

"Very well. I hope she can be back in classes next week."

"I think that's likely."

Professor Sage's wheelchair hummed as it rolled across the stone floor, and a second later, he was by my side. "Ah, you're awake. How is your stomach?"

"It doesn't feel like I'm being stabbed anymore, but it does feel like I have a horrible stomach flu." I searched the room for a trash can in case my illness went in that direction.

"Do you know what you got into? Your friends mentioned you were collecting castor beans."

"I was, but it's all kind of a blur. I must have mixed some things I shouldn't have. I can't believe how careless I was."

"These things happen, but you should know to always take extra care in the Perilous Grove. Your friends thought you might want to spend the week convalescing at home. Is that the case?"

When I nodded, he said, "I'll pack you a bag of medicines to make you comfortable and some food that should help you get back to full health as soon as you're ready for it."

"Thanks, Professor Sage. I appreciate all your help."

He nodded. "Just get better and take care of yourself. We want you back in classes soon. Take your time getting up. Callan Rhodes was here earlier. He's trying to track down what caused your illness out in the Grove. He offered to drive you to your aunt's home and quiz you further."

I tried to force a look of puzzlement onto my face. "Okay. I guess that's fine."

About five minutes after Professor Sage left the room, Callan slipped inside. More quickly than I could register, he was at my side, pressing a hand to my forehead. "You're warm. And clammy." He cursed in the cute way only magical botanists could. "I really wish we could have thought of another plan."

"Just take me away, Dr. Rhodes."

I said it jokingly, but Callan nodded and lifted me into his arms.

"Oh no. We don't need everyone seeing me getting carried out like this. Maybe I can—" I tried putting weight on my feet but immediately saw black spots.

Callan's arms were back underneath me in an instant. "Not when you're about to faint. Don't worry. Our friends made sure the central vein was clear. Hollis is doing a striptease in the teahouse."

Despite my fevered state, I choked out a laugh. "*What?*"

"He covered his chest and arms with ferns and is magically removing them one by one. Apparently, some people like to see his abs. Your friend Coral was in the front row."

I snorted. "All right, then. Sneak me out of here so Hollis can maintain his dignity and put his shirt back on."

"With pleasure." Callan pushed out of the apothecary room where I'd been recovering and—faster than I could have imagined—we were outside, darkness falling over us.

Callan settled me in the front seat of his truck so delicately that I might have been a newborn. I couldn't melt over the attention too long, though. The fever was making it hard to focus on much of anything.

"Let's get you off campus," Callan said, shifting the truck into drive. Once we were through the gate, he pulled to a stop. "Okay, Briar. You have access to your powers again. Can you try to counteract some of the poison?"

I pushed myself to sit up straighter and let out a soft moan.

"Here, take this. I think you're ready for a second dose of the brain fog reducer." He held out a glass vial, and his face was so distressed that I took it and swallowed it in full, even though the idea of drinking anything sent my stomach turning.

As soon as his concoction kicked in, the fever reduced slightly, and I took a deep, calming breath and imagined I was at the cabin on Mt. Shasta with Petra, developing counterpoisons and working on unlocking my powers. I searched through my body for the source of the poison and wrapped my powers around it. As I sliced through it, I let out a gasp, feeling its powers snap.

I sagged against the truck seat, devoid of energy.

"Briar." Callan's warm voice was reassuring. "Did it work? How do you feel?"

I nodded. "I think so. I don't feel the effects of the poison anymore. I just feel... tired."

"Here." He was opening the bag from Professor Sage. "These are going to have extremely high levels of nourishment. Get some of that in you and see how you feel."

I followed his instructions, remembering that in less than an hour, I had a flight to catch.

I ate while we drove, and twenty minutes later, we were nearing the Weed airport, with me checking my backpack for the tenth time, ensuring that the quill compass was safely within it.

"Professor Sage is a miracle worker," I said. The food had perked me up within minutes. While I still wasn't at full strength, I didn't feel like I had been poisoned in the past hour either. "And so are you. That brain fog reducer worked like a charm."

Callan reached over and ran the back of his hand from my forehead down the side of my face. "Fever's gone. Your color's back. Everything looks good."

"Are you calling me pretty?" I teased.

A smile twitched at the corner of his mouth. "Always."

Warmth kindled in my stomach. "I wish you could come with me."

Callan took my hand and squeezed it. "Say the word, and I will."

I shook my head reluctantly. "I still think this is the safest plan."

We kept our hands entwined as Callan took the exit to the tiny, one-runway airport, savoring our last bit of time together. We had sworn off kissing and publicly dating for the time being, but neither of us could resist each other's hands when no one else was around.

When we arrived at the airport, Nalin was already waiting.

I recalled my first nervous flight in the four-seater plane to the moss and tree conservatories. "Nalin's a qualified pilot, right?"

"I wouldn't be sending you with him if he wasn't. We've

trained together a bunch over the years. He is a top-tier pilot. And I came out and checked the plane this morning. Everything is good to go."

Callan's reassurance calmed my nerves—mostly. "Make some good trouble while we're gone?" I asked.

Callan's lips pulled up at one corner. "You know we will. If Feathergrass is busy with us, he won't think to check up on how you're convalescing. One last thing." Callan reached into his pocket and removed a large leaf that was rolled and tied with a piece of twine.

"What's that?"

"It's from a fiddle-leaf fig. I've enchanted it for communication."

I stared at the leaf. "Don't tell me the leaf is going to start talking to me."

Callan laughed. "I'm not aware of any Floracantus that can make a leaf do that. We can write messages to each other on it, though. Whatever I scrawl onto the matching leaf on my end will appear on your leaf and vice versa. Cell service is nonexistent at the aquatics conservatory, so we can use this to keep in touch."

"That's brilliant," I said, nestling the leaf into my bag. "I'll see you in a week."

He took my hand and ran circles around the back of it with his thumb. The tender movement conveyed more than any words could. "Have fun being a tourist. And remember..." He leaned in closer. "I'm just a leaf message away."

Chapter Sixteen

I woke to a gentle tap on my arm and salt air in my nose.

"We're here, B," Nalin said once I pried my eyes open.

"Already?" I sat up straighter, looking out the window and confirming that we were nearing a runway. "I slept the whole time?"

"Beauty sleep comes easily when Nalin's at the wheel." He flashed me a grin, and I smiled while shaking my head. "We lost three hours due to the time change, so it's nearly eight o'clock. We're landing a little early, but Nevah should meet us soon."

Nalin gently landed the plane—Callan had been right that he was a great pilot—and I peered through the windows. As when I had visited the moss and tree conservatories with Callan, we appeared to be at a private airport for magical botanists. Though it was nearly dark, glowing moonflowers and some unusually candescent tropical palm species lined the runway.

The moisture on my skin and the way my wavy hair was curling made reality sink in—I was in Florida... the other side of the country... for the first time ever. And I was there to find a book that had been missing for longer than I had been alive.

"I'll check the quill."

After removing it from my backpack, I said the Floracantus to activate the locating feature in the quill, and Nalin and I both watched as it began to spin. It barely rotated before it came to a stop, pointing east.

I let out a deep breath. "According to this, we're within twenty miles of the book."

"The aquatics entrance base is about a ten-mile drive, plus the distance to get to the conservatory itself. I think we're on the right track," Nalin said.

I nodded. Suddenly, it felt like everything I had been doing over the past nearly two years had been leading up to whatever came next. Getting invited to Evergreen Academy had changed my life, and I had a chance to help save the place that meant so much to me.

We both looked up at the shout of a familiar voice to see a figure jogging toward us.

"B!"

"Nevah!"

We hugged, and I was thrilled to see my old mentor. I hadn't realized how much I had missed her until that moment.

"Callan called with your ETA," she said.

My chest squeezed. Of course, while I had been sleeping on the plane, Callan had somehow been tracking our flight and updating Nevah.

Nevah released me and gave Nalin a welcome hug. "Great to see you. How's the academy treating you? Dr. Lemna coming down hard on all the aquatics, as usual?"

Nalin laughed. "You know it. How about you? How is the conservatory?" Nalin and I picked up our bags, and we headed toward where a white SUV was parked near the runway, its headlights illuminating the road ahead.

"It's been great so far. I'll fill you in more when we're there. You've been out here before, right, Nalin?" Nevah opened the liftgate, and we put our bags inside.

"Yeah. It's been a few years, though."

After we all climbed in, Nevah turned to smile at me as she started the car. "And it's B's first visit, of course. I've already reserved rooms for you near mine. So, tell me everything. What's new at the school?"

I filled her in on Professor East's departure and the changes at the academy as we drove on a road that was surrounded on both sides by fields of grass partially submerged in water. I could see why it was a perfect location for the aquatics conservatory. Nearly every plant around must be able to thrive in large amounts of water, making them ideal research subjects.

Soon, Nevah parked in front of a marine research facility, which advertised water excursions that benefitted local conservation efforts.

"This is it? It's just out here in the open?" I asked, surprised at how obvious it was compared to the moss and tree conservatories.

Nevah smiled and shook her head. "Not exactly. Grab your bags."

We followed her around the back of the building, and she entered a nondescript door marked Staff. She buzzed us through a security entrance with a wristband.

"We'll drop the bags here. Put your phones and anything else valuable in there." She paused at a glass window and slid it open, then typed a few numbers onto the screen, set our bags on the platform, closed the glass window, and pressed a button.

I startled as our bags disappeared into a chute below the window.

Nevah continued down the hall then exited the back door. Outside, we walked down a path along a swampy shore.

"Should I be concerned about alligators around here?" I asked, squinting at the dark water and keeping my feet clear of it.

"Nope. We planted an engineered species of seagrasses they don't like. Evergreen Academy's new director actually had a hand in its creation," Nevah said, continuing to guide us near the water's edge.

"Feathergrass?" I asked.

"Yep. I believe he patented the gene he edited."

"For a second there, I thought we had discovered his one redeeming feature," Nalin said.

"Why would he patent it? Don't all magical botanists have access to it?" I asked.

"For now," Nevah replied. "But eventually, when the human scientific market begins to catch up, he will release it there. Everyone in Florida will use it for natural gator defense on their property. He'll be rich."

"If he isn't already," Nalin quipped.

"True. Okay, this is where we get in," Nevah stopped by the edge of the water.

"In?" I looked around, confused. The only building nearby was the one we had just left, and we were well over a hundred feet away. There were no boats in sight either.

"The water, B." Nevah smiled and elbowed me. "Didn't forget how to swim, did you?"

"We're swimming?" I asked, dropping my gaze to the water, which was nearly black except for the reflections of moonlight bouncing across its surface.

"It's the aquatics conservatory. How else did you think we would get there?"

Chapter Seventeen

I breathed underwater and kicked my legs with ease, feeling as if I had a snorkeling mask and fins on. Even though I was wearing clothes, the water slid right over me, and I sliced effortlessly through it. Swimming with an aquatic affinity was always a life-changing experience, yet my few swims in rivers and lakes couldn't compare. We were in the *ocean*.

Nevah led us through a tunnel made of the woody prop roots of the mangrove trees that sank into the soil beneath us. I gracefully moved my arms through the salty water to keep up with her.

After a few moments, she paused and pointed to her right. When I followed her finger, I saw a school of gray-and-yellow fish flitting around a tree's widespread roots.

Nevah continued to point out plant and animal life as we swam for about half a mile in the dark, shallow water, Nalin occasionally darting off to swim with the fish, then she turned and touched my arm. She pointed ahead, and I saw the mangrove root tunnel was narrowing and angling down.

I took it as a sign to stay with her then followed her into the tighter space. We swam for only thirty seconds before Nevah veered upward, me right on her heels.

A tightening sensation came over me, and I could feel access to my powers cut off, instantly dissolving the connection to the aquatic plants I had been experiencing. Just like at Evergreen Academy and the tree and moss conservatories, I wouldn't be able to use my magic there thanks to the founders' curse. I refocused on Nevah, and moments later, we popped our heads out of a shallow pool.

I gasped at the sudden influx of air then pushed my hair out of my face, taking in the sight around me. "By the ferns," I murmured.

"No fern affinity expressions here, B. Welcome to the aquatics conservatory."

She helped me out of the pool of water, and Nalin emerged a few moments later, a grin splashed across his face. We were in a large glass dome, the ocean on the other side of it.

"We're underwater?" I was so surprised that my eyes must have been nearly as large as the dome. We had been swimming, but I imagined we would emerge on a barrier island. Instead, we were on the ocean floor, the sea a pool of life above us.

"Yep. The whole conservatory is down here, except for a few research outposts."

"And this is where you *live*?"

Nevah smiled. "Pretty swell, right?"

"How come all the water isn't rushing in through the entrance pool we just came in?"

"There's a special valve, made by magically enhanced plants and the mangrove roots, back there where it narrows. I tried to point it out but obviously couldn't explain it. Once you pass through there, the water is secured, and the quantity doesn't shift through the passage."

"How does our luggage get in?" I asked, remembering where we had dropped off our items into the strange chute.

"An air tunnel runs near the path we swam in. Anything that

needs to stay dry is sent in through there on a conveyor system along the sea shelf. Let's go see if they're here yet."

We collected our bags from a window identical to the one in the building where we'd dropped them off, then Nevah led us down a narrow hallway. It felt like being in a large submarine but with an aquarium viewing window above. She tapped on a door to the left, which had a water lily painted in the center. "That's my room. You'll be a few down in a guest pod."

We continued along the hallway until Nevah stopped and opened a different door, which had a seashell painted on the front.

I inhaled sharply as I stepped inside. The entire opposite wall was made of glass and had a view of a splendid coral reef. It was like a rare underwater hotel from a travel magazine. "I get to sleep here?" I asked, disbelieving.

I continued to stare through the wall, where seagrass lined the floor against the glass, and fish darted in every direction.

"When I first got here, I don't think I slept for a week. There are special lights you can turn on that don't affect the sea life but allow you to see outside at night. I couldn't stop staring."

"I wish I had my paint supplies," I said, suddenly itching for a brush or at least my sketchpad.

"I think there are some art supplies around here." Nevah dropped my bag onto a chair. "Look around and get settled. I'll take Nalin to his room. It's just three down from yours."

After sliding my backpack off my shoulders, I stood there for a few moments, marveling at the ocean.

Before long, a soft knock at the door interrupted my awe. Nevah pushed it open. "Are you hungry?"

As if on cue, my stomach growled. Even though it was well after dark in Florida, back home, it was dinnertime. I followed her and Nalin through the hallway again, bringing my backpack—and the quill—with me.

Our route returned us to the central room we had swum into then to a large commercial kitchen area. Nevah pulled a few glass containers from a fridge and got them heating in the microwave.

"Please tell me there's saltwater taffy in here," Nalin said, peeking into the cupboards.

"Plenty. And there are some seaweed crisps on that shelf there." Nevah pointed.

Once she had given us each a warmed snack pack of fish, rice, and cooked seaweed, we settled onto beanbag chairs in a private corner of the lounge area. Each of the plush seats was shaped like an open shell. The ocean overhead was slightly lit so that we could see the marine life flitting above us. Those must be the special lights Nevah had mentioned.

A kettle whistled from the kitchen, and Nevah fetched it then returned with a tray of glass jars filled to the top with loose-leaf teas and honeys. "Even underwater, magical botanists must have their tea," she said as she set the tray on the table in front of us.

A man about our age came over and kissed Nevah on the cheek. He was of Pacific Islander descent, and he squished himself into the clamshell chair Nevah was occupying.

"Briar, Nalin, this is Kai. Kai, meet my friends."

"Hey, Nalin. Always nice to meet a fellow aquatic." He turned to me. "I've heard a lot about you, Briar. Sorry our time at Evergreen Academy never overlapped."

"Same. Nice to meet you," I said, noticing he had the muscled arms of a strong swimmer.

"So, Nalin, you didn't go into much detail about why you wanted to be placed in a study here for the week or why you"—Nevah nodded toward me—"were tagging along."

I sat up straighter and rested my chopsticks against the side of the bowl then did a quick scan of the area. Aquatics didn't have access to scouting vine magic, but looking for them before sharing anything private was ingrained in me.

Nevah noticed the movement. "Don't worry. There is no one to overhear us."

I nodded but leaned in closer and lowered my voice. "Are you familiar with the *Vanished Compendium*?"

Nevah's eyes widened, and she nodded. "The fabled missing book of Floracantus."

"We think it's here. Or near here," I said. Then I filled them in on everything the Root and Vine Society had been up to the past few months, including our trip to the tree conservatory to acquire the quill.

"When we checked the quill at the airstrip, it said we were less than twenty miles from it," Nalin finished.

Nevah sat forward, her eyes shining. "Have you tried it since we got in here?"

I shook my head and tapped the small backpack by my feet. When they all nodded, I opened it and pulled out the quill, keeping it low and out of sight on the small table between us, even though the area was free of people for the night.

The quill spun ever so slightly, pointing north. The magical distance key on the quill changed to indicate that we were within two miles of the book.

Nevah frowned. "Two miles. That wouldn't be down here, then. Some of our barrier island research centers are within that range, but none of them are north of here." She glanced at Kai.

"So, it's not in the aquatics conservatory," Nalin mused. "But it's close to it. That's strange. Do you think someone buried it nearby and thought that would be safer than hiding it within the conservatory, where it might be found?"

Buried. I hadn't considered that possibility.

Kai gazed at the quill and the direction it was pointing. "I go out that way sometimes for research. There's not much out there, but we can look. We'll go first thing in the morning."

Nevah leaned forward. "With everything you told me about what's going on at the academy, it's time I filled you in on what's been going on here."

Nalin straightened, and we both fixed our focus on Nevah.

"Most members of the Magical Botanical Board of Regents also have appointments on the seats overseeing the conservatories. Here at the aquatics conservatory, we've been having more frequent visits from Primrose Marsh, the aquatics representative on the board."

"What kind of visits?" Nalin asked.

"Checking in on who we are sharing our research findings with. Wanting to know what patents we have pending. Ensuring that 'top talent'"—she made air quotes—"is recruited to work here. Kai has been under a lot of pressure." She glanced at him, her expression gentle. "He's not from a prominent family, but he has a rare gift. He's constantly being tasked with missions when he would rather focus on research."

"Rare gift?" Nalin asked then let out a soft gasp. "Can you waterbend? We heard rumors that there was someone at the academy who could do it a few years ago."

Kai nodded, Nalin looked giddy, and Nevah hurried to add, "Don't say anything back at the academy, though, okay? Very few people know the extent of his skill."

"Does waterbend mean what it sounds like?" I asked.

Nevah made a loop with her finger, and a trail of water jumped from her glass to Kai's hand, where he caught it with ease. "Most aquatics have some basic adhesion with water. But people who can waterbend can move much larger quantities of water at a time. I don't know anyone else alive who can do what Kai can do."

Nalin looked perplexed, and he stared at Kai. "Can I interview you?"

I stifled a laugh, but Kai just shrugged. "Happy to share what I can."

"Callan can sense powers, and Kai can waterbend. What other rare abilities are out there?" I asked.

"There are a few more, all incredibly infrequent in the population. They all seem to have something to do with the natural elements, which is why Callan's power sensing is an outlier," Nevah said.

Kai's eyebrows pulled together. "Is it an outlier, though? Do you know how his ability works?"

"What do you mean?" Nevah asked.

"Callan has a strong wind manipulating power, doesn't he? Stronger than most of the tree affinities? What if his power sensing ability is an extension of that?"

"How would that work?" I asked. "The wind is carrying the trace of power to him?"

Kai shrugged. "Seems possible. Has he ever explained the sensation?"

"Not really," I said, wishing Callan were with us so we could discuss it together.

"It's not like you haven't had enough mysteries to solve," Nevah said with a smile. "All right, I know you two are on West Coast time, but I'm tired. We rise early in here because the ocean rises early. Let's meet up for breakfast, and we'll get you started with wherever the quill leads, B. Nalin, I'll introduce you to your temporary research group."

He nodded eagerly, obviously looking forward to it, and stuffed a few pieces of taffy into his pocket.

"In that case, I'll see you both in the morning. Enjoy your first night under the ocean, B."

Chapter Eighteen

When I went back to the underwater pod that would serve as my bedroom for the rest of the week, I fully intended on falling asleep watching the coral reef through the wall of glass that was my window. But once I returned to the room, I couldn't stop looking at the quill. According to it, I was less than two miles from the book. Suddenly, I couldn't wait any longer.

After slipping the quill into a dry bag I found in the room, I stepped out of my pod, closing the door softly behind me. When I turned, Nevah was poking her head out of her door.

"I had a feeling you might not be able to wait until morning," she said with a knowing smile.

"Guilty." I tried to shrug casually.

"I'm not going to make you wait, but I'm also not going to let you go without backup from people who know the area. Let's go see if Kai is still awake."

When Kai opened his door, he scratched the side of his neck and glanced at a watch on his wrist. "I take it we're going somewhere?"

"Yes, if you're up for it."

Kai stretched. "I'm always up for a late-night mission. Just a sec." He turned back into his room and reemerged with a kit, including waterproof headlamps for each of us.

We knocked on Nalin's door, and he opened it, looking groggy. But his eyes cleared quickly when he saw us. "Is the mission happening tonight?" When we nodded, he said, "Meet you by the entrance in five."

Once we had all gathered, Nevah said, "We'll swim out then take a boat."

When we got in the water, Nevah and Kai took off like two fish in a race. Nalin and I were left in their literal bubbles, but I couldn't help smiling when I saw the light from their headlamps swimming circles around each other. Without going all the way back to shore, they shot upward, following a rope.

As I approached the surface, the familiar shape of a boat came into view overhead. Once inside, I pulled out the quill.

"Where are we headed?" Kai asked.

I held the quill flat in my palm. "It looks like a little less than two miles, straight north."

Kai angled the boat north, and we sped along the coastline. I wanted to look around at the beauty of the surrounding Everglades, but it was dark, and I was focused on watching for changes to the quill. "The distance meter is changing," I said after a few minutes. "Less than a mile now."

"Still directly north?" Kai asked.

"Swing it a little to the west," Nevah directed.

"Toward the shoreline?"

"Looks like it," I agreed, anticipation kicking up. Maybe the book really was buried along the beach somewhere.

A few minutes later, the boat slowed. Kai cut the engine and pointed straight ahead. "This area leads us deep into a dense patch of water hemlock. We don't go anywhere near that if we can help it."

I envisioned the cicutoxin that made water hemlock one of the most poisonous plants in North America. No wonder the aquatics botanists gave it a wide berth.

"We have some barrier cream for it, but it's back at the conservatory. With my trailing defensive affinity, I might be able to ward it off, but Kai and Nalin would be in for a rough night," Nevah said. "Let me see the quill." She examined it and frowned. "It's pointing directly in there."

"You think someone hid the book in a patch of water hemlock? If so, it's long ruined. This is one of the biggest patches of this stuff on record," Kai said, angling his headlamp toward the mass of green-and-white plants. "Plus, the inland area is oddly low in nitrogen and phosphorus levels. We did a survey of it a while back. Not very conducive to plant life."

Something in his words tugged at me. The quill was pointing directly into a patch of water hemlock, an extremely deadly plant. A *defensive* plant. Immediately, an idea clicked into place.

"I think I need to go in there," I said.

Nevah looked at me curiously but then nodded. "I'll go with you. Kai and Nalin can wait here with the boat."

"I don't like this," Kai said, still staring at the green-and-white snowdrop-like plants flanking the shoreline.

I turned to them, clutching the quill gently between my hands. "I don't think we have any other choice." I swallowed, anticipation and a twinge of nerves simmering at the suspicion that had formed. "I think this might be the entrance to the defensives conservatory."

Chapter Nineteen

"Leave it to you to find the mysterious hidden defensives conservatory when searching for the mysterious long-lost book of Floracantus, B." Nevah swiped at a piece of water hemlock that swished against her thigh.

We were waist-deep in the substance, walking along the damp shoreline. The outlines of Kai and Nalin were barely visible in the boat in the distance as they kept guard in the moonlit night. I couldn't offer an explanation beyond the fact that every instinct in my body was telling me there was something magical about the place. It was as if I were being summoned by the plants, and I couldn't resist their call.

A flash of white the size of my hand flitted in front of my face, and I jumped. I relaxed when I realized it was a moth, its white wings fuzzy. The moth continued to hover about a foot in front of me. I swished my hand at it, but the moth persisted, dodging my skin and seeming to chart a path directly in front of us.

"Are you seeing this?" I asked.

Nevah squinted at it. "Looks like a white satin moth. Their host plant is the yellow oleander. I wonder... No, that seems far-fetched."

"Nothing is too fantastical for this situation, Nevah."

"Do you think it's trying to guide us forward?"

I tilted my head sideways, studying the moth, which was heading inland. When I glanced at the quill, it was pointing exactly in the moth's direction. "Following a moth seems as good a plan as following a quill that's hundreds of years old," I said. "Lead on, Snowy."

"Snowy? You remember we're in south Florida, right?" Nevah teased.

I laughed, and we stepped carefully through the bog as we followed the moth. "Please tell me that magical grass Feathergrass patented is out here too," I said, remembering the existence of alligators once more.

Nevah shook her head. "No, but I'm checking in with the water lilies. We're clear for now."

I had no idea what she meant by that, but it was not the time to ask. The moth was veering hard to the left, and when I checked the quill again, it was too.

We were squarely inland and on mostly dry ground, though I didn't think the soil could ever fully be dry in this part of Florida. Snowy was leading us into an overgrown tunnel. Nevah and I glanced at each other, then she shrugged, and we continued forward.

"A tunnel of stinging nettles, poison ivy, and sumac," Nevah said, examining the plants around us. "Your theory is becoming more and more evidence based."

Without much conscious effort, I reached out to the plants in the tunnel, confirming that they were nearly all defensive plants. The tunnel was tight, and the plants brushed against our skin, but what would have caused red welts and painful scratches on anyone else merely glided over us like reed grass.

The tunnel continued for a few hundred feet, then the moth turned to the right.

"Whoa," I whispered, coming to a halt at the sight in front of me. We had entered a clearing that was lit by glowing moonflowers and surrounded by carnivorous plants. There were Nepenthes larger than my arms and Venus flytraps the size of pumpkins along with bladderworts, sundews, and corkscrew plants. Between them, I saw every kind of carnivorous trapping mechanism: pitfall traps, flypaper traps, snap traps, and bladder traps. Insects wouldn't stand a chance.

With a rush of concern, I searched for the moth. I spotted it hovering near a giant Nepenthes, about to slide into its pitfall trap. "Snowy, no!" I shouted, immediately gathering my power. I connected to the Nepenthes plant and said, "*Pressule.*"

The Nepenthes sealed closed, and the moth was shot away from its deadly trap in a little puff of air.

"Nice save," Nevah said, putting a hand to her chest.

I reached out a finger, and the moth rested there. Did it know how close it was to disappearing inside that plant forever? I wasn't sure if I should feel bad about denying the plant its meal, but in the moment, saving the moth had felt like the only option.

The moth flickered its wings but stayed attached to my finger, then each of the defensive plants seemed to turn toward a corner of the clearing.

Nevah gasped, and I stared in wonder. An arch made of stark-white orchids and midnight-black hellebore knotted around two cypress trees that had become illuminated, as if flicked on with a switch.

No, they weren't just white orchids. They were ghost orchids.

They were a rare species, and many an orchid hunter had attempted an ill-fated excursion into the Florida wilds to capture one.

The contrast between the white of the orchids and the black of the hellebore was striking. The ghost orchids were emitting the illuminating glow, and we stepped closer.

"What do you think?" Nevah asked, noticing, as I had, that

Snowy had not left my finger to guide us further. "Do we go through?"

I looped my arm in hers and nodded. "We go through."

Chapter Twenty

The ghost orchids and black hellebore were as still as sentinels on the cypress trees they adorned. I felt as if all the defensive plants in the area were watching our every move as Nevah and I surveyed the illuminated arch.

Nevah took a tentative step forward but then yelped when her foot seemed to get stuck in midair. "There is some kind of invisible barrier here."

I went to her side and put a hand to the air but felt no resistance. Cautiously, I took a step and passed through to the other side. My powers, which had been active on the whole walk in, instantly faded away. If I hadn't been sure before, I was now. I was in a magical botanical conservatory, and there was only one it could be. I turned back to Nevah. "That's strange. Try again."

Nevah stepped back then forward, but it was as if an unseen wall were keeping her out. "I only have a trailing affinity for defensives. I don't think I'm allowed in."

My heart sank, but I nodded. We should have seen it coming. "Why don't you go back to the boat with Kai and Nalin and tell them everything's okay? They're probably getting worried."

Indecision flashed across Nevah's face. I knew she didn't want to leave me, but waiting alone by the gate wasn't an appealing option either. And we didn't want Kai or Nalin to try to come after us through the water hemlock. "Okay, but we'll wait at the boat, and if you're not back in an hour, I'll return. Are you sure you'll be okay? Can you send a message in the leaves if you need help?"

I nodded, every part of my body feeling alive despite the lack of access to my powers. I was humming with determination. I checked the quill and found that the distance indicator was showing one hundred feet. "This is the place, Nevah. I'll be okay. I'll meet you by the water hemlock when I'm done here."

Nevah's face was tense, but she nodded. "You got this, B."

As I walked along the shaded path, I took in the assortment of plant life lining the ground and the trees on both sides and overhead. Belladonna, wolfsbane, carrion plants, black bat's flower, and doll's eye surrounded me. Japanese blood grass and tangles of strangleweed were under my feet.

The path continued to be lit by glowing moonflowers until it came to an end by the water, and a green rowboat sat there, devoid of any oars. Snowy flew from my finger to the boat, and I climbed inside.

"*Oof!*" I exclaimed as the boat began to move, and I had to steady myself to keep from tipping over the side. The grasses in the shallow water below must be tugging it forward.

As we got farther into the water, the ambient light increased. Moonflowers and floating lantern-like lotuses illuminated the swamp all around me. Once my eyes adjusted, I began to take in my surroundings, and I inhaled sharply.

A miniature living city was in the swamp, with boats that were so covered in camouflaged plant life that they appeared to be part of the land. Dim lanterns hung from each boat, and huts of various shapes and sizes littered tiny islands.

My gaze went to the largest floating hut a few hundred feet away. That was when I noticed someone coming toward me on a standing paddleboard-style raft. It was covered in moss, and the person was rowing with a tall paddle, dipping it into the water on either side of the raft.

Like the floating dwelling spaces around us, the person practically blended into the environment, a living camouflage. Everything in the area was of a similar brown, gray, and green color palette.

My stomach clenched as the raft drew closer. I had no way to steer the boat that had drawn me there, and it seemed to be delivering me straight to the stranger. Was I about to be greeted as a guest or as an invader? I slid the quill under my thigh, hoping to obscure it from view without crushing it.

"May I help you?" the person called, and finally, their face came into view as the man lifted a lamp into the air.

My brain rapidly searched for a response that would make sense without revealing my true motives. I had been so focused on following the quill that I hadn't planned what I would say or do if I encountered other magical botanists.

"I'm a magical botanist with a defensive affinity, and I was hoping to look around the conservatory," I finally said, keeping things as close to the truth as possible.

"Well, you wouldn't have gotten in here if you didn't have a defensive affinity, so that part is true. Though something is off about your powers." He studied me for several moments, and I tried not to squirm, the quill feeling like a spotlight that was going to give me away as it rested under my thigh. I hoped he was just sensing my lack of access to my powers. "Come with me," he said.

"Where are we going?" I asked as my boat began to follow the raft toward the largest hut.

"I'm going to introduce you to the curator of the defensive plants conservatory."

Chapter Twenty-One

My boat followed the guide all the way to the tiny island that housed the largest hut. When we got close to it, I realized the island was composed of tightly clustered water plants, not earth. The hut was swaying slightly as the plants drifted in place.

"One moment, please." My guide disappeared inside the hut, and I climbed from my boat to step onto one of the green floating lily pads. Amazingly, it felt solid under my feet. Snowy followed me then rested on my shoulder.

After a minute or two, a handful of people came out the door, ran their eyes over me, then got onto their own paddleboards and boats and took off toward other huts.

"She's ready for you," my guide said, pulling back a curtain of moss to make room for me.

I passed through the curtain and stepped back in surprise when I entered the room. I could tell it was the largest hut from the outside, but the exterior belied how spacious it was inside. Certainly, a trick of defensive plant magic was at work. The room was at least the size of a large pub, with a circular bar-style counter in the center and smaller gathering areas surrounding it. The space was empty, except for one woman sitting in a tall-backed chair. Were the other magical botanists asked to clear the space for us?

The woman turned, and I let out a gasp. "Petra?"

She smiled and rose, coming over to give me a warm hug. "Briar. It's a delightful surprise to see you here, though perhaps not entirely unexpected."

"What are you doing here? I thought you were in Italy for the winter."

"I have much to tell you, Briar. Are you hungry?"

With a gentle flap of its wings, the moth rose from my shoulder and went to land on Petra's.

"I see you brought Leucie back unharmed," Petra said, signaling for me to take a seat across from her.

I slid onto the seat, eager for answers. "I don't understand. Do you work here?"

Petra nodded. "I'm the curator of the defensives conservatory."

"You are?" I asked, unable to form any words more eloquent. "And you have been this whole time we've been working together?"

Petra nodded again. "Much like you, I learned about my magical botanist abilities a bit later than most. I was studying art at university in Italy, and one day while researching, I came across a book that felt warm in my hands."

My eyes widened. "That's how your powers were activated? Are you a descendant of da Vinci?"

"Yes, though from a different one of his siblings' lines than you."

"Does this mean you have all the lead affinities?"

Petra shook her head. "You're the only one I've met who can claim that trait, Briar. My defensive powers are very strong, and I have a number of trailing affinities, but for whatever reason, the traits of our ancestors that were diluted in most of us popped up again in you."

"So, if you're from Italy and learned about your powers there, how did you come to work here?"

"After college, I was part of a traveling art exhibit. We had a few stops in the United States, including one in San Francisco. It was around that time that I received a message from your mother."

I nearly slid off my seat, the world seeming to freeze. "My mom? You knew her?"

"Sadly, we never had the chance to meet. She reached out through a DNA website we had both used after she saw we were distantly related. When she learned I was in California, she invited me to your area."

I couldn't process anything except Petra's voice. I was imagining my mom planning a meeting with one of her distant relatives. Aunt Vera had told me my mom had done a DNA project in college.

"I traveled up to Mt. Shasta. She recommended we meet for a picnic lunch up on the mountain."

"It was her favorite place to paint," I whispered.

"That's what she told me. I arrived early and spent some time there. It didn't take long to realize the area was a green zone, as it was obviously amplifying my powers. By this point, I was connected to the magical botanical community near my home in Italy, and a friend there studied green zones."

Petra paused as if bracing for what she was going to say next. "Your mother never showed up, and when I tried calling, she didn't answer. After waiting for a few hours, I left. Not long after, I learned about the accident."

My hands went to my mouth. "The accident happened when she went to meet you. We always assumed she had gone up there to paint." My mind was swirling, taking it all in.

"I'm sorry to bring up these painful memories, Briar, but it is time you knew."

I nodded. "It helps a little, getting more details. It fills a hole in the picture we always wondered about. Did you ever talk to my aunt, Vera?"

"No. Your mother had told me she planned to surprise you both after she met me. She was putting together a bit of a... What do you call it? A family tree. Afterward, I thought about reaching out, but I knew you were both grieving. I hoped there would be a time when I would return to the United States, and we could meet. After my tour of the US, I returned to Italy. A few years later, the defensives conservatory began looking to recruit a new curator."

"Recruit? I've heard most of the conservatories appoint someone, typically a founders' descendant."

"The defensives community is small, and they don't always have willing candidates to choose from. Occasionally, that means tapping their research networks to find botanists outside of the United States. We serve five-year terms. My time here is almost up."

"And Evergreen Academy? How did you find out about me?"

"Professor East reached out last year about a student with incredible abilities. When he mentioned your name, I jumped at the opportunity to mentor you. Your last name was different from your mom's, but she'd told me your first name when we were corresponding, and I suspected that it was you Professor East was referring to."

"Did you hear about Professor East? How he's been removed from the academy? Have you spoken with him?"

Petra nodded. "He sent me a correspondence shortly after it happened. It's why I haven't returned to California. I apologize for not getting in touch with you yet, but I was trying to research your plant, Rosie, like we talked about."

I straightened. "Did you find anything? Can Rosie be used as a counterpoison?" Rosie had been in my family for generations, and Petra thought the plant could be the key to my getting full access to my powers back.

"I couldn't determine a species name, but she's unique and

probably thought extinct in the botanical community. I have some ideas for including her petals in an antidote. We can try that while you're here. Speaking of your being here, I think it's time to share how you came to find the defensives conservatory."

I looked up and met Petra's assessing gaze. "Do you know why I'm here?"

"I have a guess," Petra said, a smile touching her lips.

I took a deep breath. The time for catching up was over. It was time to do what I had come for.

Chapter Twenty-Two

"I'm trying to find the *Vanished Compendium*. My friends and I collected the quill that's linked to it, and it pointed us here."

Petra nodded, seeming unsurprised. "And these friends, who are they?"

"Members of the Root and Vine Society," I said, assuming she had heard of it.

She nodded again. "Ah, yes. The mission of the Root and Vine Society in recent years has been to find the *Vanished Compendium.* But did you know that when it was founded, its mission was to *protect* the book?"

My lips parted. "The Root and Vine Society are the ones who hid the book?"

"They were indeed. About a hundred years ago. But they weren't the first ones to attempt to hide the book."

"Who else tried to hide it?" I leaned forward.

"Botanists of the Renaissance period." Petra looked pointedly at me, and a shiver ran up my spine as I realized I was finally going to get some answers about Leonardo da Vinci and the Renaissance botanists.

"Certain royalties in Europe had suspicions about magic and were confiscating any 'spell books' they could find. Leonardo da Vinci and others on the magical botanist council of the region decided it was best to hide the second book so that the work that had been carefully documented wouldn't all be lost if the book fell into the wrong hands."

My mind swirled as I pictured the magical botanists of hundreds of years ago fighting to save their work.

"Around this same time, he and other powerful botanists bound up their magic within their inconspicuous botanical drawing journals. They did not want to be accused of having magic. But they didn't realize that this was going to preserve their magic in the book for future generations, which is how your magic eventually made its way to you."

My brain was sparking as I processed her words. I was piecing together things I had been wondering about, but I still had so many questions.

"What did they do with the second book? Where did they hide it? And why didn't they hide the *Compendium Floracantus*?"

"I guess they figured that if at least one book was protected, they had a failsafe against losing all their knowledge. Magical botanists didn't go underground completely. In fact, magic proliferated around that time, though they had to be careful to protect their secrets. The *Compendium Floracantus* was spread rapidly in secretive magical botanist communities with the invention of the printing press. The second book continued to be hidden and passed down through trusted members of the community, and no copies were ever made to increase discretion. Over time, magical botanists began to refer to it in rumors as the *Vanished Compendium*. Eventually, that book landed in the hands of the defensive plant founder of Evergreen Academy and the founder of this conservatory."

Petra continued, "Jean-Claudia, the defensives founder, hid the book without telling anyone where. In the meantime, she implemented a block on the quill so that others couldn't use it to find the book. Lore has it she anchored the original blocking Floracantus to a plant somehow. You must have figured out where if you got the quill working."

"Not me. A friend." My heart squeezed as I thought of Callan. I wished he could be with me to hear everything firsthand. I tried to memorize every detail to relay to him later. "It was anchored to an oak tree along a prominent nature trail in town."

Petra nodded. "That makes sense. Jean-Claudia would have centered the blocking spell in Weed because Evergreen Academy is a hub for magical botanists. I'm sure she figured many people would search for the book there, so that's where the block would be strongest. Of course, back then, more magical botanists had all the affinity powers. Today, it's a rarity, so most botanists wouldn't be able to use the quill even without the blocking spell."

"Why didn't Jean-Claudia just destroy the quill? Or hide it with the book?" I asked.

"I believe she thought, like the Renaissance botanists, that there would be a time for the book's use again. And when that time came, the right person needed to be able to locate it. The quill was a tool for doing that. Plus..." Her lips twisted into a coy smile. "Magical botanists don't enjoy destroying artifacts."

I exhaled, contemplating all she had said. It made sense, but one thing was bugging me. "You said that she thought the time would come for the book to be used again. Do you think that time is now?"

"I don't think the reappearance of a botanist with all the affinity powers is a coincidence, Briar. The power of magical botanists has been decreasing over time, but nature likes balance. Perhaps it is attempting to shift the scales again, and here you are."

I sat quietly with that statement for a moment. "So... the book. It's here?"

Petra pursed her lips. "I am not sure. The past few curators have speculated that Jean-Claudia hid it here, and we were protecting it by keeping this conservatory hidden, though none of us alive today have seen it. If the quill sent you here, then I guess their speculations were correct."

I pulled out the quill and showed it to Petra. "According to this, we're very close to the book. And it's pointing west."

Petra looked in the direction of the quill's compass arrow. "That would put the book in the library."

I didn't mean to state the obvious, but the question came flowing out of me. "Hasn't anyone ever looked in the library?"

A smile touched Petra's lips. "Let's just say the defensive library is not your... average magical botanical library."

I raised my eyebrows. "Can I see it?"

"Follow me."

Chapter Twenty-Three

We took a boat to another floating hut, which was adorned with trailing lily of the valley flowers. When we stepped inside, I looked around in confusion. Instead of being filled with books like the libraries at Evergreen Academy and at the tree conservatory, the space was overflowing with defensive plants.

Wild vines snaked across the fronts of shelves of potted plants, as if daring someone without a defensive affinity to take a pot.

"Umm... where are the books?" I finally asked.

"The plants like to hide them," Petra said. "Try the quill again."

To my surprise, the quill spun slowly to the left, and I walked forward, following its direction. The space was filled with thousands of plants. And if our evidence had led us in the right direction, one of them was hiding the *Vanished Compendium*.

The quill led me toward the center of the maze of a library, until it was pointing directly at a striking mulberry tree. The quill began to emit a soft glow. I studied the tree, which was covered in rich red and black berries.

"Isn't this the tree da Vinci depicted in one of his murals?" I asked.

"You've been studying," Petra said with a nod. "The Sala delle Asse in Milan. He was captivated by the tree because its leaves were used to make silk. I wonder if this hiding place was intentional."

I approached the tree and laid a hand on its trunk then jumped back as the bark began to peel outward. Moments later, a book tumbled from inside the tree. I gasped and hurried to grab it before it could fall to the ground.

"I wondered how that would work," Petra said. "Every plant in here delivers its book a little differently and under varying levels of coaxing."

"Should I open it?" I asked, a surreal sense of excitement coursing through me.

"The book came to you, Briar. Every decision from here on out is yours."

With a deep breath, I took hold of the thick cover, which was free of dust—presumably absorbed by the mulberry tree it had been living in—and looked at the first page.

It was blank.

I flipped to the second page. Also blank. More quickly, I swiped through the entire book. "There's nothing here," I said, panic beginning to set in.

Petra stepped closer. "Are you sure?"

"I don't see anything on the pages."

"If there's one thing a defensive affinity should always remember, Briar, it's that things aren't always as they appear."

I sucked in a breath. "You think there could be some kind of invisible ink on the pages?" I asked.

"I'd be disappointed if there wasn't," Petra said, a note of excitement in her voice. "And I have a few ideas of how to make it appear."

Chapter Twenty-Four

"I see something!"

Gray ink was materializing on the first page of the *Vanished Compendium,* as if seeping out of the parchment.

Petra and I sat crouched over the book in the strange defensive plant library, having just completed our third attempt at drawing out the invisible ink.

A title scrawled into view:

To make

"This was reenchanted into English at some point," Petra observed. "Maybe by Jean-Claudia."

"Why is it titled 'To make'?" I asked. "Shouldn't it be called *Compendium Floracantus,* Volume Two or something?"

"It is curious," Petra agreed.

I turned the page, and we repeated the process of making the ink visible.

The word at the top read Aldrovandi.

"Aldrovandi?" I asked.

"It's a name. I have a feeling we're about to discover who authored the *Compendium Floracantus* and the *Vanished Compendium*. There have been theories, of course, but it's never been confirmed. They didn't put their names in the first volume."

"Probably didn't want it traced back to them if it fell into the wrong hands, since they were letting the first book be distributed among magical botanists."

Below the name, a list appeared of steps and ingredients as if portraying a recipe, but it was written in convoluted language.

"Are these instructions for something?"

Petra pursed her lips. "I'm not sure. It doesn't look anything like the format in the original *Compendium Floracantus*."

We turned the page and repeated the process. The word at the top of that one was Cesalpin.

"Another name," Petra murmured. Another riddle-like list appeared below, with similar but slightly different instructions, none of which made sense.

I touched Petra's arm, my heart racing. "Cesalpin was the last name of the tree affinity botanist who helped us break the Floracantus on the tree that was blocking the quill's locating features."

"That doesn't seem like a coincidence," Petra said. "I am not surprised that another Renaissance-era descendant knew the Floracantus that would help you with the tree. Do you think he knew anything about this book?"

I shook my head as I recalled my conversation with Oren. "Just old family tales and rumors, like much of the society."

We continued page by page until a name appeared that made me suck in a breath—da Vinci.

"Leonardo da Vinci was one of the authors of the *Compendium Floracantus*?" I breathed.

"The timing makes sense," Petra said. "Most scholars date the book back between five and six hundred years."

My eyes jumped to the few lines of text below my ancestor's

name. Like the notes on the other pages, it had been enchanted into English.

> *With two hands, we gather power.*
> *Bring each botanical gift to center.*
> *Lay to canvas. Sprinkle light. Make the new creation bright.*

I pondered the text, trying to make sense of it. "Do you understand this?" I asked after a few moments had passed.

"It reads like a riddle. Da Vinci was known for creating those, I believe. They called them prophecies and used them to entertain courtiers." Petra's head tilted slightly as she studied the page. "I think they were known to be a bit of a stretch, though. This might prove rather hard to interpret."

"But what are these riddles for? Did each Renaissance botanist leave the instructions for their favorite Floracantus in riddle form?" That idea didn't seem right.

Something tightened in my chest as my stomach sank. The *Vanished Compendium* wasn't what we'd thought. It was marvelous, to be sure, and a priceless piece of magical botanical history. But unlike the original *Compendium Floracantus*, it clearly wasn't stuffed full of ready-to-use enchantments. Would it still be able to help us save the academy?

Petra continued to flip through the pages until she finally revisited the first one. "To make," she said then looked up, staring into space. "I wonder..."

I waited, letting her work through her thoughts.

"I wonder if these are instructions for how to make Floracantus."

My brow furrowed. "*New* Floracantus?" The idea went against everything I had learned about magical botany.

"The botanists who wrote the original *Compendium Floracantus* must have made them somehow. It would make sense that they would want to preserve that process and hide it more securely than the other book. Someone with the power to discover and make new Floracantus could change the world."

"And you think they wrote those instructions in riddles so they couldn't easily be copied if the book were discovered by the wrong person?"

"That could very well be the case," Petra said.

"I wish I had more time to review this with you," I said, my heart sinking at the thought of leaving. But Nevah was out there in the boat, likely worried something had happened to me. I wasn't sure how much time had passed, but it felt like more than an hour.

"Didn't you say you were here for a few more days? Go reassure your friends you're all right then come back tomorrow. We still need to work on unblocking your powers using the Rosie recipe, and this may be the perfect place to do it." She closed the book and pressed it into my hands.

"It is yours now," Petra said, and I felt a twist of discomfort at the words. The book didn't belong to me. It belonged to all of us, just like the original *Compendium Floracantus*. If only we could figure out how to use it.

Chapter Twenty-Five

When I broke free of the maze that led to the defensives conservatory and returned to the water hemlock-covered portion of the coastline, my backpack began to rustle. Startled, I slid it off my shoulders and checked the *Vanished Compendium* for signs of movement. The book was still and calm, exactly as a book should be.

I frowned and felt around my bag until my hand landed on the rustling leaf wrapped in twine. *Of course. A message from Callan.* I removed the twine and unrolled the leaf to read the hand-written words upon it.

> Got the feeling I should write to you. Still up?

My chest squeezed at the thought that Callan was thinking about me from across the country. Maybe he somehow sensed that I hadn't gone to bed and had set off to find the book instead.

I thrust my hand around in my bag until it landed on a pen then scrawled a response below Callan's message.

Still up. Lots to tell you. Nevah said there's a satellite phone, so I'll call you in the morning to explain.

A few moments after I had written it, my message dissolved and another appeared.

You really know how to keep a man in suspense. Talk to you tomorrow.

I waved my arms at Nevah and Kai, and they began to maneuver the boat in my direction.

"Thank water lilies. I was getting ready to go after you." Nevah reached out a hand and pulled me into the boat. "So, what happened? Were there people there? Did you find the book?"

I filled her, Kai, and Nalin in on all that had occurred inside the defensives conservatory as we made our way back toward the aquatics conservatory, the ocean rippling underneath us in gentle, rocking waves.

"I can't believe you found the *Vanished Compendium*," Nevah said, a quiet awe in her voice as we reached the spot where we would leave the boat.

"I'm not sure what to make of it, though. What if we can't solve the riddles? Or what if the instructions aren't what we think they are?" I gazed at the dark water, barely seeing it.

"Think about it, B. Why would they go to this much work to protect this book if the contents weren't extremely valuable? I think Petra's theory is strong. We should focus on the fact that each Renaissance botanist seemed to have their own method for creating Floracantus. Did that mean they could only use the method they developed? If so, the only riddle we need to worry about in that book is the one for your ancestor, da Vinci. If we can figure it out, you might be able to use it."

I considered Nevah's words and hoped she was right. We secured the book in a dry bag, and Nevah enhanced it with aquatic protection charms, though I could sense that there were plenty of protective enchantments on the old book already. We swam back to the aquatic conservatory and went to our separate rooms.

I headed straight for the shower, which was filled with plants and fragrant herbs. The shampoo smelled of rosemary and ginseng. If the spa-like shower experience didn't make my hair as smooth and shiny as Nevah's, nothing would. I breathed in the dried lavender that hung in the bathroom while I dried off and felt my eyes grow heavy.

After I lay down in bed, I watched the sway of the seagrass on the ocean floor, which was lit by the dim yellow lights embedded around the conservatory dome. The leaf on my nightstand rustled, and I rolled over to look at it. When the message appeared, it immediately put a smile on my face.

Sweet dreams, tourist.

Chapter Twenty-Six

Nevah had been right—the ocean woke up early. The coral reef that had been calm when I went to bed was full of movement as the various creatures that called the reef home went about their daily tasks. The eels and groupers I had spotted the night before were gone, and more brightly colored creatures had taken their places. Butterfly fish skimmed the water, searching for breakfast, and blue tang added a shock of electric azure to the scene.

As I prepared for the day, I wanted nothing more than to share the results of the previous night's adventure with Callan.

The common area of the conservatory was much busier, too. Botanists dressed in wetland working attire were drinking coffee and tea and loading dry bags with gear for their studies. I spotted Nalin in the corner, following instructions from a woman with silver hair. He must have been preparing to go on his research assignment already.

Nevah met me in the kitchen area and offered me a blended green drink. "Wolffia smoothie. Have you ever had one?"

When I shook my head, she said, "Full of health benefits. I like to mix mine with cherry juice."

I took a sip and savored the new flavor. "Pretty good. What is Wolffia?"

"It's an enhanced version of *Wolffia globosa*, an aquatic plant that has protein and other nutrients in it. So, I'll give you a quick tour today before you head back to see Petra, but I imagine you want to call Callan first."

"That would be great. I didn't get to say much in the leaf messages, so I'm sure the man is on pinecones and needles."

Nevah laughed. "I'll show you to the call room."

Once Nevah got me situated with the satellite phone, she left me to speak with Callan in private. He answered after three rings.

"Rhodes," he answered.

"Hey, it's me," I said, smiling at the sound of his voice.

"Are you on the satellite phone?" he asked, his tone softening. "You sound distant."

"Well, I *am* underwater. You could have warned me about that one. Where are you?" Evergreen Academy had a no-cell-phone rule.

"I went out for an early treewalk, waiting for your call."

I glanced at my watch. It was nine a.m., meaning it was six in the morning in California. *How early had Callan woken to answer my call?*

"Well, I have good news."

"You found it?"

"I found it. But it's not exactly what we were expecting. It's not a book full of Floracantus like the *Compendium Floracantus*. Instead, it seems to be a book of riddles written by a bunch of the Renaissance botanists."

"A book of riddles?"

"Petra has a theory. It's a pretty big leap, but if she's right, the book could still be very important."

"Petra's there?" Callan asked, sounding confused. "Where did you find the book exactly?"

I took the next ten minutes to explain everything that had

happened, from arriving at the aquatics conservatory to following the quill to the water hemlock to entering the defensives conservatory and finding the book with Petra.

"So all this time, you've been working with the defensives' curator for your field studies assignment? You never cease to impress, local," Callan said.

"It's not like I had any idea! I don't know when or if she would have told me if this mission hadn't led me to her."

"And she really didn't know the book was in the defensives conservatory?"

"She said there had been suspicions over the years but nothing concrete. And the way the plants in that library are possessive about the books, well, I'm not surprised no one has done a deep search in there based solely on rumors."

"Tell me more about the riddles in the book."

I pulled it from my bag and opened it to da Vinci's page then read the text aloud.

> *With two hands, we gather power.*
> *Bring each botanical gift to center.*
> *Lay to canvas. Sprinkle light. Make the new creation bright.*

Silence followed on both ends of the phone for a few moments as Callan and I sat there, thinking through the possibilities within the cryptic words.

"Make the new creation bright," Callan repeated. "If Petra's theory is correct, that has to reference creating Floracantus, right?"

"Seems likely. Which would make the rest of the riddle instructions. But it doesn't seem like much to go on."

"The first two lines could be somewhat straightforward. Use both hands. Call on all nine affinity powers."

"But what about 'lay to canvas' and 'sprinkle light'? Da Vinci was a painter, but what would that have to do with this?"

"I'm not sure," Callan admitted. "Since da Vinci was known

for writing riddles, it could be helpful to study some of them to learn his style."

It was a good suggestion, and I brightened at the idea. "I'll do that as soon as I get back to the academy."

"Now that you've found the book so quickly, what will you do with your remaining days at the conservatory? Can you tag along with Nevah?"

"Actually, Petra invited me back to the defensives conservatory. She wants to pick up where our field studies left off."

"I can't believe you got to see the mysterious defensives conservatory. What was it like? Was everyone's hut covered with defensive plants to keep others out?" Callan joked.

I laughed. "No. It was surprisingly peaceful. Like being at a high-class nature retreat in the middle of nowhere."

"Interesting. I'd better get back to the academy. The rest of the school will be waking up soon, and I've been trying to make regular appearances so Feathergrass doesn't go looking for me or you."

"Thanks for holding it down for us. I'll see you in a few days."

"Stay safe. And if you find any more books that are hundreds of years old and highly coveted by the society of magical botanists, give me another call."

"I promise." I grinned as I hung up the phone.

Chapter Twenty-Seven

For the next few days, I left the aquatics conservatory before the sun made its way over the ocean, before most of the other researchers rose, and took the boat to the water hemlock patch. The defensive plants along the hidden path to the conservatory seemed to show off for me, and I noticed new species each time I went through.

Spending time at the defensives conservatory was like an extended and more immersive version of my field studies. Each day, I interacted with a selection of the unique defensive plants before Petra and I set in to work on my powers.

We tried several recipes that included rose petals from Rosie, but so far, none had released the poison that was stifling my powers.

"Did you feel anything?" Petra asked after I'd ingested our third recipe of the day. She had included a pressed-oil version of the petals in the most recent experimental antidote, which was more concentrated. It made the hut we were working in smell like a perfume store that only sold rose-scented formulations.

I tilted my head to the side, deciding how to explain what I was feeling. "Yes. It's like the time in the cabin on Mt. Shasta when I felt like we were getting close. The petals from Rosie seem to almost be... relaxing my system. I'm not sure if it's a placebo, but I feel calmer than when we usually do this. Almost like I took a muscle relaxant."

"That's interesting," Petra said. "Even if it is just a placebo, like you say, you are obviously very used to the scent of Rosie, and that may naturally be calming your body down."

"I don't think I'm going to have any luck cutting through the bonds on my magic when I'm this relaxed. It might even be having the opposite effect of what we want."

Petra studied my face as if I were a complex puzzle. "The opposite effect of what we want... Perhaps we do want you relaxed. If you were fully relaxed, others could attempt to undo the bonds on your magic. I wonder if we could try to... What do they call it? Tag-team it? This conservatory houses the most defensive botanists you'll find at any one place in the world. If we all worked on undoing the magic of the defensive founder, perhaps here, in this other place she built, the effects of the Floracantus will finally come loose."

"Let's do it," I said, sitting upright. I wasn't sure whether it was my relaxed state or the eagerness to try something new that told me we should do it, but either way, we were running out of time to keep tweaking the antidote. I couldn't return to the academy with a book of unsolved riddles and nothing else to show for it.

Petra nodded, and I waited in the hub while she gathered eight other magical botanists.

"That makes nine of us in total. The same number as there are affinities. Seems like good luck, I think."

"Magical botanists operate on science, not luck," one botanist chastised her in a voice that sounded practical rather than reproachful.

"Perhaps you're right, Yew, but thanks for joining, regardless," Petra replied. "On the count of three, I would like you all to target the founders' poison in Briar's magic. If you sense it, try to counter it with your own magic. Briar, make sure you don't block any of us. Hopefully, Rosie will help with that. Let our magic work and help us if you can."

I nodded, bracing myself as questions ran through my head. *Will this hurt? Do I care?* I had poisoned myself to get here. *Could this be any worse than that?* I inhaled the fragrant scent of the roses in the hut and let Rosie work her relaxation magic in my bloodstream. "I'm ready."

"One... Two..." Petra began. On "Three," I felt a cool liquid sensation as other defensive magic began to search my body for Jean-Claudia's curse. Thankfully, it wasn't painful, and I tried to give in to the calm I was already feeling, guiding their magic toward where the poison had a hold on mine. Soon, I could sense the other botanists' magic beginning to work on the poison, tugging and slicing. I focused on breathing and letting their defensive affinities work.

After about two minutes, I felt something snap, and I gasped as tension released like a pressure valve, the feeling of the poison's effect on my magic completely gone.

"I think... I think it worked," I breathed. Immediately, I felt the other botanists back off, the coolness of their magic leaving me.

"Test it out," Petra said.

Another botanist handed me an angel's trumpet the size of a desk lamp as a test subject.

I said the first Floracantus that popped into my mind. "*Flos flori.*"

Before the words were out of my mouth, I knew it had worked. My power was humming through my veins again, and I felt intimately connected to each of the plants in the surrounding area. The lemony smell of the angel's trumpet filled the entire hut, responding to the Floracantus I had used.

"I'd say it worked," Petra said with satisfaction in her voice.

"Thank you all." I looked around the group. "This means the world."

A few people gave me smiles, but most were already heading back to their research.

"Congratulations, Briar," Petra said. "And just in time. I'm sure you'll find a way to solve the riddle and use the book."

"I really hope so."

Petra studied me for a moment before speaking again. "When I discovered my relation to da Vinci, I began to research his history, as I know you have also done. I found there was a phrase he used to describe how he approached the world. He called it *saper vedere*. It means 'knowing how to see.' He wanted to know everything about the world, and his incredible achievements in art and science can be attributed to this."

"*Saper vedere*," I said slowly, trying out the words.

"You have that vision, Briar. I think it's been instilled in you since you were born. I suspect that it's not a coincidence you grew up in Weed. Perhaps your family—your ancestors—could subconsciously sense the school's magic, even though their own magic was locked away. That may be what kept your mom and aunt there too. I have a feeling they experienced a connection to the place that they couldn't explain. Even though da Vinci tied up our family's powers in his journals, that spirit of curiosity about the world passed through your blood."

I glanced at Leucie, who was resting on Petra's shoulder and gently flapping her wings as I considered Petra's words. The idea was so beautiful that tears pricked my eyes.

"You think I have what he had? He was one of the greatest artists and inventors in history."

"Perhaps anyone can have that, whether or not they are related to him. You told me you are an artist, that you've been seeing the world through your art since you were a child. Your art—and exploring the images in da Vinci's book—is how you ended up activating your powers without even realizing it. I know magical botanists are people of science but..." Petra paused, seeming to consider how to phrase her next words. "We also know that there's more mystery and wonder to this world than humans can even imagine. Everything I've come to know about you tells me that the wonder and curiosity within you will lead you to discover the secrets of da Vinci's riddle and much more. After all, it's brought you this far."

I swallowed the lump in my throat. I couldn't form any words of protest, because I desperately hoped it was true.

"Thank you, Petra. For everything. Will I see you back at the academy?"

Petra shook her head sadly. "With the departure of Professor East, I think it's best that I stay away for now. Besides, my reason for being there is now accomplished. You have access to your powers. You're more skilled in defensives than most botanists I've met. I think your field studies were a success, don't you?"

I nodded, but I fought back a wave of sadness, as I wasn't sure when—or if—I would see Petra again.

Seeming to read my mind, she said, "It's been my pleasure working with you, Briar, and I hope our paths will cross again. I have a feeling that life will lead you back here one day."

"I hope so, too, Petra. Thanks for everything."

"No matter what happens next, you're always welcome here. We're family." Petra smiled then nodded toward Leucie, who was hovering over the boat, ready to lead me out of the conservatory.

I climbed into the tiny vessel that had been transporting me the past few days and used my powers on every passing plant as I said farewell to the defensives conservatory.

Chapter Twenty-Eight

As I returned to the aquatics conservatory, I was buzzing with energy and a sense of connection to the aquatic plants both in and above the dome—confirmation that the restored access to my powers at the defensive conservatory hadn't been a fluke. I could feel the difference as soon as I swam through the barrier. The bonds on my magic were gone, and I had full access to my powers.

I was practically floating as I told my friends.

"Well, hot water lilies. Now that you have your powers back, Briar, if you're up for it, I have a mission for you tonight," Nevah said.

"What kind of mission?"

"The aquatics representative on the Board of Regents is supposed to be here for an aquatics conservatory meeting." Nevah's eyes were bright. "I think we should listen in."

Kai asked, "You sure?"

Nevah nodded. "It's all hands on deck now. The Root and Vine Society is doing what it can at the academy, but changes have spread to the conservatories too. Knowledge is power, and we need more of it."

"How can we listen in?" I asked.

"They hold the meetings in a small outer dome. There's only one way in and out," Kai answered.

"So how are we going to spy on them?" Nalin asked.

"Remember how I told you Kai has the ability to waterbend? With the right trick of the light, he can swim us in without anyone seeing us," Nevah said.

"Have you tried this before?" I asked.

"Waterbending? Or spying on a council meeting?" Kai asked, a touch of humor in his voice.

"Both."

"I've done waterbending plenty of times. Nevah and I have successfully spied on one meeting. When rumors started flying around that Feathergrass had replaced Professor East at the academy last week, we had to listen in on the special session they called."

I relaxed a little.

"I only had to bend the water around two of us that time, so it might be more challenging with four, but I'll make it happen." Kai's confidence was reassuring, but the operation was still risky.

"Make that three," Nalin said. "I have plans with my research group this evening."

"What happens if we get caught?" I asked.

"To you? Probably nothing other than getting sent out of the conservatory, which you're planning soon anyway. You're not under their jurisdiction. Kai and I could lose our positions here," Nevah said.

I stilled. "Are you sure you want to risk that?"

"Absolutely." I could hear the resolve in Nevah's voice. "This fight isn't just for the academy. Changes there mean changes for all of us. We've already witnessed it happening. And if the higher-ups won't share information, we'll have to get access to it ourselves."

"But you're a founders' descendant. Why aren't they sharing information with you?" I asked.

"It's a good question. Information is being held within tight circles these days. It feels ominous. You heard about the changes at the moss conservatory?"

I nodded. "I was there when the vote happened. They only want founders' descendants to be in charge."

"That hasn't happened here yet. But I wonder if it's only a matter of time."

"Well, if you two are willing to risk your positions here, I'm in."

~

AFTER WE SAID GOODBYE TO NALIN, KAI AND NEVAH led the way to the miniature dome where the council meetings were held. We slipped into the water tunnel to swim in, and Kai raised some crystals that he held in his palms.

As Nevah and I glided through the water, I blinked several times when I realized her form was disappearing. Kai's water-bending light tricks must be working. We continued through the tunnel, and when we got to the end, I stayed in the water, just as Kai and Nevah had prompted me to do.

A circle of aquatics botanists sat in the room, trays of fresh seafood on the driftwood table in front of them. From the way the conversation was going, the meeting had already started. The sounds were muffled, but then Nevah swirled her hands, and their voices began to pass smoothly through the water.

"Plans are in place to take back control of public lands from the humans. We have a bill in the state legislature, and when it passes, it will hand stewardship to our nonprofit," one of the council members said.

I tensed. What did that mean? Which public lands were they taking over?

"We expect similar bills to pass in surrounding states. Soon, magical botanists will have control of most state and national parks," another explained.

Murmurs spread throughout the room.

One woman spoke up. "Will these lands continue to be open for human tourism and recreation?"

"For now. But ultimately, most of these will close for private stewardship. It's time we took a more aggressive approach to conservation of our plants' habitat."

I swallowed. I understood that magical botanists wanted to protect plants and their homes, but cutting off access from humans was too much. How could humans ever be motivated to care for their natural environment if they could never witness some of the most beautiful, well-preserved places in the country?

"At that point, we'll have full access to these habitats. We expect research to accelerate at a rate not seen in the modern era. Feathergrass expects patents to be processed more quickly, and we'll be able to roll out some of our findings to the public. Strategically, of course."

Feathergrass. Of course he was involved. The advancement of science was great, but at what cost? Why couldn't we advance the science while still allowing nonmagical people access to the beautiful species we cared about so much? And was Feathergrass more concerned about conservation or about profit?

"When will this take place?"

"The legislative session begins in March. We estimate most changes will begin occurring in the fall or next year."

March was only six weeks away. Everything was happening too quickly. I had only just found the *Vanished Compendium*, and I didn't know how to interpret the riddles within it.

We continued to listen until the meeting began to wrap up, then we hurriedly returned through the tunnel under the cover of Kai's waterbending abilities.

"*Seven bubbles,*" Nalin cursed once we'd filled him in on the meeting. "They really want to take over all the public lands?"

We all sat in Nevah's room again, the coral reef outside putting on a spectacular show.

"I understand why some would think that's a good idea, but do they think the humans are just going to let it happen? Like us, many of them have a deep connection to those places. Closing them to the public is not a viable option," Nevah said.

"I agree," I said. "In California, public parks are a major part of our identity. Even if they manage to get a bill through under the guise of moving the parks under the management of a nonprofit, do they think they're just going to put up a Closed sign outside of Yosemite and people will be okay with it?"

Kai shook his head. "This could be dangerous. Botanists have always worked with humans when possible. This would be a massive shift."

"What can we do about it, though? The legislative session will begin in March." I ran my hands across the cover of my notebook, trying to let the soft fabric comfort me. What I really wanted was to talk to Callan. Maybe he would see a way out of the situation.

"We have to change the direction of leadership," Nevah said. "That way, even if these bills pass, magical botanists can change their minds on how they intend to manage the land."

"And how do we change the direction of leadership?" Nalin asked.

"By becoming more powerful than they are." Nevah looked pointedly at my backpack, where the *Vanished Compendium* was stored. "It's more important than ever that you figure out how to use it, B. Nalin, we'll have the plane charged with biofuel for you so you can get into the air first thing tomorrow morning."

We each looked around the circle, meeting one another's eyes. The countdown was on. It was time to head back to Evergreen Academy. And when I got there, I would have access to my powers.

Chapter Twenty-Nine

"So, you found the long-lost book and the long-hidden defensives conservatory. Remind me never to underestimate you, local," Callan said when he picked me up from the airport. He pulled me into a hug that went on so long that I wondered if the night sky was going to blush.

"I'm as surprised as anyone."

He released me from the hug then helped me carry my bag to his truck. We said goodbye to Nalin then got on the road.

"How was everything at the academy while we were gone?" I asked.

"All the students are sour on Feathergrass, which is no surprise. He manages to suck the fun out of everything." Callan paused before speaking again, easing the truck onto the freeway that would take us into Weed before we exited for the forest and back to Evergreen Academy. "I stopped at Professor East's SCC office yesterday."

I sat up straight and whipped my head toward him. "Was he there? What did he say? *How is he?*"

Callan shook his head. "He wasn't there, and the door was

locked. But he keeps enough trailing plants inside that I was able to summon one through the door to unlock it."

"You broke into Professor East's office at SCC?" I was equal parts surprised and impressed.

"Desperate times. Plus, I think he'd approve."

I nodded. We agreed on that. "So, did you find anything? Any evidence of where he went?"

"Nothing on Professor East, but I found a folder in his desk. It was concealed well, tucked inside his biology planning papers from last year. There was the student roster, which included your name—that's what tipped me off that maybe he had left it for us—then a nondescript folder. When I pulled it out, it contained Alex's file."

"By the leaves!" I exclaimed. With all the excitement of the Florida trip, Alex had taken a back seat in my mind. "What was in it?"

"The SCC records were pretty uninteresting. They contained the address in San Diego he enrolled under, presumably a fake. There was a copy of his grades. He was keeping them up enough to stay enrolled but was obviously not putting in more than a passing effort. But one thing of note was that he didn't enroll in any classes for this spring."

I frowned. "He's not coming back to SCC? Why? Do you think he knows we saw him at the tree conservatory?" Even as I asked it, I knew that didn't fit with the timeline. Alex would have needed to enroll in spring classes before the winter break.

"My guess is that he completed what he was sent here to do."

I frowned, my stomach sinking as I remembered. "Activating Aunt Vera's powers."

Callan nodded then reached over and squeezed my hand.

I chewed my lower lip. "Who do you think sent him?"

Callan took a deep breath, and when his words came out, they were quiet. "I'm beginning to wonder if it was my parents."

I kept my mouth shut, not surprised by the revelation but heartbroken that Callan had to come to such a conclusion.

"He's a tree affinity, so he must have been working for someone there. Who would have been motivated to poison the shield? Who benefits from its being compromised?" He ran a hand through his hair. "The faulty shield was the springboard for getting more power at the academy. It's one of the reasons Feathergrass was able to replace Professor East. My mom is the tree representative on the Board of Regents. She and Feathergrass have been friends since their days at Evergreen Academy. It all fits."

I nodded and looked out the window, barely seeing the familiar trees of the forest leading to the academy. Everything he said had been piecing itself together in my mind as well.

"The timing works. Feathergrass is successfully installed at the academy, so Alex is no longer needed here to do their dirty work," I said. "Do you think they'll still try to use my aunt?"

"I think we had a bit of luck there. Wyatt got his hands on the quill—the real one, as far as any of them know—before the board could. While I don't agree with the DBI on everything, I don't think their intentions for the quill or the book are as self-serving as those of the influential members of the board."

"So if our assumptions are correct and they activated my aunt's powers so that she could use the quill, and now they no longer have access to the quill, they should leave her alone?" The idea made me hopeful, though I still felt unsettled.

"It seems like it. I can't see what else they would use her for. If they manage to get the quill back from the DBI, which is unlikely, they could try to have her use it. Obviously, they would learn that it wasn't the real quill then. But hopefully, we'll have made our move long before then."

I nodded, strumming my fingers against my thigh. The best way to protect my aunt was to act first. Once we revealed our hand, the board would have no use for her.

Callan cleared his throat. "The most important things now are that you returned safely, we have a new lead, and the Root and Vine Society is ready to fight."

"Well, then, I think you're going to like my next bit of news," I said, my lips twisting into a smile.

"*More* news?" Callan asked, raising an eyebrow. "You were only in Florida for a week."

"In my field studies last term, Petra and I were working on a way to unblock my powers."

The truck slowed as Callan let his foot off the gas.

"When I was at the defensives conservatory, she had the idea to have nine defensive botanists work on undoing the bonds on my magic."

"And?" Callan glanced at me, and at the twinkle of hope I saw in his eyes, I couldn't drag it out any longer.

"It worked. They undid the bonds of the poison on my powers. We tested it at both conservatories, and I had access to my magic in each after the procedure. Going back to Evergreen Academy will be the final test."

Callan tapped his palm against the horn in excitement, and birds flew out of a nearby tree. "Are you serious?"

"As serious as cedar," I said, grinning.

Callan's face was pure joy, and his smile was one of roguish delight as he said, "Feathergrass is never going to see you coming."

Chapter Thirty

The wisteria flowers leading into the Evergreen Conservatory emitted a familiar calming fragrance as the Root and Vine Society gathered a few nights later. The aliveness of the place was a reminder that spring was coming, and perhaps the winter of Evergreen Academy under Feathergrass's rule could come to an end sooner than anyone expected.

"Sooo," Hollis said, flopping onto a smooth boulder as if it were a pool chair. "Heard you have some big news for us, B. In addition to getting access to your powers back."

A few cheers went up around the room, and I did a little pose and smiled to show my gratitude.

"I did regain access to my powers. For now, that's a secret just for this group. But the biggest news is about the book. You've probably all heard by now that I found the *Vanished Compendium*. I can't say where, exactly, but it was hidden in Florida, near the aquatics conservatory."

Petra hadn't needed to remind me that the location of the defensives conservatory was secret from all nondefensives and that, even though the conservatory moved around, I wasn't to share its current location with anyone unless strictly necessary.

The eyes of every member of the Root and Vine Society, plus Yasmin, Coral, and Aurielle—our newest informal recruits—were plastered to me.

I took a breath and continued. "The book seems to be a sequence of riddles created by the Renaissance botanists who authored it. There is a theory that the riddles contain the instructions for creating new Floracantus."

Everyone stilled. They had known I found the book, but that was new information.

"So it wasn't filled with ready-made Floracantus, like the *Compendium Floracantus*?" Laurus, the herbs affinity botanist, asked.

"It wasn't. Which came as a big surprise, obviously."

"You really think there's a way to make new Floracantus?" Meadow asked.

"It's never been done in recent times," Callan said. "But the botanists who created the *Compendium Floracantus* obviously had a method for doing so. It seems plausible that these riddles could contain instructions for this process."

"We think that each botanist had their own recipe for making Floracantus. It was likely that only their family line could use the method, which is why making new Floracantus eventually ceased when the Renaissance botanists tied up their magic in their journals. Over time, they had fewer and fewer descendants with access to their magic, and the book of instructions was well hidden. Which means we need everyone's help to decipher the riddle that was created by my ancestor, Leonardo da Vinci. I don't want to share the book publicly until we figure that out."

"That's the plan, then? Share the book publicly?" Kaito asked.

"I think that's what our community deserves, but we can vote on it." I searched the room and, one by one, each person nodded.

Callan stepped forward. "For security purposes, we won't be sharing printed copies of da Vinci's riddle—the one we need to solve for Briar to use—but it's short. I expect you all can memorize it, if you've ever survived one of Dr. Lemna's tests."

A ripple of laughter relieved some of the tense excitement filling the cave.

Callan nodded to me, and I recited the riddle a few times, until everyone confirmed they had it memorized.

"In regard to the other riddles in the book, written by other Renaissance botanists, if you ever want access to any of them, please let me know," I said, wanting my friends to have all the information. I planned to share the Cesalpin riddle with Oren as soon as I had a chance to visit his tree house above the Wildflower Trail.

Kaito spoke up first. "We appreciate it, but we think your plan to focus on da Vinci's riddle is a good one. The others aren't useful to us without someone who can use them."

Murmurs of agreement spread through the cave.

Meadow peeled a piece of moss from the back of her hand and tossed it in my direction. I caught it and set it on my wrist, where it immediately formed a delicate bracelet. "So, B, what's the first Floracantus you're going to create when we crack this riddle?"

I played with the moss on my wrist, unsure of the answer. "I hadn't thought about that. I'm focused on figuring out if this book is even what we think it is."

"Well, start thinking. I'm picturing one that moves all the pollen from the flower gardens into Feathergrass's hair, dying it yellow." Meadow smirked, and our friends laughed.

The conversation popcorned around the room, each person sharing something they thought I should do to Feathergrass to drive him out of the academy.

When we'd shared enough potential antics, Callan spoke again. "All good ideas, but in the meantime, we have our own sabotage to do that doesn't involve new Floracantus."

Hollis rubbed his hands together and leaned forward. "Put me in, coach."

"We want to avoid trouble, so don't do anything that can lead directly back to you. But get with your affinity group friends and get creative. We need Feathergrass to know that we're united if he decides to do anything big against the academy."

As the other members of the Root and Vine Society left the cave, they were all brainstorming ideas. Callan hung back, so I did too. When we were alone, after Hollis shot a wink over his shoulder at us, Callan spoke.

"What Meadow said about the first Floracantus you create, then everyone sharing their ideas after... I just wanted to remind you that this power is yours."

"I—"

He silenced me with a touch of warm air to my lips. "I know. You want to share this knowledge with everyone. And you will. But the truth is the rest of us can't create new Floracantus. Only a person with all the lead affinity powers can do that. Which means the Floracantus you choose to make—if any—are yours to decide. Yours to discover."

Discover. I liked that word much better than *decide.* I had been making too many decisions lately. "Thanks for the warning," I said, though I was grateful for how he seemed to read my every concern.

"Don't worry. I'm not leaving you high and dry. But remember to trust yourself. Everyone else already does."

"Are there any scouting vines in here?" I whispered, though I knew the answer. The Root and Vine Society wouldn't be meeting in the Evergreen Conservatory if it weren't thoroughly cleared of the little plant spies. I took a step closer.

"You're killing me, local," Callan whispered back, our faces only inches apart.

My breath caught in my chest, and all I could do was watch those long, dark eyelashes as he studied me, a slight smile pulling at the corner of his mouth. I knew what he meant. We had both agreed—reluctantly on my part—to keep our romantic distance until the showdown with the Board of Regents was over. But the problems within the society of magical botanists only seemed to be getting more complex, not simpler. *How long will we have to wait?*

At that moment, a trio of fireflies dove from the ceiling, whizzing right through the tiny space between our faces.

I jumped backward. "I think we have chaperones," I said, laughing.

Callan smiled, but I caught a flash of longing in his eyes before he cleared his throat and nodded toward the pool of water that would take us out of the cave. "After you."

Chapter Thirty-One

When I went to the teahouse the next morning, some kind of tournament was in motion. The sun from the giant glass walls cast soft morning light upon several pairs of students who sat across from each other at the tables. Each set of students had a square dish between them, filled with soil and two opposing plants.

"What's going on?" I asked Yasmin as I brewed a cup of strong coffee.

Yasmin had been watching our classmates, and she smiled. "They're playing Roots and Xylem. I think humans have a version called Shoots and Climbers?"

"Ladders," I said, letting out a soft laugh.

"Most magical botanists play it as kids. The goal is to get your plant all the way through the soil and across the dish. But dice rolls allow each player to do different offensive or defensive Floracantus, which can set your plant back."

"Sounds fun. Do you know who started it?"

"Apparently, it was Hollis. All that talk of us working together and showing the affinities are united must have inspired him. I guess nothing does that better than a game we all have a nostalgic attachment to. They upped the stakes with the rules a bit, though, and there have been some nail-biters. I heard some people stayed up all night playing."

I took a sip of my coffee and watched as a first-year harvester student rolled her tomato seedling around an herb affinity's bush of oregano. "Are you going to play?"

"I'm sure I'll get in on the action at some point," Yasmin said, her eyes bright. "You want to sit and watch a round?"

I shook my head. "Maybe later. I want to get some sketching in before class." I patted my bag, where my art materials were stashed.

"Have fun," Yasmin said, moving back toward the Roots and Xylem game stations.

I was glad the other students had found an outlet from the tension surrounding Feathergrass's presence at the school, which was floating around the academy like pollen on a windy day. But my mind couldn't stop working on the problems in front of us and the puzzle my ancestor had created. Callan's words from the night before played in my mind as I walked to the gazebos. *Which means the Floracantus you choose to make—if any—are yours to decide. Yours to discover.*

I wondered how da Vinci and the other Renaissance botanists determined what Floracantus to make. They had created an entire book full of them. Was there a method, or did they do whatever came to mind when working with a particular plant? The best way to connect with my ancestor might be to lean into my favorite hobby, one that seemed to run in the family.

I settled into a hammock hanging between two trees near the pond and let my mind wander, getting lost in the movement of the pencil across the page. I must have been subconsciously connecting with the vines in the trees as I worked because I felt a tickle as a tendril of ivy snaked around my shoulder.

"Oops," I said, straightening and looking around. Thankfully, the area was clear of other botanists, but I would have to be more careful. Aside from Callan, only the members of the Root and

Vine Society knew I had my powers back. I wasn't used to being able to access them on campus, and it was a secret I needed to keep for the moment. Apparently, the plants had other plans. I carefully lifted the ivy from my shoulder and reattached it to the tree.

After finishing a sketch, I reached into my bag, retrieved one of da Vinci's notebooks, and spent some time imitating his style. As I worked, and scribbles turned into full-fledged art, I reflected on the fact that drawing was creating. *Is that how he eventually got the idea to make Floracantus?* It was all so long ago, the history so secretive and lost to time, that we would probably never know. Too bad there wasn't a long-lost library full of references to the Renaissance botanists somewhere.

I sat bolt upright, the hammock rocking underneath me.

"I can't believe that slipped my mind," I said, hurriedly collecting my items and racing back to my room. When we had traveled to the tree conservatory a few weeks ago, I stopped in one of the tree library hollows and stealthily borrowed a book.

With all the drama that had followed, including Callan almost getting caught by his brother, Wyatt, me stealing the quill, seeing Alex, Wyatt coming to the academy and our giving him a dummy quill, Professor East getting kicked out of the academy, meeting Oren on the Wildflower Trail and unblocking the quill, traveling to Florida to both the aquatics and defensives conservatories, then finding the *Vanished Compendium* and having a new riddle to solve... I had forgotten that I was a *double* thief at the tree conservatory.

I breezed into my dorm, my heart racing as I hastily sought the travel backpack I had brought to the tree conservatory. After removing the quill on our return, I had cast the backpack into my closet and hadn't thought about it since. I yanked it open and pulled out the contraband book.

"You're one forgetful criminal, Briar," I said.

When I opened the book, that warm feeling returned to my hands again, as if the pages were emitting the warmth of a gently roaring fireplace. If it were an old book of da Vinci's that he had infused his magic into, it made sense that I would have that reaction. It was extremely similar to what I had experienced the first time I picked up one of his books, though the sensation had barely registered then.

I skimmed the pages, noting the faded text and images on some pages and others that were blank. My heart rate kicked up again as I thought about the invisible ink that had been used on the *Vanished Compendium*.

Had this book faded because of time, as I thought when I first borrowed it, or could there be more to it? Were the words and pictures worn, or were they... hidden?

"What are you hiding?" I asked, running my hands tenderly across the old pages.

At that moment, Yasmin stepped into the room. I must have been quite the sight, sitting crisscross on the floor, hunched over the book with an undoubtedly wild look on my face.

"Umm, B, is everything okay? Did Feathergrass unveil a new rule?"

I shook my head and smiled excitedly as I held up the book. "How much time do we have before class? Want to help me uncover some invisible ink?"

Chapter Thirty-Two

"Soil and rhizomes," Yasmin muttered, using a magical botanist phrase I had never heard from her before. "I can see it." We were both sitting on our bedroom floor, da Vinci's book open in front of us.

The concoction we had created to draw out the invisible ink was working. Ink began to fill each page as we added the tincture, just like it had at the defensives conservatory.

"How many secret messages in books do you think da Vinci left like this?" Yasmin asked, her eyes glued to the parchment.

"I don't know, but let's hope this one isn't written in riddles like the *Vanished Compendium*."

We scanned the first page together.

"Doesn't look like it. In fact..." Yasmin let out a sharp breath then rose and went to her desk. She returned with her copy of the *Compendium Floracantus*. "These are laid out just like the pages in here."

I took another look, comparing the two books. She was right. "Does this mean da Vinci created some Floracantus that never made it into the *Compendium Floracantus*?"

"Perhaps. Maybe he created them after the book was

published. He could have been working on a second volume, like we thought the *Vanished Compendium* was meant to be. Or maybe these are ones he was just experimenting with and weren't intended for publication." Yasmin ran her fingers across the Latin that spelled out the Floracantus on one of the pages.

"Want to try it?" I asked, knowing she was eager to.

"Let's see..." Yasmin flipped through a few pages, turning each as delicately as if she were holding a piece of razor-thin glass. "Here's one that seems to apply to ferns." She studied the page then turned to one of the ferns hanging in the corner of the room.

"*Fiet indicum*," she said.

We both watched in amazement as, one by one, the fronds of the fern turned from bright green to deep purple.

"He created a Floracantus to turn plants purple?" I asked. "I wonder if it was for art. I remember reading that purple dye was difficult to come by back then. Indigo dye came from *Indigofera tinctoria*, but I don't know how common the plant was. If he could readily make the dye from ferns or other plants, he would never have to worry about running out."

Yasmin was still staring at the fern. She walked over to it and felt the leaves. "Remarkable."

"Is there a Floracantus in here for how to reverse it?" I asked, turning to the next page. "I guess we don't want Feathergrass knowing about this just yet."

Indeed, on another page, da Vinci had created a Floracantus to return any plant to its standard color. Perhaps he hadn't wanted to be caught with unnaturally purple ferns either.

An hour later, we had reviewed the entirety of the book. Only the first dozen pages contained Floracantus. The rest held drawings or remained empty. I wondered whether da Vinci's work on the book had halted when the Renaissance botanists paused their magical innovations and sent the *Compendium Floracantus* and *Vanished Compendium* into hiding.

"Most of these have to do with color or light or other physical properties of the plants," Yasmin mused. "I think you may be right in suggesting these were his own experiments for the sake of improving his art."

"Da Vinci had so many interests. It makes sense that he would overlap his studies and inventions."

"This is an incredible find for the magical botanist community, B," Yasmin said, her voice slightly shaky. Her hair was mussed, as if she'd run her hands through it while we worked. "Even if you had never found the book in Florida, people would have thought this book was the *Vanished Compendium*."

I gasped. "Yasmin, you're a genius."

She narrowed her eyes at me. "What are you plotting?"

I considered what the next few weeks at the academy had in store, and a smile touched my lips. "I have an idea."

Chapter Thirty-Three

"Are you ready for tomorrow?" Yasmin asked, her voice low. We were sitting at our usual table in our prop design class. The spring production of *A Midsummer Night's Dream* would debut in a few weeks, and we were finalizing the forest and the light-up flower we were responsible for creating. At other tables, students were testing out the fairy face masks, a lion's head, and other costume elements.

I set down one of the tree branches and stretched my arms over my head. The other students were chattering away at their own tables, paying us no attention, but Yasmin and I were always careful when discussing magical topics at our nonmagical college.

I lowered my voice to respond, "As ready as I can be. February fourteenth is going to be interesting this year. The Floral Fete can never be a normal event, can it? Last year, there was the truth-serum-spiked cupcake incident. This year, I'll be the one causing chaos."

"Yours is good chaos, B. Everyone will be excited. Just wait." Yasmin examined the flower in front of her. "You don't think anyone is going to notice this is magically enhanced, do you?"

I had used my floral affinity to modify a real flower and cause it to light up with bioluminescent genes, but as far as anyone in our class knew, the prop was made of realistic fabric and battery-powered lights.

A student's phone pinged across the room, then we heard a soft shriek of joy. "Early decisions are in for some of the state schools!"

Yasmin looked at me. "What's that about?"

"Some colleges do early admissions, where you find out if you were admitted before the normal admission date later in the spring."

"Does your art school do early admissions? Have you heard anything?"

"I haven't checked my personal email in a while." I pulled out my phone.

"It's not like you've been busy or anything," Yasmin teased.

I scrolled through some junk emails, then I saw it—an email from the art school I had applied to in the fall. "They emailed me," I said, a strange sensation filling me.

"What does it say?" Yasmin leaned in.

I clicked on the email and read the message. "I got in." I waited for the moment of exhilaration to come over me, but instead I felt... confused.

"Congratulations!" Yasmin said before seeing the look on my face. "Or... not?"

"No, I'm glad I got in. I know I always would have wondered, 'What if?' if I hadn't applied. But with everything that has happened and how much I care about the new society I'm part of now, it just doesn't feel like the right path anymore."

"If you don't go to art school, is there something else you want to pursue?" Yasmin asked.

"Honestly, I don't know. I still love art, obviously. And I love botany now too. And I've been enjoying art history as we research da Vinci. I just don't know what I'm actually *meant* to do."

"Are you asking for advice or looking for a listening ear?"

I shrugged. "A little advice couldn't hurt."

"I think the fact that you just said what you are 'meant' to do rather than what you 'want' to do means a lot. You're the first one of us in a long time with all the affinities. There is so much you could be meant for. And uniting the different affinity groups through sharing this centuries-old knowledge you've found... That's a pretty good start."

I contemplated her words. "But what should I do after this year at the academy ends? I feel like I have a purpose now, but if we somehow stave off Feathergrass's changes and return the academy to its former glory... then what?"

"I know you'll figure it out. A girl with as many interests and skills as you have will do well wherever you end up."

"How about you?" I asked. "Is the plan still to work at a field station in San Antonio?"

"Yes, if possible. I've always known I wanted to work at a field station back home and hopefully do an internship there. The downside of being so sure is that I don't exactly have a backup plan."

I nodded, knowing exactly what she meant. Until I'd learned I was a magical botanist, my every intention was set on attending the art school where my mom had been a student. There was no plan B. But I had since discovered a whole new magical world, and deciding what should come next somehow felt harder than ever.

We ceased our conversation when we saw our prop design instructor approaching our table. She examined the flower Yasmin was holding. "That's quite impressive. I can tell you two put a lot of time into it. It's so... realistic. I think the actors and the audience are going to love it." She nodded her approval then moved to the next table.

Yasmin and I looked at each other, barely able to suppress our laughter.

Chapter Thirty-Four

After the prop design class, I said goodbye to Yasmin and walked to the nearby Wildflower Trail. The surrounding forest felt different since I knew a magical botanist lived within.

Once I was sure I was alone, I climbed into a tree and tree-walked in the direction of Oren's tree house. The forester was sitting on the small porch with a thermos in hand and a clipboard on his lap. He waved when he saw me.

"Is now a good time?" I asked, signaling to his clipboard.

Oren moved it aside. "Yes. I was just taking a break from my tree density surveys. We're thinning this year for fire protection. Wasn't expecting to see you so soon. Are you still on your quest for the book?"

"Yes and no. We found the book, but we're working on interpreting its contents." I filled him in on everything I knew about the book so far then turned to the page with the name Cesalpin at the top. "I believe this was written by your ancestor."

Oren ran his fingers over the name. "This is incredible."

I nodded. "Did you know you were descended from the Renaissance botanists?"

"We had a general idea of our heritage, but we never knew the history you just shared. They bound up their magic in books when they were hiding from the rulers? That means one of our family books must have activated my magic."

Oren rose, and I followed him into the tree house, which smelled of citrus and sweet olive. He scanned a shelf of books carved into the tree and pulled one out. The cover looked similar to the da Vinci botany journals I had encountered.

"Possibly this one. I think it's the oldest book I have, and it's been in our family as long as I can remember." He tilted open the cover. "No author listed, but the writing matches Cesalpin's riddle in your book."

"Lucky your family managed to hold on to that," I said, thinking of how, if my family had one of da Vinci's books at some point, they had lost it at least a few generations back. "And you're sure you don't have all the affinity powers?"

Oren closed the book and shook his head. "No. I attended Evergreen Academy and took all the affinity tests like everyone else. My lead is trees, and I have a strong trailing for harvesters, the same as most of the rest of my family."

My shoulders deflated slightly, but I tempered any disappointment. Petra didn't have all the affinity powers either, so it seemed it was rare even among the Renaissance families. Or perhaps they were just beginning to reemerge.

I held out the *Vanished Compendium*. "I have a group of friends working on deciphering the da Vinci riddle, but I wanted to make sure you had access to yours."

Oren took the book from me and read over his ancestor's riddle several times, and I assumed he was memorizing the text, as I had with da Vinci's riddle.

"Any ideas?" I asked.

He shook his head. "No, but I'll work on it. This must be how my great-grandfather made the Floracantus we used to break the blocking spell in Frank. I know he had several affinities, but he must have had all of them if he was able to make new Floracantus."

Oren returned the book. "If my magic works like yours does, I don't think I'll be able to make new Floracantus with just my tree and harvester affinities. But still, I'd like to solve it. Maybe the remaining affinities will recur in my family line someday. I'll send you a leaf message if I figure anything out. Thanks for sharing this with me."

"Of course. We Renaissance botanist descendants have to stick together."

Chapter Thirty-Five

When the morning of the Valentine's Day Floral Fete arrived, the halls of Evergreen Academy seemed more vibrant than usual. After weeks of underhanded sabotage of Feathergrass's continued oversight of our classes while trying to keep our studies and research priorities moving forward, we were all ready for a "normal" Evergreen Academy experience.

When I opened the door to let Coral and Aurielle in, a heart-shaped piece of greenery flew into the room and landed on my shirt. When I examined it, I realized it was composed of two simple tree leaves that were fused together in a nearly perfect heart.

"The tree affinities are floating those throughout the building. Can't let the florals have all the glory today, I guess," Coral said.

We worked to put the finishing touches on our outfits, makeup, and pinup-style curls. The era we were channeling with our outfits was 1950s and '60s floral fashions, and Yasmin had raided the costume closet for us.

"You know things are going to go sideways after your reveal, B," Coral said, touching a bit of cream rouge to her cheeks.

"Yes, so let's try to enjoy the party until then," I said, my stomach slightly unsettled at the thought of what I was going to do.

"Professor Sage kept a close eye on all the food preparations, so there should be no carniolica-spiked cupcakes this year," Aurielle said. She had chosen adorable high-waisted capri pants and an off-the-shoulder floral top, and she was rocking the pinup curls in her mousy blond hair.

"Thank ferns for that. The last thing we need is for members of the Root and Vine Society to be spilling their secrets to Feathergrass." I did one final check in the mirror. My dress—which was solid red on the top—was tight fitting through the bodice then exploded into a fluffy skirt of turquoise blue covered in real red and pink flowers. My lips were as red as the poppy anemones.

Well, even if everything about my plans went sideways and Feathergrass kicked me out of school, at least I would have one last epic fashion night at an Evergreen Academy party.

We filed out of our dorms, joining the stream of students in floral attire, headed to the flower gardens. I tried to focus on the beauty of the moment, on the way the flowers seemed to bloom from every surface, rather than on the nervous bees in my stomach.

I was searching the fields of flowers and tables, wondering if Callan had arrived, when a hand tapped my shoulder. I turned to see Callan extending a flower-shaped cupcake my way. "In case you wanted to get anything off your chest," he said, a knowing smile gracing his lips.

I shook my head and couldn't help laughing. "Aurielle already told me Professor Sage checked all the food. No truth serum in the cupcakes this year."

I took in Callan's outfit. He was wearing navy pants, suspenders, and a bow tie. His white shirt was rolled up to the elbows, displaying his tattoos. I swallowed. He looked *very* handsome—front-cover-of-a-vintage-men's-fashion-magazine handsome. I never imagined *suspenders* would be the thing to take me down, but there was a first time for everything.

When I came back to my senses, I saw that Callan's eyes were flicking to my lips. "Do you like the red?" I asked.

His eyes darkened. "You have no idea, local."

Coral turned away from the conversation she was having and slipped an arm through mine. "Sorry, have to steal her. She promised we could enjoy the party before she flips this whole academy on its head."

Callan gave a slight incline of his chin. "She's all yours. For now."

My stomach flipped as he kept his eyes locked on mine, walking backward a few paces before turning away to join Hollis.

Coral said, "Breathe, darling. We all know he looks good in a suit. Let's get some rose water lemonade to cool you off."

We meandered around the party, eating, admiring the gorgeous lengthy garlands the floral affinity students had made of braided-together flowers, and socializing as if everything were normal, until the time finally arrived for us to gather around the floral students' displays.

In past years, students had wandered through the displays as part of the party. But Feathergrass wanted things to be more academic, so we would each be presenting our design in front of the gathered crowd.

"Welcome, everyone. It's time to see what our floral affinity students have been up to this year. As it's our most abundant affinity, I hope your creations will impress us with their ingenuity. I'll be teaching a class on acquiring patents next year, and I will be watching for items I think could make good candidates." Feathergrass concluded his introduction and stepped aside.

Next to me, I could practically feel Coral restraining herself from rolling her eyes.

"Patents?" Aurielle whispered, her voice sour.

I knew what she meant. It went against everything Evergreen Academy stood for, which was the open sharing of knowledge in our community and, over time, the distribution of our most helpful finds in the human world. Extreme profit was never intended to be part of it. The plants worked with us for free, so why should we profit from their splendor?

One by one, floral affinity students showed us what they had put together for the Floral Fete. A few had made skincare products and healing ointments, but most of the presentations were valuable because of their beauty. They presented pressed flower displays of the most delicate flowers, dishes with real flowers embedded into the ceramic, jewelry, hair pieces, and more. The creations were stunning reminders of the beauty of nature and how little we magical botanists had to do to enhance it. In a way, the floral affinity students were putting up their own acts of resistance by demonstrating it.

I watched Feathergrass's face throughout the presentations and could see that he was underwhelmed. *What was he expecting? Flower-fueled rockets?*

Finally, it was my turn. Professor Tenella had ensured I would be the last to present. While we hadn't filled her in on what I was doing, for her own protection, I had a feeling she knew I was up to something, and I felt that her playing along indicated she supported it.

I stepped forward and retrieved the large bouquet I had stashed with the other floral presentations. I moved it to the small garden table used for the presentations and let the flowers rest there for a moment. Finally, I spoke.

"My presentation is going to be a little... unusual," I began. "The flowers you see here are carrying something precious." I untied the ribbon around the bouquet, and the flowers fell outward, revealing da Vinci's book, which I had taken from the tree conservatory. I let my eyes flick to Feathergrass, who had zeroed in on the book like a hawk. *Good. Let him think this is what I want him to think it is.*

"I recently came into possession of a book from the Renaissance period. It is by one of the authors of the *Compendium*

Floracantus, and it contains Floracantus none of us have ever seen before."

Gasps spread throughout the crowd, and a few people took a step forward, as if they wanted to touch the book.

"There are about forty Floracantus in this book. Many of them have the function of changing the appearance of a plant or enhancing beauty, which is why I thought it was fitting to share it at the Floral Fete, a celebration that has historically been a reminder of the beauty plants provide to the world."

Feathergrass's attention hadn't shifted.

"The book will remain here at the academy, under a phytoglass display, for all to enjoy. I know this is a large find for the magical botanist community, and I want all of us to have equal access to it."

At that, Feathergrass strode forward and reached for the book as if to remove it from the table. But when he made contact, he drew his hand back with a sharp hiss.

"Careful," I whispered. "The book doesn't take well to strangers." I kept my face straight, but internally, I smiled at the look of disdain on his face, deciding it had been worth it to stay up far too late enchanting the book with powerful defensive spells.

Feathergrass's lips pressed into a thin line before he relaxed his features and attempted to pull himself together. He turned to the crowd. "We can all agree this is an amazing discovery. It will need to be authenticated and stored for its own protection."

A few students protested with groans.

I spoke again. "Unfortunately, the book cannot be moved. As part of its defenses, it will stay on this table." I reached underneath the stand and pulled out the phytoglass cover then settled it over the book. "The pages will flip every few minutes so students can study them as they wish. This knowledge—created by my ancestor, Leonardo da Vinci—is for *all* of us. Trust me when I say it is authenticated, as you will soon find out when you begin to try the new Floracantus for yourselves."

A vein was pulsing in Feathergrass's neck, but otherwise, he kept his outward appearance surprisingly calm as he spoke again. "Well, I believe this concludes our floral presentations. Everyone, please disperse and enjoy the rest of the party."

I looked out into the crowd and caught Callan's eye. He nodded, and I could see pride there. Step one was complete.

Feathergrass moved closer to me as the crowd began to dissipate. "This is a clever little stunt, Briar, but don't think it will be allowed to stand. The Board of Regents will want that book."

"Then they can come here and view it. I meant what I said. The book is available to everyone."

"You didn't really think you could find the *Vanished Compendium* and get to keep control over it, did you? You're a *student*. Others of much more stature will decide what happens to it. And rest assured you'll be questioned about how and where you found it."

I didn't correct him. We wanted him to think the book was the *Vanished Compendium*, and he was buying right into those plans.

"If someone wants this book, they are welcome to try to take it," I said, my voice calm and crisp. And with that, I turned on my heel and walked away, my floral skirt bouncing all around me.

Chapter Thirty-Six

As the hubbub from my reveal of da Vinci's book at the Floral Fete died down and botanists dispersed to wander through the flower gardens and eat, dance, and enjoy the unusually warm February night, Callan took my hand and pulled me under an arbor of apricot-colored weeping begonias. His hand was warm against mine, and some of the nervous tension that had built up during my bold display in front of Feathergrass eased.

"Seems like he bought it," Callan said.

"He did. Did you see how quickly he tried to take it from the table?"

"Those must have been some powerful defensive charms you put on it."

I nodded. "I may have stayed up a little too late last night working on it. Having access to my powers on campus again is proving to be exceedingly useful."

Callan took my finger and raised his hand, prompting me to do a little twirl in my flouncy dress. "I never thought I liked this era of fashion, but you may have changed my mind."

"What do you think of the skirt that defies gravity?" I swished the bobbing skirt back and forth, and some of the flowers rose slightly before settling against the fabric once more. "As long as the wind doesn't pick me up and float me off somewhere like one of those flying fairy dolls, I kind of like it."

Callan stepped closer, and I felt a touch of wind against the back of my neck. "You don't want the wind to take you places? Because that could be arranged."

My cheeks heated. "I guess it depends. Where would your wind take me, Callan Rhodes?"

He was getting ready to respond when an origami paper tree floated through the air, and seemingly instinctively, Callan caught it on an open palm.

"Where did that come from?" I asked.

Callan was silent, staring at the tiny folded tree in his hand.

I stepped closer, my instincts kicking in. "What is it?"

"We used to make these and send messages to each other down the hall when we were kids," Callan's voice was soft, his jaw stiff as he swung his head around. "Wyatt is here somewhere."

"Here? At the academy?"

Callan unfolded the meticulously crafted tree, and I leaned over to see handwriting scrawled across the paper.

You know where to find me.

"I take it you know where he's waiting?" I asked.

Callan nodded before stuffing the tree into his pocket. "He's in the secret room upstairs. Only tree founders' descendants can open it. It would be the safest place for us to meet if he didn't want to be overheard."

"Do you think he came for the book I just put on display? How would he even know about it?"

Callan's eyes were slightly narrowed. "I'll go talk to him. Whatever he wants, it's better to deal with it sooner rather than later."

"I'm coming with you," I said, already beginning to walk toward the academy's entrance.

"Briar—"

"Remember what you told me? You wanted to protect me from your family until I had access to my powers back. And now I do. You don't need to protect me any longer."

He sighed and ran a hand through his hair. Then he let out a deep breath and met my eyes. "You're right. I think you may have been right from the beginning. I can't keep you safe by hiding you away from them. Instead, they need to see that we're stronger together."

Then, to my utter surprise, he inclined his head toward the building, signaling for me to join him. "Besides, after that display against Feathergrass, I don't think anyone could underestimate you, local."

I fell into step beside him, my heart racing with delight at the shift that had just occurred and anticipation of why Wyatt had come. We went up the stairs, my retro skirt bouncing all the way, until we paused outside the secret wall panel near his dorm.

Callan cupped my face in his hands so gently that his skin hardly touched mine. "I've been stronger ever since I met you, and that's never going to change. Whatever my brother is about to say or do, I want you by my side."

I slipped my hand into his as he touched his birthstone pendant to the spot below the wall sconce and the hidden panel door swung inward. "Then lead the way, Callan Rhodes."

Chapter Thirty-Seven

We climbed the narrow stairs that took us into the secret alcove at the top of the academy building, my nerves skyrocketing as we neared the top. The last time I had seen Wyatt, he came to take the quill from us. Was he here to commandeer the book we just put on display? If so, how could he know about it already?

When we reached the landing, Wyatt was waiting, his arms crossed. Just like the first time I had seen him, I noticed the physical similarities between him and Callan and the subtle ways they were different. Wyatt's five o'clock shadow had filled in a bit more since our January encounter.

"You wanted to see me?" Callan asked by way of greeting.

"Have a seat," Wyatt said, gesturing at the cushiony chairs.

I sat immediately, hoping to ease some of the tension in the room. Callan didn't follow right away, but once Wyatt sat across from me, he took the chair between us.

"Good to know you still remember our old code. It's been a while."

Callan gave a short nod. "It has."

Wyatt let out a deep sigh. "Look, I understand why you're on guard right now. I know we aren't as close as we used to be, Cal. I'm afraid that's a symptom of my taking the job..." He cast a glance toward me, hesitating.

"She knows you work for the DBI," Callan said.

Wyatt's eyebrows rose slightly, but then he nodded and continued. "A lot of this work requires us to purposefully maintain distance. I don't love that, but it's an important job, and I feel called to do it. However, what I've been working on and what you two have gotten involved in have overlapped for a while, and I think it's time to clear the air."

I straightened, eager to ask what he was referring to, but I held back. He was Callan's brother, after all, and it felt right to let him take the lead.

After several moments of silence, Callan spoke. "What do you think we have 'gotten involved in'?" He made air quotes.

"Perhaps it's best if I start at the beginning." Wyatt shifted slightly in his seat, but there was a practiced evenness in his voice. "Last year, the DBI received intelligence that the verdant shield was faltering. We sent one of our newest agents, undercover, to investigate."

I sucked in a breath. "Alex?"

Wyatt's usual stoicism slipped momentarily, and I could see his shock. "You knew he was a magical botanist?"

"It's a fairly recent discovery," I said.

Wyatt's eyebrows were still slightly elevated, but he didn't ask for more details. "His objective was to keep an eye out here and alert us if the progression of the deterioration worsened."

Callan fisted a palm against his thigh. A few vines from the upper parts of the wall stretched out their tendrils, as if flexing in response to him. "And part of that objective included getting friendly with Briar and dating her friend?"

Wyatt winced, and I could tell the lapse in control had caught everyone in the room by surprise. The vines relaxed. "That was not part of the original mission. I'm afraid Alex may have gotten a little... overzealous in his approach to monitoring the situation."

"Then why did he enroll at SCC instead of Evergreen Academy?" Callan asked.

"Alex was a student here not too many years ago. The instructors would have recognized him. Enrolling at SCC gave him plausible cover to be in town and to engage with some of the dual-enrolled students from SCC and Evergreen Academy if needed."

"You expect me to believe that his selecting Briar as his target was mere chance?" Callan's voice oozed disbelief.

"Not mere chance, no. We gained intelligence early in the school year that a new student who was local to the area and unfamiliar with our world had joined. She seemed like a promising dual-enrolled student to keep tabs on, as she was unlikely to be suspicious of a new friend seeking her out at Siskiyous Community College."

I tried not to be offended by that, and Wyatt wasn't wrong. I *hadn't* suspected Alex in the least, not while we'd still been friends anyway.

"And what about dating her friend Maci? Didn't that seem a little over the line? Or are there no professional boundaries at the DBI?" Callan asked.

"As soon as I found out about that, I recalled Alex from the field immediately. It's why he never returned from winter break. Trust me. The DBI is handling it, and he will receive plenty of training before—if—he's allowed back into the field."

I could tell Callan wanted to ask more questions, to grill Wyatt further, but I was ready to move on. Neither Maci nor I was damaged by Alex. There were more important things to discuss. "So, if Alex wasn't the one poisoning the shield, did you get intel on who was?"

Wyatt cast his gaze to Callan before refocusing on me. "Unfortunately, yes."

"Who was it?" I leaned forward. The question had been hanging over my head for so long.

Wyatt cleared his throat before answering. "It was our mother."

Callan's shoulders tensed then drooped, as if he'd just received news he was expecting but hoped would never come. "We thought Alex might be working for her."

"That was a good guess. It wasn't her directly," Wyatt continued. "She arranged for a student here to do it. It's my understanding that student got expelled for spiking cupcakes at the Floral Fete last year, but by that point, the soil was already severely compromised."

I sucked in a breath. So it was true. Callan's mom had hired or convinced a student to poison the verdant shield. But the student *hadn't* been Alex. He had been working for the DBI all along.

Another thought occurred to me then, and my fingers formed fists, which I hid by stuffing my hands under my legs. If Alex had been working for the DBI when he attended the wedding, it meant the DBI were the ones responsible for activating my aunt's powers.

"Why did Alex activate my aunt's powers?" The words shot out of me before I could stop myself.

Wyatt winced almost imperceptibly, and again, there was a touch of surprise. He obviously hadn't come into the meeting aware of how much Callan and I had pieced together about his agent. "That decision came from... higher up. Once word got out into the society that you were a descendant of Leonardo da Vinci and had all the lead affinity powers, the DBI began digging into your family tree."

At the affronted look on my face, he put up his hands. "Standard practice. Your aunt was your only close living relative on the da Vinci side. The DBI has always had a division working on finding the *Vanished Compendium*—a different division from the one I work in—and they saw their opening. An agent, code name Cobralily, gave Alex the directive to get a da Vinci journal to your aunt. It was shortly after that when I learned how close Alex had gotten with your friend and I pulled him from the academy mission."

My mind was spinning as I processed all that had been happening behind the scenes for the past year and even longer. I still didn't know what I was going to do about my aunt's powers and whether I should tell her. We were both in a terrible position, and the DBI had put us there against our wishes.

"Is my aunt off limits now, or is the DBI's *Vanished Compendium* team still after her?" I asked, trying to keep my voice calm.

"She was still being considered as a remote option, but now that you just put that book on display..." He let the implication sink in. "I don't think they have a need for her. Why stealthily acquire a book when it's already public for the world to see?"

I relaxed a little at the confirmation of what we had hoped.

"And if my word means anything to either of you, I'll do my best to ensure that the *Vanished Compendium* team pulls your aunt's name from the files."

Callan glanced at his brother but remained quiet.

"I would appreciate that." I took a deep breath. Since the questions about my aunt were out of the way, I wanted to circle back to the revelation about Wendy Rhodes and the Board. "Why did your mom arrange for the shield to be poisoned? Was it to gain access to the school?" I asked, remembering Callan's hypothesis.

Wyatt nodded. "Seems like it. Look around. Feathergrass, our mom's close friend and ally, is now in charge of the academy. The Board of Regents has more influence than ever. My best guess is that they created the appearance of things breaking down at the academy so they could swoop in and gain more control."

"Creating a problem so they could be the ones to fix it," Callan murmured, giving a light shake of his head. "Unbelievable."

"Who all knows about this?"

"Just a few officials assigned to this task force at the DBI.

Given the identities of those involved, we've had to tread carefully."

"Does Mom know that you know?" Callan asked.

Wyatt shook his head. "We've been cautious in our information gathering. As far as we can tell, she and Feathergrass think they're in the clear."

"When you came for the quill, what was your goal?" Callan asked, and I could hear multiple questions being asked in one.

Wyatt's words were even and measured, as if he'd been planning how to explain it. "We knew we had to keep the quill out of the hands of any members of the Board of Regents, since we didn't know who could be trusted at that point. The *Vanished Compendium* recovery team was breathing hard down our necks. Mom or Feathergrass getting their hands on the *Vanished Compendium* would lead to far fewer options for us. You two and whoever you have been working with had more intelligence than we did on that front." Wyatt gave me a nod that seemed strangely like approval.

"So you haven't been working against us?" I asked.

"Not directly. Does the DBI think college students were the best ones to be in charge of the quill and the fate of the *Vanished Compendium*? No. But as it turns out, you all may have been better caretakers than we could ever have been."

"What is the DBI's endgame?" Callan asked.

"Believe it or not, the DBI believes in a free intellectual and academic community here at Evergreen Academy and at our research conservatories. We believe magical botanists operate best by taking a light hand in society whenever possible, not by extending our control in the bolder ways the Board of Regents seems to want."

"So we're on the same side?" I asked.

"If by 'side' you mean supporting the academy—and our society—and the traditions and conservation efforts that we have been fighting for in the shadows for years, then yes, we're on the same side. But what I need to know now is what the two of you have planned next. I take it sharing that book today wasn't the only trick up your sleeves?"

I cast my eyes to Callan, and he studied my face for a moment before turning to his brother. "You've come here with a nice story, Wyatt, but why should we trust you?"

Wyatt leaned back, trying to force a casual posture, but he ran a hand through his hair, something I had seen Callan do multiple times when he was hesitating on what to say or do. Finally, he spoke. "The origami I sent you was an olive branch. Growing up, that meant something." His voice, which had softened, held a meaningful tone, and for a moment, I felt like an intruder on a private conversation.

Callan touched his pocket. "A truce."

"We sent it when we wanted to clear the air after a fight. While we haven't been fighting, exactly, I know I haven't been around much. I left you to the mercy of Mom and Dad and all the pressure they've always put on you with your magic-sensing powers when I joined the DBI. The olive tree is my way of saying... I'm sorry. I want to make this right. And I want to work together."

"And if we share our plans with you, what do we get in return?" Callan asked.

Wyatt crossed his arms. "I can give you Professor East. And we can help you put him back in charge at Evergreen Academy."

Chapter Thirty-Eight

"So, this other book, the real *Vanished Compendium*," Wyatt said, mulling over everything I had just told him, "it's written in riddles?"

The three of us were still in the secret tree founders' descendant room, our heads huddled together, over an hour after Wyatt's surprise arrival.

Once Callan and I agreed to bring Wyatt into our plans—at least partially—the atmosphere had relaxed a hair. For the moment, we were all on the same side, and that side was going to do whatever it took to protect Evergreen Academy and all that we loved about it.

"Yes. We're working on trying to solve the one from da Vinci."

"Feel like sharing?" Wyatt asked.

I looked at Callan, who nodded. I was the only one who could use da Vinci's riddle, if we managed to work it out, so I didn't see the harm in Wyatt knowing it.

I recited, "With two hands, we gather power. Bring each botanical gift to center. Lay to canvas. Sprinkle light. Make the new creation bright."

Wyatt contemplated it for a moment. "Have you tried following the instructions verbatim?"

Callan rolled his eyes. "Of course she has."

"Here. I'll show you." I took an empty journal from the bookshelf and spread it open in front of me. "With two hands we gather power." I raised my hands over the journal. "Bring each botanical gift to center." I tapped into all nine affinities. "Lay to canvas." I set my hands on the notebook. "Sprinkle light."

Callan stepped aside so that light from the overhead window filtered directly onto the page. "And before you ask," he said, "yes, we have tried other sources of light."

"Make the new creation bright." I thought through a simple idea for a Floracantus, inspired by the bonsai tree in the corner of the room. I envisioned its branch structure flipping, turning into the mirror image of itself. But as I thought it, no magic moved from my hands to the page. The bonsai didn't change. There was just... nothing.

"We've tried having her write out instructions. We've used painting canvas instead of a journal. Something seems to be missing," Callan said.

"I see. Well, continue to work on it. What is your plan, when you decipher it?"

I appreciated the way he'd said 'when' and not 'if,' but I was not quite so confident. "If we can decipher it and it truly contains instructions for making new Floracantus, then we plan to use that as leverage against the Board of Regents."

"How so?" Wyatt asked. I could see the gears in his head turning as he strategized various scenarios.

"We've been thinking through ideas," Callan said. "We could hold on to the book until they agree to our terms. Briar could create a Floracantus that could sway their hand somehow. We're still deciding."

Wyatt nodded, then he looked at me and tilted his head

slightly. "What if we did something that changed the balance of power at the school? Something that would bury two weeds with one shovel."

"I'm listening," I said.

"What if you use the book to reset the verdant shield?" Wyatt's voice was low, and his eyes never moved from my face.

"How would that even work?" I asked.

Callan glanced at me, and I could tell by his expression that the proposal had him intrigued.

"The verdant shield was set up with a Floracantus by the combined magic of each of the founders. If you could override that Floracantus with a new one—one you create—the founders' descendants would no longer have such a grip on the academy."

Callan turned to his brother. "How do you think the Board of Regents would react to that?"

"The verdant shield is the ultimate source of authority that founders' descendants have always had over the school and the professors. Most of the board members are founders' descendants. If they were taken out of the charging equation, things could shift around here and quickly. That would have ripple effects into the broader society. We would just be bloodlines then and not hoarders of power."

I swallowed. The fact that Callan and Wyatt were willing to do something that reduced their own power in society had not escaped me. Both brothers turned to me as if asking a silent question.

"It *would* solve the problem of the current shield's weakening that's happened over time and accelerated with the poisoning last year. Do you really think it's possible?" I asked. "The original Floracantus was established by nine founders all working together. It was an incredible show of magic. Even if we could figure out how to make a Floracantus, how could I muster up enough power to replace that?"

Callan touched a hand to my knee. "I've been telling you, local, you're more powerful than you know. If you can figure out how to make the Floracantus, I believe you can do this."

I nodded. If Callan believed it, I could too. I considered Wyatt's suggestion, and the more I mulled it over, the more sense it made. But there were so many unknowns. We didn't know how to interpret the riddle. We didn't know how to make new Floracantus. And if we figured it out, we didn't know how long it would take to make a Floracantus that could replace the one on the verdant shield. And if I managed to make it, how would I get access? Feathergrass had locked down admittance to the charging circle except for founders' descendants on the solstices and equinoxes.

"*If* it were possible," I said, "when would we do this? The board's control over the academy is growing daily. And the spring equinox is my last charging date here as a student."

"Then the spring equinox, it is," Wyatt said.

I balked at him. "That's only five weeks away."

"Then I guess you'd better get to work solving that riddle."

With that, Wyatt stood, and I knew there would be no changing his mind. We had set a date, and we had to find a way to make it happen.

"As for the book down there in the flower gardens..." Wyatt nodded toward the window. "I'll have a word with Feathergrass. The DBI is officially classifying all information about where or how it was found. If he asks you about it, remind him of that."

I nodded, glad to avoid an interrogation from Feathergrass.

"When will we hear from Professor East?" Callan asked.

"He'll make himself known when the time is right. I'll keep him apprised of important updates. For now, he's busy working his contacts and trying to stop the land grabs from humans."

"Tell him good luck," I said.

If Professor East was working on the rest of the society while he couldn't be with us, the Root and Vine Society could work on preserving the integrity of the academy in his absence.

Doubts about my powers whirled in the back of my mind, but I couldn't help seeing the merit in the plan and being bolstered by the fact that both Rhodes brothers believed it could be done. If we could pull it off, it would be a miracle. And a miracle was exactly what Evergreen Academy needed.

Chapter Thirty-Nine

On an early March morning, a few weeks after the Floral Fete and all of Wyatt Rhodes's many revelations to Callan and me, Feathergrass called the students and faculty of Evergreen Academy into the teahouse for an announcement.

The place was already half full of botanists playing Roots and Xylem, which had only grown in popularity since its introduction. Some of the tree affinities had created a tournament board on a thin tree ring they hung on the wall, and names were being crossed off one by one as they worked toward an overall winner.

"What do you think it's about this time?" Coral asked.

"Maybe someone is getting in trouble for sealing Feathergrass's office door closed with moss last night," Yasmin said.

I shot a glance at Meadow. I had seen her do that move before and fully endorsed its use on Feathergrass. However, I didn't want her—or any other student—getting caught.

My classmates outside the Root and Vine Society seemed to have been emboldened by my open defiance of Feathergrass at the Floral Fete. In the few weeks since, acts of resistance to his meddling in the curriculum had popped up everywhere.

When he went to review an affinity studies session at the pond, the aquatics created waves lapping nonstop against the shore, effectively keeping him away from the studies they were conducting underwater.

The herbs put something in his food that caused him to sneeze for a full minute every hour. The man seemed to have several allergies, and the herb affinities students had learned how to sneak them into his food in small doses. He must not have caught on that food was the source yet, since he was still eating the provided meals.

The most courageous group had to be the grasses, who were standing up to a man with their own lead affinity. The previous week, they'd introduced a reversible but dramatic disease to a strain of ornamental grasses, which kept Feathergrass busy trying to undo it all the way until the previous day.

Members of the Root and Vine Society had spotted Feathergrass trying to remove da Vinci's book from beneath the phytoglass multiple times, but my defenses were holding. Beyond that, the members were keeping our heads down. We were attending classes and trying to give the appearance of normalcy so that Feathergrass wouldn't have a reason to suspect us more than any other student.

"Today, I'm announcing the arrival of a special plant," Feathergrass said, his words effectively quieting the room. "The Dandelion of Desire is on loan from the grasses conservatory."

Coral gave a soft gasp then rubbed her hands together. Based on the similar reactions around the room, most of the other magical botanists knew what Feathergrass was referring to.

"Any student who catches another conducting any level of sabotage of my curriculum reviews and reports it to me will get to use the Dandelion of Desire."

A nervous silence spread across the room. It was the first time Feathergrass had publicly acknowledged that any sabotage was occurring.

Coral immediately quit rubbing her hands together, her face turning sour. "He wants us to turn on one another."

"Guess he doesn't know our student body very well," Yasmin whispered firmly.

"All reports will be kept in confidence, so you may share what you uncover with me without fear of revenge from your classmates," Feathergrass said. "The Dandelion of Desire will be stored by the charging circle, under the protection of modified giant hogweed. Anyone who thinks of accessing it without my supervision will walk away with a nasty noticeable rash. For those who would like to notify me of anything for their chance to use the Dandelion, I've added a letter slot to my office door. Place a note through there, and I will seek you out. That is all. Enjoy your evening."

Coral pointed a finger at her tongue and made a gagging expression.

"It's too bad he couldn't have brought the Dandelion of Desire to use as a reward for something actually important, not ratting one another out," Aurielle said.

"What is the Dandelion of Desire?" I asked. "And why do people want to use it?"

"Have you heard the stories about blowing on a dandelion to grant a wish?" Yasmin asked.

I nodded. "Sure. I did that all the time as a kid."

"Well, the Dandelion of Desire is where that myth came from," Yasmin said.

My eyes widened. "It grants a wish?"

Yasmin shook her head. "Well, it doesn't exactly do that. That's how humans have twisted the legend. Or maybe how we intentionally twisted it for them. Instead of granting a wish, it magnifies your magical power on the next Floracantus you use. So for magical botanists, that's like being able to grant a wish, as long as your wish has something to do with using your powers."

"Wow," I said, startled. "It's like an energy drink for botanists?"

Yasmin laughed. "Something like that. But most will never get to use it in their lifetime. They're super rare and tightly controlled by the grasses."

"Why the grasses?" I asked.

"Humans consider the dandelions an herb, but in our society, the dandelions fall under the purview of the grasses. We assume it's because of their root systems and ability to add nitrogen and minerals to the soil," Aurielle explained.

I had experienced the magical botanist classification system differing from that of humans before. Considering what Yasmin had said, I wondered what I would do with increased power if I ever had the chance to use a Dandelion of Desire. I certainly wouldn't be using the one at the school.

"Do we think anyone is going to take Feathergrass up on his offer?" Aurielle asked as we shuffled out of the teahouse to head to the library.

"I sure hope the students here are better than that," Yasmin said. "But I guess we're going to find out."

Chapter Forty

When the weekend arrived, I took a break from the sabotage and secrets at Evergreen Academy to spend an evening with my aunt. Bryce was out with friends, so my aunt and I were crafting homemade pizzas before watching a rom-com. The aroma of spring flowers floated in through the open patio door. Since the weather was warming, my aunt had moved most of her flowers outside, and I assumed Bryce was grateful to have some surface space back.

As we put the pizzas in the oven, my aunt turned to the one large bouquet remaining on the counter, whose blooms were currently evenly splayed between both of us. I had been watching them all evening as they'd subtly flipped back and forth between me and my aunt.

When I got up from the counter, the flowers tilted back toward my aunt. I hadn't realized she was watching them, too, until she pointed and said, "There! See?"

"See what?" I asked, wondering if there was a bug on the bouquet.

"The flowers have been moving," she said, squinting at them.

I froze, a giggle of sheer panic coming out of me.

"I know it sounds crazy," Aunt Vera said, "but I've been noticing it for weeks. At first, I thought I was imagining things, but with you here, it's even more obvious. They've been subtly shifting in the vase."

I swallowed, words trapped before the point of forming anything intelligible in my brain. Aunt Vera knew something was going on. Was it time to tell her? And if I told her, what then?

While I was running through my internal freak-out, Aunt Vera pointed the oven mitt at me. "You know something."

I put my hands up. "No, I don't!"

"Oh yes, you do, Briar Rose. I've been able to spot your tells since the first time you ate the last of the ice cream then pretended to know nothing about it. What is going on?"

I dropped onto the barstool, my bottom hitting it with a loud thud, as any will to continue keeping the secret departed. It was time. Aunt Vera deserved the truth.

"Aunt Vera, there's something I need to tell you. It's about Evergreen Academy and about... you and me."

She paused for a moment before leaning on the counter across from me. "What is it?"

"You and I are... special." I cringed at the word. I should have practiced what I would tell her if the moment ever came. Instead, I had been blissfully ignoring it.

"Special?"

"We have... powers." I grimaced. *I am* horrible *at this*. "Maybe it will be better if I show you." I picked up one of the flowers and, keeping an eye on my aunt, said, "*Petale expandere*." Immediately, the flower expanded its petals in every direction.

Aunt Vera's eyes widened. "How did you do that?"

"It's magic, Aunt Vera. We have plant magic. You and I and a small percentage of the population can work spells on plants."

"I'm a flower witch?" Aunt Vera asked, raising her hands to look at them.

I let out a choked laugh. "I guess you could call it that. In our family line, we have powers—affinities are what we call them—toward all kinds of plants. I don't know whether you have all the affinities or not. You seem to be particularly drawn to flowers, so maybe you just have a floral affinity." My mind spun as I thought through the genetic possibilities. My aunt had been a twin. Was her magical DNA split between her and my mom?

"I knew something was going on," Aunt Vera breathed. "Once I started going all feral for flowers after the wedding, I sensed something was... different about me. I began to pay closer attention to them, and they always seemed to bend toward me and toward you. And now you're telling me I'm a flower witch."

"We're called magical botanists, technically." I tried to smile. It was hard to tell if she was taking the revelation super well or if she was in complete shock.

"Bisnonna always said we had magic in our family. She was serious? This is real? Do that spell thing again."

"It's real," I said then demonstrated a few more basic Floracantus, causing the flowers to grow, shrink, and—when I tried a Floracantus from the new book of da Vinci's—causing a petunia to turn from white to purple.

At that, Aunt Vera put her hands over her mouth. "I feel like I'm hallucinating, but this affirms what I've been feeling these past few months. You've known about this since you joined Evergreen Academy?"

"Yes," I said, preparing my apology. "Professor East said I couldn't tell anyone. The academy is extremely secretive. I wish I could have told you. I'm really sorry, Aunt Vera."

She shook her head. "Don't be. I'm not sure I would have believed you until I started experiencing it myself. Professor East... He's the one who called me last year, wanting to ask a few questions?"

I nodded.

"Why did I start experiencing my powers last fall? What changed?"

"You came into contact with something that unlocked your powers, just like I did. It's a trait of our family line."

Aunt Vera poured herself a glass of wine and beckoned me to the couch, where she sank into one of the deep, cloud-like cushions. "I think it's time you tell me everything."

∼

I spent the next hour filling Aunt Vera in on everything from the moment I had seen something strange in the microscope in Professor East's class at SCC through an overview of my recent classes. I left out the Root and Vine Society, the *Vanished Compendium*, and the extent of the threats to the academy. The last thing I needed was for her to be concerned about anything in the world she had just learned about.

I waited in tense silence for her response. My aunt was rarely quiet for so long.

Finally, she let out a soft "huh."

"Huh, that's interesting? Or huh, you think your niece has gone crazy?"

"It's more of a huh, that feels right."

I let out a breath of relief.

"Thanks for telling me. I'm happy to know my dealings with the flowers weren't all in my imagination."

"You certainly have a floral affinity. I can run all the other tests on you to see if you have affinities for other plants, like I do."

Aunt Vera surprised me by shaking her head. "No, I don't think so. I haven't felt a connection to any plants except for the flowers. And maybe a little something when I'm baking. That would mean I had a... What was it? Herbs affinity?"

I nodded.

She continued, "But I don't want to get tested for the rest. Despite how fascinating this is, it doesn't change much for me. Bryce and I just started our life together, and it's a good one. I can already tell that what you've been learning at Evergreen Academy is going to take you far away from here. I suspected that before I began to connect with the flowers. And I'm happy for you. You're a lot like your mom in that way. But me? I'm content right here."

Something like relief coursed through me, with a sprinkle of disappointment that Aunt Vera didn't want to know more. I couldn't imagine not learning everything there was to know about my affinities. But our life paths were different, and I respected that.

"I'm not saying I'll never ask for details down the road, especially if plants start growing out of my ears or something. But for now, I trust you, and I believe everything is how it's meant to be."

"Okaaay," I said. "But if you do ever decide to add a florist business to your café, I think it will be wildly successful."

Aunt Vera glanced at the bouquet on the coffee table, which was arcing toward both of us. "You don't think the clients would wonder what was with *that* little trick?"

"You'd be surprised what people don't notice if they aren't looking for it."

Chapter Forty-One

The sweet scent of almond blossoms floated through the tree house window, a reminder of how close we were getting to the spring equinox. While a weight had come off my mind when I told my aunt about her powers, the days since had been filled with new blooms sprouting everywhere, a living countdown to my one chance to save the academy.

That night, as Callan and I sat in the tree house, the stress of it all was clinging to me. Not even the orange blossom tea was calming my nervous system. For our plan to work, I would need to be skilled in making new Floracantus by the spring equinox. But Leonardo da Vinci's riddle, despite how simply it read, was proving to be difficult to unravel.

The Root and Vine Society had spent countless hours reviewing his known riddles and answers to try to get a feel for his style, but we could never quite crack the code. I had even tried reciting the riddle verbatim, backward, and searching it for anagrams, but nothing had worked.

The sound of a page flipping caught my attention, and I watched as Callan scanned an aged sheet of an old book. We were poring over the private journals and known works of da Vinci, looking for any scrap of information that could help solve the riddle.

As it neared midnight, I slammed my notebook shut. "We're not getting anywhere." I sighed, which turned into a yawn.

"What's infuriating is that the riddle sounds so simple, yet it's too vague to do anything with," Callan said, echoing the thoughts I had been having.

"Exactly. We don't have enough information to make the riddle usable."

"Too bad we don't know any descendants of the other Renaissance botanists in the book, besides Oren," Callan said. "We could see if any of them still hold knowledge of how to create a Floracantus. These riddles have been locked away in this book, but that doesn't mean there isn't some familial knowledge out there somewhere."

"Too bad Oren didn't know anything more about the Floracantus we used to unblock Frank. He seems nearly as in the dark about his family history as I am." I let my mind skim over Callan's words again. "Familial knowledge..." I said, the term unlocking something in my memory. I sat up straighter, all traces of tiredness gone.

"What are you thinking?" Callan asked, catching on to my body language. He was sitting on the stool next to me, and he turned away from the book he had been combing through to face me.

"Do you remember our first year at Evergreen Academy, when Eli used a Floracantus from his tribe to increase the nutrients in the soil and get the recharge to hold on the verdant shield?" I asked.

Callan nodded. "Yeah. He had to go back to his tribe for healing because it took so much magic out of him."

"But what about the Floracantus he used?" I asked.

"What about it?"

"It's not one from the book of Floracantus. It's one that only his tribe has knowledge of," I said, saying the last sentence with added emphasis.

Callan straightened, understanding dawning. "You think Eli's tribe can make Floracantus?"

"Not necessarily anymore, but maybe they could at one point. Just like science and art developed independently in different regions of the world before international travel, Floracantus could have been developed by Native Americans similar to how they were by the Renaissance botanists."

"That's brilliant." Callan snapped his fingers. "We've been approaching this in a very Eurocentric way. But there might be local knowledge right here."

"Do you think Eli would be willing to share what he knows?"

"He might not personally know much, but there seems to be some generational knowledge passed down through his family. If we explain what's at risk at the academy, maybe they'll share."

"Do you know how to get in touch with him?"

Callan nodded. "I'll see if he'll meet with us. But not at the academy. The last thing we need is Feathergrass catching wind of it. If Eli is available this weekend, could he meet us at your aunt's café?"

"I think—wait." I went through my mental calendar. "You know the play Yasmin and I have been creating props for in our prop design class? *A Midsummer Night's Dream?* This is opening weekend, and we have to be there."

Callan shrugged. "That could be the perfect cover. I can see if Eli can meet us there."

I nodded. "That's a good idea. We'll just be old friends meeting up for a play. It's worth a shot anyway."

"It was great thinking. That's what it was," Callan said. "We haven't been getting anywhere with da Vinci's riddle. And we're running out of time."

"Then let's hope Eli knows something."

"I guess we can stop with the books for the night." Callan

closed his and used his wind powers to whisk them into a basket and secure them in a hidden compartment of the tree house. He picked up his mug—his orange blossom tea was loaded with honeysuckle, of course—and held it up. "To finding answers."

I clinked my mug against his. "To finding answers."

We were suddenly very close, our knees touching as we faced each other. I tilted my mug to take a sip, and Callan's eyes were locked on my face. They dropped momentarily to my lips, and his Adam's apple bobbed before he cleared his throat and took a sip of his own drink.

"Did you mean what you said when Wyatt was here?" I asked, my voice barely above a whisper.

We had rarely been alone since the Floral Fete, both of us busy with classes, Callan balancing two field studies assignments to keep up appearances for his mother, and meeting with the Root and Vine Society to research as a group. Now, we were researching as just the two of us, and I was hyper-aware of how adorable Callan looked when he was slightly sleepy and on a post-idea high.

"Which thing?" he asked, running a hand through his hair.

I set my mug down on the table and trained my gaze on him. "The one where we're stronger together."

"Ah, that thing." He hooked a foot on the leg of my stool and pulled me closer in one swift movement so that I was a breath away. "I definitely meant it."

"Does that mean…" I touched a finger to his forearm and traced a vine along it. "That kissing is no longer off limits?"

Wisps of wind caressed the back of my neck. "Do you want kissing to be off limits?"

"I've *never* wanted kissing to be off limits."

My attention suddenly shifted to a voice calling from outside the tree house.

"Rhodes! You up there?"

Callan called back without ever taking his eyes off my face. "Everything okay, Leif?"

"Feathergrass is doing random room checks."

"Thanks. I'll be right there."

I gasped, pulling back and sitting up straight. "Room checks? What is he checking for?"

"Evidence of the pranks that have been pulled on him lately, maybe. Or just flexing his power after you showed him up at the Floral Fete. Why? Have something in there you don't want him to find?" he teased, and I wanted to wipe the smirk off his face with the kiss we'd just been talking about, but I needed to get back. Clearly, the tree affinities wanted Callan there to supervise too.

"No, the *Vanished Compendium* is secured with both of our protections in the secret room, but Yasmin is going to have a heart attack if our room gets searched. Even though she's one of the most rule-following people I know, this is going to stress her out. I want to be there for moral support."

With a reluctant sigh, Callan scooted back his stool, putting space between us. "Sounds like Leif is on edge too. Can I walk you back to your room?"

"Only if you can keep up." I winked then dashed out of the tree house and onto the nearest branch.

"Cheater!" Callan called, and I could hear the laugh in his voice as he came after me.

Chapter Forty-Two

When opening night for *A Midsummer Night's Dream* arrived, Yasmin and I finished arranging the props backstage, told the actors to break a leg, then headed to the box office to meet the rest of our party. The theater was buzzing with the anticipatory energy that would persist until the curtains were opened and the show began. Guests flowed in a steady stream from the ticket counter through the doors to the auditorium.

Callan and Eli were already there, a little overdressed for a community college play, but they blended in with the other college students well enough.

"Hey, Eli," I said, greeting him with a warm smile. "How has life outside the academy been treating you?"

"Pretty good. I've been working with a homeopathic doctor in the area. We've been doing some good work." Eli looked just as I remembered, with a topknot of dark hair, warm brown eyes, and a stature that would make anyone think he was a professional body-builder, not one of the area's best medicinal healers.

"Putting that famous herbs affinity to good use," I said.

Eli shrugged, but there was a smile behind his eyes. "Trying to.

It's hard enough for people to get medical care here, especially in some of the more remote areas. Whatever I can do to help."

"Speaking of," Callan said, nodding toward a space in the corner of the lobby. We went to it and huddled together. "Do you have anything you can share with us?"

"Some," Eli said to Callan before turning to Yasmin and me. "Rhodes told me you're researching the familial connection to making Floracantus, and you remembered the one I used last year."

"That's right," I said, leaning forward. "Can you tell us how it works?"

"The Floracantus I used for increasing the nutrients in the soil is one that my people have used as long as I can remember. Each year, we give our soil a boost with that magic. It's one of the reasons we've been able to grow most of our own food despite the soil quality not being great on the tribal lands.

"But when I was twelve or so, I was warned never to use it in front of outsiders. That's when I learned that the Floracantus we used wasn't in the *Compendium Floracantus*. It was created by one of my ancestors at least a century ago, probably longer."

"Are there other Floracantus your tribe created?" I asked.

Eli shook his head. "That's the only one I know of. There were more at one point, but as our people were displaced and we moved around, those traditions were lost. The one for the soil quality is the only one we managed to maintain."

I swallowed, considering his words. "I know it's a long shot, but do you know anything about how the Floracantus were created back then?"

"Not much. But there is one thing I can tell you. My older relatives talked about a specific plant that was important to our tribe. It was an herb that was native to the region. Oral tradition said that the plant had something to do with how the Floracantus was created."

Callan's expression told me he was paying close attention,

considering every word Eli said. "A specific plant? You don't know which one?"

Eli shook his head. "Sorry, no. I don't know if it's even growing in our area anymore."

"Do you know what they did with the plant? What kind of role it played in the process?" Yasmin asked.

Eli shrugged. "I always heard that they had to activate the magical genes in the plant and that the genes were dormant otherwise. Lore has it they did it by adding extra fertilizer to the soil. I don't know what the composition was specifically. But all the stories claimed the new Floracantus couldn't be created without the activated plant."

I considered his words. Would I need to use the same plant? As soon as I'd thought it, I discredited the idea. It didn't seem likely that Leonardo da Vinci had used the same plant in Italy that Eli's ancestors had used in Northern California.

"Whatever plant this was, I'm sure your family kept a close eye on it?" Callan asked.

"I'm sure they did. But like I said, I don't know the current status of it."

Yasmin gasped, and each of us swiveled our heads toward her. "Your family keeps a close eye on a plant, B."

"What are you—oh!" I exclaimed, catching her meaning. "Rosie?"

Yasmin nodded. "Think about it. The plant has been kept in your family for generations. None of us has been able to identify it. What if it's actually been in your family for hundreds of years?"

"You think someone transported it across continents?" I asked.

"Maybe. All they would have needed is a cutting. Perhaps the plant grew somewhere in the United States too. Without knowing what it is, it's impossible to say for sure. Think about it. How many families do you know that keep a family plant?"

Callan and Eli raised their hands, and Yasmin waved them off with a shake of her hand. "Okay, magical botanist families are obviously an exception. But your family didn't know they were magical botanists for at least a few generations. So why were they carefully preserving Rosie?"

My pulse was racing. Yasmin was right. She had to be. "Yasmin, you're brilliant. I'll swing by my aunt's house tonight to take a fresh cutting, then we can experiment with trying to activate it."

"It's a solid lead," Callan said, clapping Eli on the shoulder.

"Thank you so much for your help, Eli," I said. "This is far more information than we started with."

"I'm glad I could help, even if I couldn't provide specifics. My tribe is aware of what's been going on at the academy and in the Society, and they're prepared to isolate themselves even further if things in the Society don't settle down, but we younger generations don't want that. I hope to be practicing medicine with this guy one day." He nodded toward Callan.

An usher came our way then, signaling that the show was about to start. The four of us went inside and found seats together.

As the play unfolded, I tried to stay in the moment, marveling at the amazing work of the acting students and appreciating the way the props and costumes we had been creating for months came together to bring the show to life. When our flower prop had its big moment, I leaned in a little closer.

Cupid's bow struck the flower, and as we had planned, the touch activated the little cells inside the flower, and they lit up, running tiny lights of electricity through the petals and stem. Yasmin elbowed me and smiled at the gasps of delight from the audience.

When the show ended, we stood with the rest of the crowd, clapping loudly until the curtain was closed. When I finally couldn't be patient any longer, I waded through the crowd toward the exit, eager to get to my aunt and Bryce's house.

Callan and Yasmin were right on my heels when we reached

the parking lot and said goodbye to Eli. We didn't have a moment to spare.

It was time to figure out what, if anything, our family rose bush was hiding.

Chapter Forty-Three

"Are you going to sneak up and take a cutting, or are you going to tell your aunt what you're doing?" Yasmin asked as we pulled up in front of Aunt Vera's home.

"I don't see Bryce's car, so it's just my aunt here. I'll tell her so she doesn't think someone is trying to raid her flower beds."

"Want us to come?" Callan asked.

When I nodded, we left the car and walked to the house. Callan and Yasmin waited by Rosie while I went in the house and found my aunt watching television.

"Hey, B. I didn't know you were coming over tonight," she said, pausing her show.

"Sorry, it wasn't planned. I'm here for Evergreen Academy reasons. Can I take a cutting of Rosie?"

Aunt Vera stood up, looking intrigued. "Are you going to use your flower witch skills?"

I laughed. "Magical botanist skills, Aunt Vera. Want to help? We could test out what we're trying to do here if you have any fertilizer."

"I have a few bags in the garage. Take your cutting and come right in." She glanced out the door and waved at Callan and Yasmin.

I took the cutting, and soon, we were all gathered around the dining room table. "We're trying to activate some genes in Rosie," I explained. "She's been in our family a long time, and we think she might be an ingredient in some magic we're trying to do."

"Really?" Aunt Vera looked surprised. "I guess I always wondered what the history was behind her. The only thing we were told growing up was that we couldn't let Rosie die, and we had to keep her in the family."

Callan, Yasmin, and I exchanged meaningful glances. That boded well, based on what Eli had told us. I took some of the fertilizer and spread it onto the soil containing the cutting.

"Eli didn't say if there would be any outward appearance of the genes activating," Yasmin mused.

"True." I took that as my cue to connect with the flower on the cellular level. After a minute of searching Rosie's cells, I didn't notice anything out of the ordinary.

"Maybe we need to play with the soil concentration. More nitrogen, less phosphorous, that sort of thing." Callan reached into his backpack and pulled out a notebook then quickly drew a perfectly straight table with names of common soil nutrients in its columns.

"Is *this* what you do all day at Evergreen Academy? Take measurements and create graphs? I thought magical training would be more exciting," Aunt Vera said, though she was eyeing Rosie with interest.

I laughed. "There is plenty of work involved in magical botanist training, but I can assure you there are exciting parts too."

We got to work, with me manipulating the soil and checking the flower's cells for any reaction while Callan recorded null result after null result. After fifteen minutes, my aunt brought us all glasses of spring cider, and we took a short break.

"You're exceptionally good at working with soil, B," Yasmin said.

I shrugged, surprised by her words. "Maybe it has something to do with having all the affinity powers."

Yasmin bit her lower lip before saying, "Maybe."

I stared at Rosie, searching through her cells. The lack of any changes was strange because of the fertilizer. "Maybe it's not the quantities that need adjusting," I said after thinking it through. "Perhaps I need to work on her uptake mechanism. Maybe in her dormant state, Rosie doesn't take up nutrients correctly."

"Good hypothesis," Callan said.

I zeroed in on the plant's roots and xylem, gently modifying them with a common Floracantus to increase nutrient uptake. Only a few seconds passed before Rosie's bright-pink flowers emitted a soft glow.

Aunt Vera gasped, Yasmin clapped, and Callan gave me a high five.

"I take it back. That was exciting," Aunt Vera said, running her hand along one of the glowing petals. "How did you do that?"

"I can teach you one day, if you'd like."

"I'll think about it. What happens now?"

"Now," Callan said, grinning at me, "Briar is going to test out your family's ancient powers."

Chapter Forty-Four

"Any specific requests for the type of Floracantus I try to make first?" I joked, trying to ease some of my tension. I was in the Evergreen Conservatory with Callan and the rest of the Root and Vine Society. With everyone gathered, my nerves were showing their pesky faces as I wondered if I could successfully make a new Floracantus.

"Whatever you want, B," Aurielle said encouragingly.

I surveyed the cave and found the lily of the valley flowers I had grafted there after my initiation into the Root and Vine Society. "Maybe I'll try making those glow, like the genetically modified moonflower plants."

Callan nodded as if he liked the idea. "Do you have a name in mind for the Floracantus?"

"Does it need to be in Latin?" Meadow asked.

"We think it could be any language. Eli's family Floracantus wasn't in Latin," Callan said.

"But since this is through my family line, which historically used Latin to create Floracantus, I'm going with that just to be safe," I explained.

"I'm dying to see how this works," Heath said, his eyes alight.

I had memorized da Vinci's riddle, so I recited it for the group:

> *With two hands, we gather power.*
> *Bring each botanical gift to center.*
> *Lay to canvas. Sprinkle light. Make the new creation bright.*

I walked them through the process we had worked out in my head. "For the 'lay to canvas' line, we're using the Floral Fete book as a template. It was full of Floracantus done solely by da Vinci, and it was written in a notebook, so that's the type of 'canvas' I'm using."

Coral opened my notebook on the ground in front of me.

I took a deep breath, glad for all the Latin studies I had done, and recited the words in my mind, envisioning them forming on the pages of the journal.

"Lay to canvas. Sprinkle light. Make the new creation bright," Aurielle quoted. "I've got the candles." She reached into her bag and pulled out a candle and some matches.

"Everyone ready?" I asked.

I was met with nods and a slow clap of encouragement from Hollis. It was now or never.

After opening the notebook, I hovered my hands above the pages, keeping my focus trained on the lily of the valley.

Callan stepped forward and nestled the cutting of Rosie in my hands.

I drew on all of my nine affinity powers, taking care to intentionally connect with each one. They felt stronger since my trip to the defensives conservatory, when the poison on my powers had been dissolved.

"Ready for the light?" Aurielle asked. When I nodded, she lit the candles and held them inches from me, bathing the journal in a soft glow.

I recited the new Floracantus in my mind once more, maintaining my connection with both the lily of the valley plant and all of my affinity powers.

At first, I thought nothing was happening, but then I felt movement in my fingers. When I looked down, Rosie's glowing petals were arcing toward the page of my notebook, as if wanting to dive into it. I remained still, and with a ripple like a drop of rain landing on a lake, the petals hit the page and absorbed into it, disappearing. Light flickered across the journal.

Around me, my friends gasped. I forced my concentration back onto the Floracantus I was trying to make and pulled the lily of the valley back into my vision. I connected with each of the cells and thought of them glowing as brightly as the moon.

"Did it work?" Aurielle asked.

My heart racing, I looked at the journal and saw the Floracantus I had been repeating in my mind written on the page in a looping cursive. "It's there," I whispered, a smile touching my lips. It had worked. "*Petale candenti.*"

When I spoke the words aloud, every tiny white bell of the lily of the valley flower lit up like streetlamps in winter.

My friends gasped again, and I released Rosie, not wanting to crush the rest of the activated cutting.

Hollis, who had been unusually quiet for most of the ordeal, let out a low whistle.

"It worked," Coral said, her voice shaky. She was beaming at me.

"And the new Floracantus just... exists? I feel like that defies the laws of physics." Laurus said, scratching the side of his neck with a pencil.

"You know we've been working toward this for weeks, right?" Meadow asked, giving Laurus a sideways look.

"Yes, but it wasn't real then."

"How do you think the original Floracantus were made?" Yasmin asked.

Laurus put his hands up. "I know. I know. It's just weird that this Floracantus that didn't exist now does."

"Physics and magic can coexist, Laurus," Meadow said, flicking a piece of moss in slow motion at him as if to demonstrate it.

"This is going to be revolutionary. We've never been able to get flowers to glow without genetic modification," Aurielle said, her attention still on the shining white orbs.

I looked at Callan, who smiled.

We took another moment to marvel at what had just happened before Coral asked, "So, what next? What type of Floracantus could you make that would be most successful in taking down Feathergrass?"

I paused, lacing my fingers together in front of me. It was time to share the idea that Wyatt had suggested. Callan and I had kept it to ourselves until we solved da Vinci's riddle.

I cleared my throat and said, "I want to make a Floracantus to reset the verdant shield."

Silence filled the room, and a smile pulled at the corner of Callan's mouth.

Hollis quit playing with the fern he had been annoying Coral with and turned his full attention to me.

"What do you mean?" Yasmin asked.

"The founders used a Floracantus to put the shield in place, including stipulations that only founders' descendants could recharge the shield. What if we were able to change that?"

"You really think you can create a Floracantus to reset the verdant shield?" Ravenna asked. "Isn't that going to be much harder than making petals glow?"

"I'm going to practice and work on harder manipulations, but I have to believe it can be done. Wyatt—Callan's brother—was the one who suggested it. He thinks it's possible, and he's pretty well acquainted with the verdant shield. We'll need to do more research on how the shield was set up. That book Meadow stole for her Root and

Vine initiation might have some information. We can't guarantee this will work, but we need to try. Part of what the society is doing that we disagree with is consolidating power into the hands of founders' descendants. If we can remind them of why Evergreen Academy was created in the first place—to be somewhere for *all* magical botanists to study together, then maybe we can turn things around."

"It's a bold plan," Hollis said. "I like it."

Meadow nodded. "I've been reading the book about the founders. It's proving to be pretty illuminating. The shield design was initiated by Douglas Vitalis, Callan's ancestor." She nodded toward Callan. "And it was put in place by all of them, using a protective Floracantus from the *Compendium Floracantus*. The mechanism that made it so only founders could recharge it was implemented by the defensives founder, Jean-Claudia Callahan. The poison from her magic was what Briar experienced when she tried to help charge the shield last year."

"So are we all going to need to help reset the shield?" Heath asked.

"According to the book, it was a time-consuming process for the founders to all merge their magical abilities like that," Meadow said. "There's no guarantee we will get that much uninterrupted time. And none of the founders had all the lead affinity powers like Briar does. Theoretically, she should be able to do it all herself. Especially if she's using a similar but new Floracantus of her own creation."

A few nods came from around the group, but I could tell some of them wouldn't be fully convinced until we successfully pulled it off. I couldn't blame them, because I felt the same way.

"Do you have a plan for how to get to the charging ring? Feathergrass still has it locked down," Hollis said.

"Not yet. We'll have to get creative in figuring out how to distract him."

Playfulness lit up Hollis's eyes when he nodded in approval at my response.

"And we'll have to do it quickly, since the vernal equinox is just around the corner," Callan said, stepping forward and effectively calling the meeting to a close.

After a few more side conversations, the members of the Root and Vine Society left the cave in waves, heading off in different directions. We didn't need other students tracking us down and reporting what we were doing so they would get to use the Dandelion of Desire.

When just Callan and I remained, I stared at the lily of the valley flowers, which were still glowing in the cave from my Floracantus.

We were one step closer. We had solved the riddle. I could make new Floracantus. Wyatt's plan was out in the open, and our friends were on board.

When I turned to Callan, he was studying me.

"Do you really think we can pull this off?" I asked, voicing the concerns I hadn't wanted to express in front of the others. "What if I can't figure out how to make the right Floracantus to replace the current one?"

"I know you can, and you *will*." Callan took my hand. "We're going to figure out how to make a Floracantus to reset the verdant shield, then on the vernal equinox, the Board of Regents is going to find out *exactly* how powerful you are."

I nodded at him in response, the cave seeming to clear of everything else as we looked at each other. I had a newfound power, one that had been lost—at least in my family—for generations. And I was going to do whatever it took to use it to help save Evergreen Academy.

Chapter Forty-Five

"Capture the Roses is going to operate a little differently this year." Feathergrass stretched his arms wide, as if he were an orchestra conductor.

The students and faculty of Evergreen Academy were gathered at the edge of the flower gardens, preparing for the annual Capture the Roses competition. I thought back to the previous year, when I had been put on Callan's team. With Callan and Eli as co-team captains, we had secured a victory.

"To allow you all to stretch your skills to the best of your abilities, there will no longer be only two teams. Instead, there will be eight," Feathergrass continued.

I listened carefully, though I was pretty sure I knew where he was going.

"Each affinity group will have its own team. Team captains have been pre-selected by your instructors. The team that can hold on to its rose for the longest will earn twenty points. Claiming the roses of other teams earns you ten points each. The group with the most points at the end gets a special prize."

His designation of eight teams instead of nine felt like a subtle insult. I was the only defensive affinity student at the academy, and as far as most people knew, I didn't have access to my powers, making me effectively useless in the game.

"What kind of prize?" The question came from a student by the snapdragons, the bright blooms of which came up to our shoulders and extended around the floral affinities, nearly caressing them.

Feathergrass paused for a moment, waiting for total silence. "The group that wins will receive special access to use the Dandelion of Desire on the spring equinox. I will enchant the area where the Dandelion is stored to allow access to that affinity group's students for one night only."

"Hot fronds!" Coral whispered loudly.

Seeming to sense the excitement stirring among the students, Feathergrass spoke again. "Each member of the group will have the opportunity to use the dandelion, though the more people who use it, the less potent the power enhancing properties will be." Feathergrass waved a hand, and the grasses in the nearby meadow shimmied, creating a tune, as if playing walk-up music for us. "Everyone, please sort yourselves into your affinity groups. We will begin shortly."

"Which group are you going to join, B?" Yasmin asked.

I barely heard her, my thoughts spinning from what Feathergrass had declared. I needed to find Callan. "I'll be right back," I whispered.

When I spotted where the tree affinity students were gathering, I moved to Callan's side, trying to blend in with the other students. "Did you hear what he said?" I asked, casting my voice low.

Callan nodded. "Yep. You know what it means?"

"Someone from the Root and Vine Society needs to win the contest. Getting to the Dandelion of Desire ensures us access to the charging circle on the spring equinox."

Callan shook his head. "*You* need to win. You're the one who has to reset the shield."

"How about I join the trees? If I work with you and we win, we'll both get access to the charging circle."

He conceded the point. "True. But then every other tree affinity will get a chance to use the Dandelion of Desire too. It will dilute its powers and put students we don't want near the charging circle while you reset the shield. But if you win as a defensive, you'll have no other students to split the power enhancement with. It's your best guarantee that you'll have the place to yourself, have a power boost, and orchestrate the *entire* visit to the charging circle to your liking, without others intervening."

I inhaled deeply, knowing he was right. "Feathergrass probably thinks I'm sitting this one out because of the lack of access to my powers."

Callan's smile was radiant, excited with a touch of competitive spirit, as it spread across his face. He leaned closer to whisper into my ear, "Then the time has finally come to show everyone what you can do."

As the students sorted themselves into their affinity groups, I made my way toward Yasmin, Coral, and Aurielle.

"Joining us?" Yasmin asked.

I shook my head and quickly whispered the plan. My friends gave tight nods of agreement in return.

"Incoming," Coral hissed, nodding behind me.

When I turned, Feathergrass was approaching. "Ahh, Briar. Joining the ferns today? I thought you might choose the trees. I guess it doesn't much matter, since you won't be able to use your magic to participate. A shame."

I straightened, drawing my breath and quieting the power within me. When I spoke, my voice was steady. "I'll be representing the defensives."

Feathergrass's eyebrows rose. "Indeed? And how will you be competing? You have no teammates and no access to your powers."

"I guess I'll just have to give it my best shot," I said before skipping off to claim the ninth encapsulated rose, which was midnight black.

Once the captain from each team was clutching their rose container—I saw Callan holding his—Professor Tenella raised her voice. "Good luck, botanists," she called, and the affinity groups began to disperse to separate parts of the grounds, like nine petals of a flower extending in different directions.

I knew immediately where I would hide my rose. Being a solo competitor, I couldn't leave affinity classmates behind to protect it while I sought to steal the other roses. So I would have to put the plants to work.

When I reached the Perilous Grove, I debated my options. Several plants could serve as a deterrent for my rose, but only one could truly hide it. I knew because the same plant had delivered me my field studies invitation envelope the previous fall.

I approached the massive corpse flower and whispered, "*Apertum.*"

Slowly, the plant opened its red and green spathe. Inside, there was plenty of room to nestle my rose within its tissues. Once it was situated, I said, "*Pressule.*" The corpse flower closed its leaves again, the rose disappearing completely inside.

Satisfied with the hiding spot, I turned to the other plants in the Perilous Grove and implemented the Floracantus I hoped would keep my rose safe while I scoured the forest. "*Protegere.*" Protect.

"Now you just have to figure out how to steal as many other teams' roses as possible all by yourself. No big deal." Still, as I said the words, I smiled. I had access to my powers on campus, and it was time for Feathergrass—*for everyone*—to find out.

Chapter Forty-Six

Gathering my power, I used my connection with the trees and their interconnected root system to locate the other roses, just as Callan and I had done during Capture the Roses the previous year.

The trees came through with the intel, and soon, I had a mental map of where each rose was stashed. For the most part, the roses were scattered all over campus, and it was fairly clear which affinity group each belonged to based on location. Like me, it seemed the other affinity groups had gone to areas where they thought they would have an advantage.

I hoped that didn't mean Perilous Grove would be an obvious target. Most students would think I would have no access to my powers, and they might assume my rose would be an easy take. Well, I just had to count on my lack of presence in the grove and the help of my defender plants to hold them off for a while.

Next, I had to decide where *I* wanted to start. I had Root and Vine Society friends in each affinity group. They might catch on to what I was doing and help me somehow. Based on who I'd seen holding roses when we spread out, the only members of the Root and Vine Society selected as team captains were, predictably, Callan, Hollis, and Meadow, the three founders' descendants. The other selected students I didn't know as well, which meant I didn't know if they would fight against me in the game. I had to assume they would. The Dandelion of Desire—and bragging rights—was no small prize.

I decided to start where I felt I had the best chance of success then proceed from there. Hollis was team captain for the ferns, and Yasmin, Coral, and Aurielle were all with him. They were the smallest affinity group besides mine. Numbers wise, my odds were best with that group.

I used my tree GPS sense to head for a heavily fern-laden area in one of the thickest parts of the forest. Debating between sneaking in or approaching with my hands up, I yelped when ferns snaked around my ankles. Then I heard laughter coming from the surrounding grove. The ferns relaxed, and my friends emerged from their hiding spots.

Hollis balanced the encapsulated rose casually in one palm. "We thought you might head here first," he said, a lazy smile on his lips.

"Oh, don't tease her, Hollis," Coral snapped. She marched over to him and took the rose from his hands. Her face twisted into a smile I knew well. "Besides, it's her against all of us. She doesn't stand a chance."

Then she said more quietly, "Use your wind power to take it from me, in case anyone is watching."

I raised an eyebrow but quickly caught on to the ruse. If our instructors were watching, the ferns couldn't roll over without a fight, even if it was a fake one. I called on my wind powers and sent it toward Coral. She stumbled backward, and the rose slid out of her hand. My wind was there to scoop it up, drawing it toward me. I was so busy concentrating I almost missed Hollis putting out an arm to steady Coral.

Ferns were tickling my ankles again—Yasmin, Aurielle, and the others were putting up a half-hearted fight—but I used my own fern powers to get free. I sent a blast of air toward Hollis for good measure, because I knew his ego wouldn't let him be seen holding back. Once he was out of the way, I said, "*Petale expandere.*" The rose grew until it popped its bubble, and the flower was officially claimed.

One down.

The ferns came in close in a huddle.

"Where to next?" Yasmin whispered.

"I was thinking I'd try for the mosses. Their rose is on the north side of the forest."

Hollis nodded. "Good. Meadow should be able to help."

"Should we come with you?" Yasmin asked.

I shook my head. "No. That would be too suspicious."

Hollis spoke up again. "We'll get one rose to help your odds. Only one. Tell Meadow to do the same."

I nodded, catching his logic. "Okay. Who do you want to go after?"

"Cassia, the team captain of the herbs, has been deliberately hiding the best pastries from me at dessert lately. Must be jealous of all my charm." Hollis smiled casually. "I think I'd like to get a little payback."

"Have fun, then. And good luck."

"You, too, B," Yasmin said.

With that farewell, my friends were running off behind Hollis with the other fern students.

As I made my way north, treewalking to speed things up, I passed over the harvesters below. It appeared they were being attacked by the aquatics. The river that helped water the agricultural fields was sloshing violently, muddying the ground nearby.

I didn't have time to watch what happened. The mosses were my next target, and I had to hope Meadow wasn't camouflaged as an earthen goddess like she had been during Orchard Lantern Tag the previous fall.

As I reached the northern part of the campus, the trees thickened again, sunlight barely slashing through them. The north side of each tree was covered in moss, and I knew I was getting close. I used my moss affinity to carefully remove the substance from the tree I was standing in then covered my arms and hair with it. If it had worked for Meadow, maybe it could work for me.

The moss began to stretch out, creating a cool, slightly damp sensation as it crept across my bare skin. I pulled it back as it neared my face. I wasn't *that* committed to my camouflage.

The tree network told me the rose was close. I looked down and scanned the forest floor but didn't see anything. If moss affinity botanists were there, they were hiding well. Or maybe they had taken the tactic I had—hidden their rose then gone on the offensive against other groups.

I began to treewalk again, stepping so lightly that the branches barely moved. The forest was thick enough that they didn't need to. "Where are you?" I whispered, straining for any sign of the rose.

After a few minutes of delicate stepping and searching in the nearly silent forest, I spotted a patch of glowing moss on the ground.

Goblin moss.

I wondered if it was naturally occurring or if the moss affinities had put it there. Cautiously, I climbed down from the tree and approached the moss, still not seeing anyone. The eerily glowing vibrant moss was leading into a small cave I hadn't noticed before. It was feeling more and more like a trap, so I backed off and prodded the goblin moss with my magic.

A Floracantus was working on it, causing it to glow extra brightly. The magic had been applied recently, which meant the mosses were hoping to lure people into the cave. *Then what?* I wasn't going to fall for it and find out. Instead, I changed direction and circled to the back of the small cave, examining the moss's cells as I went to see where the interference ended.

Just as I was about to give up and go after another affinity, I looked up and saw the rose attached to the tree above me, its outline almost invisible through the moss that encased it against the tree branch. "Clever," I said. They must have found a way to mold down the encasing to the shape of a rose.

Using my moss powers, I stretched out a hand and directed the moss to pull back. The fluffy green material slid to the left and right, and the rose fell into my hands.

Clapping began behind me, and I spun around to see Meadow—or at least, Meadow's face. The moss that had been covering her began to peel back until she came into clearer view. "Nicely done. I was kind of hoping you'd fall for my cave trap, but I guess I'm glad you didn't."

I shook my head, smiling. "And what would have happened to me if I had gone into the cave?"

"Let's just say moss can function like quicksand if you know how to work it right."

I raised my eyebrows. "Remind me to never cross you."

"You wouldn't dare," she said. "Now hurry up and claim that rose so I can go join the rest of the mosses."

"Where are they?" I asked before saying, "*Petale expandere*," and claiming the mosses' rose.

"They're scoping out the grasses' hiding space. I'm sure Feathergrass is hoping the grasses will win, so I'll be happy to take them down."

"Perfect. Hollis wanted you to get one of the other groups, but it sounds like you're way ahead of him."

"You got ferns already? Who did they go after?"

"The herbs."

"That leaves trees, aquatics, harvesters, and florals. Where are you headed next?"

"I saw the aquatics in a pretty intense battle with the

harvesters. I'm going to avoid those two and see if one of them takes the other's rose." I contemplated my next steps.

"Don't act like you're deciding. Say hi to Rhodes for me." And just like that, moss crept up Meadow's arms, camouflaging her to the forest once again.

"Good luck!" I called then climbed into the nearest tree.

Callan, here I come.

Chapter Forty-Seven

I hurried directly from where I had retrieved the moss's rose to the tree houses, a slight smile touching my lips. The trees' rose location hadn't been sent to me through the tree network. Apparently, they were protecting their own. But it was as good a place to start looking as any.

I was about one hundred feet from Callan's and my tree house when a cool breeze touched the back of my neck. I froze and spun around. Callan was a few feet behind me, leaning against the tree as if he were out for a casual stroll.

"Out here alone? Where are the rest of the trees?" I called.

"They're on the offensive. They trusted me to handle defending ours."

"And will you?" I asked with a slight smile touching my lips. "Defend it?"

"We're going to have to put on a little show so any observers think I gave you a run for your money. I do have a reputation to protect, you know." His voice was so quiet, the breeze still caressing the back of my neck, and I shivered.

"Is that so?" I asked, cocking my head. I doubted Feathergrass had eyes on either of us up in the trees, but the idea of a little sparring with Callan was too enticing to turn down. "What are you going to do to me, Callan Rhodes?" I teased until a gust of wind swept me off my feet and positioned me in a tree twenty feet away.

I could see Callan's smirk from across the thicket. "Maybe that?"

With my own wind manipulating powers, I ferried myself down. Waving my hands, I pushed Callan flat against a nearby tree, wrapping tendrils of air around him like he had when he was hiding me from his brother in the tree conservatory. "Now, where is the rose hiding?" I asked.

The branches of the nearest trees began to grow and bend, stretching toward me. I jumped as one brushed my arm, and I said a Floracantus to fight them back. When I looked up, Callan was free of his air bonds and nowhere in sight.

"*Leaves*," I muttered, though a shiver of anticipation went through me. It felt right to be sparring with my former tutor once again. And it had been so long since I used my powers freely on campus. I was ready to see what I could do.

"Over here, local," Callan called, and I turned to see him standing near a tree about ten feet away.

Instead of fighting back immediately, I paused to sense for the rose through the trees, trying to dig through the trees' defenses. If my instincts were right, it was hiding in our tree house. And Callan was standing directly between it and me.

I moved toward it, but Callan's reaction was quick. "Careful, local. What tree is this?" he asked, using wind to hold me in place.

"What?" I asked, confused.

"What tree am I standing under?"

I studied the stately tree. "Lodgepole pine, but wh—"

Tiny seeds flew at my head, pelting the air around me like an airsoft gun. I shrieked and ducked behind the nearest tree.

"Leaves," I breathed again, my heart racing. Then I remembered lodgepole pine was a host for *Arceuthobium americanum*, a dwarf mistletoe whose mitochondria could heat up, build pressure within its fruit, and send the seeds out in an explosive onslaught.

It was amazing that none of the seeds had hit me. Or was it? Did Callan use his wind powers to control the seeds so they would only pass close by me? Either way, it was time to fight back.

Sure, I was sparring with the most powerful tree affinity botanist in generations, but I had *all* the affinity powers, and I needed to remember that. I formulated the steps in my head then attacked.

The tree vines moved toward Callan, which he fought off with ease. But I sent grasses and ferns for his ankles and flower petals floating through the air to block his vision. Moss snaked across his wrists, molding him to the tree behind him. I noticed he was smiling as I continued the assault.

After I called on nearly every nearby plant to tie him to the tree, I stepped in close, so that our lips were inches from each other. "Wanna tell me where that rose is now?" I asked.

"Nah. I quite like being interrogated by you," Callan whispered, his eyes blazing.

My breath caught, and I froze, until vines snaked around my ankles, and I had to jump out of his reach. He had distracted me—much too successfully. *Stay focused, Briar.*

"I think the smooth talking has got to stop," I said lightly before pulling a particularly aggressive Venus fly trap from my bag. I had grabbed it as an afterthought when leaving the Perilous Grove.

I used my wind manipulating powers to hover it in front of his mouth. "If it sees your tongue, it's going to have it for lunch."

Callan's eyes widened with delight, but he didn't say anything. He remained anchored to the tree by the many plants I had tangled him up with.

I climbed the tree and entered the tree house. Sure enough, the rose was there, floating in its capsule above the worktable. When I approached it, I noticed a leaf in the shape of a heart underneath.

I bit down a smile as I grabbed the rose and said, "*Petale expandere.*" The capsule exploded, and I had my third rose. I waited until I got back down to the ground to release Callan from his bonds.

He rolled his wrists as if he had been imprisoned for hours then ran a hand through his hair. With a whisk of wind, a vine snaked around my waist.

He used the vine to tug me to him, both of us leaning against the tree. "I told you that you were powerful, Briar Rose."

"Thanks for always believing in me," I whispered.

"Think Feathergrass is watching?" Callan asked, playing with a lock of hair by my face.

"Honestly, I couldn't care less if he is."

Callan's smile tugged at the corner of his mouth. "If he wanted a show, you gave him more than he bargained for." And with that, his lips were on mine.

The rush of the game, of capturing the rose, and of being among the trees with Callan, his sandalwood and peach smell somehow still cutting through all the natural forest fragrance around us, had my head spinning as soon as our lips touched.

I could feel leaves swirling around us, Callan creating a miniature tornado, locking us in place and locking the rest of the world out.

Who cares about Capture the Roses? Who cares about Feathergrass? This is the moment I want to live in right now.

Finally, after several moments of bliss, Callan pulled back. The leaves floated for a half a second more before falling slowly to the ground. Callan rested his forehead against mine, his hand still cradling the back of my neck. "Leaves, local."

"Want to do that again?" I asked hazily.

Callan caressed the side of my neck before stepping backward. "You know I do. But let's finish this. Then we can do that whenever you want."

I raised an eyebrow. "Whenever?"

He smiled playfully but directed me back to the game. "Which roses are still in play?"

"I think florals are. Aquatics and harvesters were battling each other. Meadow's group was going after the grasses, and the ferns were going after the herbs."

"One of my scouting vines reported the aquatics took the harvester's rose just before you got here. Then they got the florals."

"So the aquatics have two. If they beat our friends to either the herbs or the grasses and manage to hold on to their rose, we're tied." I stuffed the tree rose into my backpack with the others, preparing to move.

"I'll get their rose while you go back to defend yours. Everyone who lost their rose already is going to be coming for you."

"Right," I said, having nearly forgotten my defense in all the offense I'd been doing. Well, faux offense.

"Whatever you do, hold on to your rose. I'll join you when I can." And with that, Callan Rhodes was climbing back into the trees, disappearing into the forest.

Chapter Forty-Eight

After watching Callan depart, I hurried back toward the Perilous Grove, my heart rate increasing as I got closer. Sure enough, some of the defeated affinities were coming for me, hoping to reclaim a portion of their points. While the trees, ferns, and mosses were nowhere to be seen, several herbs, grasses, harvesters, florals, and aquatics were making their way toward the grove.

"Fronds," I murmured, debating how I was going to fight them all off at once.

Just as I was clearing my brain to strategize, I heard a whistle to my right, from the forest floor.

"Hollis!" I shouted. "Did you get the herbs' rose?"

"Of course. And mosses are on their way back from taking the grasses' rose. What's the plan?"

"I have to hold them off until Callan gets the aquatics' rose. It's the last one in play." When Hollis nodded, I headed straight for the center of the Perilous Grove. A few students were inside, sporting a mix of rashes and swollen skin.

"Looking for my rose?" I asked, stepping into the grove.

A floral student tossed a packet onto the ground, and wildflowers sprang up around my feet. I gently sidestepped them.

"Are you sure you want to fight me in here?" I asked the group as my defensive plants continued to reach out and irritate the students who were searching them for the rose.

One girl pulled back her finger with a hiss of pain.

"We didn't know you had access to your powers," a first-year harvester student said.

"Surprise," I replied before stretching out my arms and calling a few of the plants toward me, forcing the students closer together in the grove.

"My team captain sent me out here, but I didn't know it was going to be like this," a grasses student said, jumping sideways when a thorny nettle nearly scratched his foot.

"It's not too late to turn back." I moved to reveal a clear passage out of the grove behind me.

The botanists looked at one another, and after one last poke to each of them from the nettle, they ran past me and out of the grove. Well, that had been easier than expected. There were perks to being the only defensive botanist on campus.

"Thank you," I said to the plants.

When I had the place to myself, I spun around, connecting to the plants around me and focusing on what it felt like to be using all my powers, fully unleashed.

In that moment, I had confidence that maybe I *could* create a Floracantus to reset the verdant shield. I had been practicing every day, and so far, I had created four new Floracantus, all of which were recorded in the journal I was using as the conduit. And while it still felt like a miracle each time I created a new Floracantus, the feeling was also becoming familiar and comfortable.

I tried out the Floracantus I had made on the lily of the valley flowers in the grove. "*Petale candenti.*" They began to glow, and I smiled. It was reassuring to know that the new Floracantus were still working.

When I heard footsteps, I quickly whispered, "*Petale neutrus,*" reciting another Floracantus I'd created, which undid the effects of the first. The lily of the valley's white petals returned to their normal state.

"Briar!" Aurielle called. "Callan got the aquatics' rose. The game is over. You won!"

I smiled with relief. She hugged me then asked, "Where is your rose?"

I led her to the corpse flower and beckoned it to unfurl. Once it had opened, I lifted my rose out.

"Genius hiding spot," she said. "I know I sure as spores wouldn't be sticking my hand in there."

"That's what I was banking on." I thanked the corpse flower then turned back to Aurielle. "Time to claim the win."

Chapter Forty-Nine

The post-Capture the Roses celebration dessert was an experimental soufflé from Professor Sage and the other herbs affinities. The flavors were combinations of chocolate, cheese, peach, raspberry, and other decadent fruits fresh from our orchards. Pairing it with academy-made ice cream or mochi, the students lounging in the teahouse were in heaven.

I had barely taken two bites when Feathergrass approached our table. "Briar, may I have a word?"

"Yes," I said, leaving my bowl with Yasmin for safekeeping.

She mouthed, "Good luck."

"Congratulations," Feathergrass said, ushering me into a seat in Professor East's former office. While a few of the vines that had previously lined the walls of the room were still present, our scouting vines mixed among them, some had been replaced by pots of ornamental grasses, giving the impression we were at a fancy garden party. "That was quite the feat. Winning Capture the Roses as a team of one. I don't know if it's ever been done before."

"Yes, well, defensive affinities do have a bit of an advantage in that game."

"I suppose they do," Feathergrass admitted. He leaned back.

"But the real question is: When did you get access to your powers on campus again? And how did you do it?"

I had been expecting the question and had prepared my answers. "Not long ago," I said. "I've been working on increasing my defensive skills in my field studies assignment this year. Eventually, it got to where I was able to break the bonds on my magic." There. Simple enough and true enough.

"Hmm. I didn't realize that was a focus of your field studies assignment." He studied me. "Your field studies advisor hasn't checked in with the academy since before the winter break. Can I assume you haven't had a field study since then?"

"That's correct," I said. My time in Florida didn't count.

"Their name isn't listed in your file. The entire thing was marked Classified by Professor East." Feathergrass tapped a pen to the table as if trying to work something out. "Who is your mentor?"

"I'm afraid I can't share that information."

"I am the director of Evergreen Academy now, Briar. Field studies are within my purview."

"If the files weren't declassified for you, then it is not in my power to do so."

Feathergrass frowned. "Field studies are a requirement for second years, and if your advisor is no longer participating, we will need to find you a new assignment for the remainder of the year."

I straightened, nerves churning in my stomach, which I tried to settle. Perhaps this didn't have to be a bad thing. I was open to a new field study assignment. But Feathergrass might put me on a project that would take me away from all that I was doing with the Root and Vine Society. We were so close to the spring equinox and I couldn't afford a distraction.

"Perhaps I could join one of the studies that are already running, since it may be difficult to find a new advisor and project at this point in the year," I suggested.

Feathergrass tapped his pen against the desk a few more times then rose. "Let me think on it. In the meantime, I will be sharing the development of your powers with the Board of Regents. I'm sure they will be most interested by this news." He opened the door for me.

When I stepped outside, I was still processing the conversation. Feathergrass hadn't seemed angry that I had my powers back. I wondered if that meant he hoped I was on his side of the philosophical table. If so, what kind of field assignment would he place me in? And what would the Board of Regents—Callan's mom, specifically—think about my overcoming the curse of their ancestors, the founders?

Would they finally leave me alone, or would this development make them want to get access to my powers even more? Would I be forced to reveal the identity of my field studies advisor? Wyatt had successfully helped quash questions about the origin of the fake *Vanished Compendium* that I had debuted at the Floral Fete, but my secrets were stacking up and likely pushing Feathergrass's bounds.

When I returned to the teahouse, Yasmin passed me my soufflé and mochi. "Everything okay? Did Feathergrass interrogate you about your powers?"

"He says I need a new field studies assignment, since my advisor is uncommunicative. And he tried to press me on who my advisor was."

Coral snorted. "He'd lose his mind if he learned your former advisor was the curator of the defensives conservatory."

"That he would," I said, smiling slightly at the thought.

"Did he say what your new project will be?" Aurielle asked.

"He's going to think on it. And he's telling the Board of Regents that my powers are unlocked."

"Of course he is." Coral rolled her eyes.

"I just hope he finds me a field studies assignment that isn't completely for the board's agenda." I took a bite of the soufflé, my mood instantly boosted by the explosion of flavor.

"Whatever it is, you won't have to do it long. After the spring equinox, there's only one term left," Yasmin said.

"You know you don't have to listen to him, right?" Coral asked.

We all turned to her.

"What do you mean?" I asked.

"You're probably the most powerful magical botanist alive. And you've just proved that your powers aren't restricted on the academy or conservatory grounds anymore. No one can *make* you do anything, B. Not even Feathergrass."

Yasmin and Aurielle both turned to me, wide-eyed, and Coral smirked. "You know I'm right."

"Even if that's true, I have to keep up the ruse that I'm playing nice. At least until the spring equinox. Which means I'll take on whatever field studies assignment Feathergrass wants to give me, even if it's only for two weeks."

"Okay," Coral said, sighing. She pointed her spoon at me. "But after that, you'd better show Feathergrass who's boss."

Chapter Fifty

The day after the game of Capture the Roses had revealed my renewed access to my powers to the entire school, I decided it was time I attempted to make the Floracantus that all my practice Floracantus were building to.

I needed to create a verdant shield that would replace the one currently protecting the academy. It was a much larger task than anything I had done so far, and my palms were slightly sweaty as I arrived at the caves of the Evergreen Conservatory.

Only Callan, Meadow, and I were there. Since Meadow had scoured the book about the founders, we hoped she might have some insights into the shield's creation that would help me.

"I have no idea how to start," I admitted once the three of us had gathered with my conduit notebook and my cutting of activated Rosie.

"How have you started with the other Floracantus you've made?" Meadow asked.

"I connect with a plant and think about what I want to make it do. But this is different. Do I connect with the soil? The plants? Do I need to connect with all the plants I want to protect?" I didn't say it aloud, but the task seemed impossible.

"The original verdant shield is tied to the soil," Meadow said. "When the founders placed their hands in the charging circle, each imbued a tiny bit of their own power. I don't think this Floracantus is going to be like the others. Instead of concentrating on a plant, you need to tap into each of your powers and direct them into the soil."

I nodded, grasping onto the sureness in her words. "Any other tips?"

"The original Floracantus was invented by the tree founder, so you may need to use a little more tree affinity power compared to the others. I imagine the defensive founder instilled a good deal of power, too, since the shield keeps humans from seeing the truth."

"Got it," I said, sounding surer than I felt.

I knelt and touched my right hand to the ground. Callan had created a stone circle to imitate what the experience at the charging circle would be like. My left hand held Rosie over the notebook. With so many moving parts, it was difficult to focus on any one thing, but I closed my eyes and tried to push out thoughts of anything but creating a new Floracantus.

I dug inside myself, as Petra had taught me to do, and felt for each of my powers. One by one, I pushed them into the soil. Floral affinity... harvester affinity... grasses affinity... aquatic affinity... tree affinity. There, I paused and took extra time, making sure to incorporate the network component of trees. Moss affinity... herbs affinity... fern affinity... and finally, defensives affinity. I focused on the protective traits of defensive plants, trying to imagine them forming a shield around the Evergreen Conservatory.

Once I felt I had done all I could do, I whispered the words I had planned for the Floracantus. "*Terram protege.*"

A few of Rosie's petals fell from my hands, and when I opened my eyes, there was a small, shimmering clear shield—nearly invisible—around the stone circle and my notebook.

I experienced a strange mixture of thrill and disappointment. Some kind of shield had been created, but it was tiny. I had been hoping to create one around the entire conservatory. Instead, it was only a few feet in diameter.

"Are either of you seeing that?" I asked.

"Seeing what?" Callan looked around.

"There's a shimmering—" The shield dissolved. "Never mind. It's gone."

"What did you see?" Meadow asked, and I explained.

"So it seems like it only lasted a few seconds," I said, trying not to let my disappointment ring too loudly in my voice.

"But you did create something," Callan said. "Maybe it requires some practice."

I frowned, unsettled by that answer. "None of the other Floracantus I created required practice."

Meadow was sending moss up and down her arm, as if using that to help her sort her thoughts. "It is strange. It seems the components are there, but it's not quite strong enough."

"Maybe Callan's right. I'll just have to keep practicing."

We cleaned up and headed back to the academy.

As we went through the flower garden, Yasmin rushed up to us. "Feathergrass is looking for you, B."

"What is it this time?" I wasn't in the mood for another interrogation. Then dread pooled in my stomach. "You don't think he knows what we were up to, do you?"

Yasmin's brow furrowed. "We've been careful."

"Want me to listen in through the scouting vines in his office?" Callan asked.

"Yes, please," I said, relaxing at the thought that I wouldn't have to try to relay back whatever Feathergrass said word for word.

"Can I come?" Yasmin asked him. "I've always wanted to see how the listening side of those worked."

"Sure," Callan said.

They both wished me luck, and I walked up the stairs to meet Feathergrass.

When I was admitted to Feathergrass's office, he picked up the conversation as if we had never left off. "I've found you a new field studies assignment. You were lucky that someone in a very prestigious position recently became available and volunteered to take you on."

I relaxed slightly. He wasn't on to us. "What kind of study is it?" I asked, equal parts cautious and curious.

"Like your previous one in defensives, it is classified. Your new advisor has a trailing affinity for defensives, but they have a broad variety of experiences that we hope will complement your skill set."

I glanced out the window, which was cracked open, inhaling the sweet spring air and the fragrance from the flower gardens below, letting it calm my nervous system as I wondered what Feathergrass had planned for me.

I told myself it was only for two weeks, then I could get out of it if I wanted to.

Feathergrass signaled toward the door. When it opened and I saw who stepped inside, I had to sit on my hands to hide my surprise—and recognition.

"Briar, this is Wyatt Rhodes. He works with the Department of Botanical Intelligence."

Chapter Fifty-One

It took me a moment to recover from the shock of seeing Callan's brother in Feathergrass's office under official circumstances, but I pulled my face into an expression of polite interest. "Hello," I said, rising to shake Wyatt's hand.

When Wyatt took it and said, "Nice to meet you," he confirmed what I'd suspected. Feathergrass didn't know we had already met.

"Mr. Rhodes will work with you to ensure that your training meets the expectations of our society," Feathergrass said. "I'm afraid that without having the identity of your prior field studies instructor, we have to assume your field study sessions have been unconventional up to this point."

I tried not to let my face sour.

"Yes. I'll make sure her skills are on track for what the society needs from her," Wyatt said. His voice was serious, but I caught a touch of irony in it.

"Good. Well, then, don't let me hold you up." Feathergrass rose, and Wyatt and I made for the door.

"I'll expect regular reports," Feathergrass said.

Wyatt nodded.

When we were outside the office, Wyatt walked casually down the stairs. I followed, wondering what on earth he had planned. Once outside, we walked to the edge of the forest, and Wyatt put up a wind sound barrier around us like I had witnessed Callan create.

"So," I said, ready to find out what Wyatt was doing here. "Are you going to try to tell me it's a coincidence you're my new field studies advisor?"

A smile pulled at the corners of Wyatt's mouth, making him resemble his brother even more than usual. He quickly wiped it away. "Not a coincidence. I volunteered."

I narrowed my eyes. "Why? I'm sure the DBI has more important things to worry about than my field studies."

"As I told you before, the academy is a top priority for the DBI. If the students here aren't happy, they lose their motivation to do work that matters after they leave. The principles of the DBI align with those of the academy. We don't want to see any major shifts here. Having an agent in place will give us direct access to the academy, should the need arise."

I recalled how Alex had been the agent dispatched before and tried not to get upset. At least Wyatt wasn't trying to hide the DBI's involvement this time.

"This gives me an excuse to be in the area and on campus more regularly," Wyatt continued. "It will also provide opportunities to interact with you and Callan without raising suspicion. I can help make sure everything is in place and monitor the situation on the spring equinox. Have you planned how you will get access to the charging ring?"

I hesitated. Wyatt didn't know that I had won Capture the Roses, which was going to grant me access to the charging circle and use of the Dandelion of Desire, which would boost my powers. But it was the final ace up our sleeve. I wasn't sure if I should share it.

As if reading my thoughts, Wyatt asked, "Still don't trust me?"

"It's just better if as few people as possible know what we have planned."

To my surprise, Wyatt nodded approvingly. "Good. You're thinking like a DBI agent."

I laughed. "Don't get any ideas."

Wyatt put up his hands. "Just saying. We're always recruiting, if you're interested."

I raised my eyebrows. The DBI was seemingly one of the things that had driven a wedge between the two Rhodes brothers. How would Callan feel if he knew Wyatt was suggesting I work there too?

"Thanks, but I don't think I'm built for undercover work," I said, my mind flitting uncomfortably to Alex again.

Wyatt seemed to sense the direction of my thoughts. "We do a lot more than that. Much of intelligence work looks boring from the outside. Some of our best agents spend most of their time in the conservatory libraries, studying texts and missives and botanical evidence that isn't available to the public. Others monitor intel from scouting vines or botanical plant smuggling checkpoints throughout the country. These agents are the backbone of our work."

While I had to admit that spending my work hours in the conservatory libraries was a pretty enticing job description, I was not entertaining the idea at the moment. It was time to figure out how Wyatt and I were going to spend our field studies sessions together, even if it was just for show. "So, do you have a field studies assignment for me?"

"Not exactly. It's been a long time since our society has seen a botanist with all the affinity powers. Your potential is huge but somewhat of a mystery. What is it you see yourself contributing to our society?"

I stilled, the question catching me off guard. With Callan, it was so clear that he was going to be creating lifesaving medicines that would change the world. He already had several developments in the works that would improve human lives when it reached them. But I had always intended to be an artist, and artists impacted the world in different ways.

They took little pieces of themselves and molded them into something they hoped was challenging or comforting, affirming or thought-provoking, subtle or bold, and they sent it out into the world, praying the person it was meant for would stumble across it exactly when they needed it.

I was still trying to figure out how that life goal and my new life as a magical botanist aligned. As I looked at Wyatt, I let an idea that had been forming in mind since my most recent chat with Aunt Vera come to the surface.

Evergreen Academy lived on the outskirts of Weed. The locals never experienced it, and they never could. But what if they could experience something else, something that shared a fraction of the magic we have here?

I decided to throw my petals on the table. If Wyatt wanted to use me for access to the academy, perhaps I could get something out of it in return. "I want to create a botanical garden," I said.

Wyatt looked surprised, but he merely said, "Go on."

"Here in Weed. Something run by the students. Nothing obviously magical but something that will allow the residents of Weed to enjoy a sample of the plants we grow here. We need these sanctuaries, these natural spaces, to remind ourselves who we are. I didn't truly find myself until I came here. I want a version of that experience to be available to everyone." Plus, it would fly directly in the face of everything the Board of Regents was trying to do, which was get humans out of natural spaces.

"Interesting," Wyatt said. "And who would own this botanical garden?"

"It would be a nonprofit. Evergreen Academy could start it with a donation, then it could run off an endowment plus volunteers. The volunteers could be a mix of locals in Weed and students from the academy. It could be part of the service work we do on the equinoxes or an optional service rotation for students. If the model works, botanists could form similar partnerships with their local communities around the country."

"And if Evergreen Academy doesn't provide the seed funds?"

"Then we'll find another way," I said, confident. "If we have a handful of magical botanists involved in cultivating the plants, then the major hurdle will be acquiring a location."

"And do you see the DBI playing a role in this?"

"The board is trying to take control of public spaces from humans and give it to magical botanists. But a project like this could show them the value of getting humans *more* involved with plants, not less. You all could study the impacts. Run influence campaigns. Do whatever it is you do. But if your agency's mission is to protect plants for future generations, then I don't see how a project like this wouldn't align with that."

Wyatt studied me for a moment, and I took a deep breath. I had dumped a lot on him without intending to, but I didn't regret it. I had meant every word.

"Done," Wyatt said after a long pause.

"Done?" I blinked. "Which part?"

"All of it. The DBI will provide the seed money. We'll help acquire the land in town. In return, you and other students here get it off the ground this term. I want the gardens open to the public by midsummer. This is a pilot project, like you said, so make it a good one."

My mouth fell open, and I rushed to close it, but it was hard to hide my astonishment. "Just like that?"

"When the DBI sees a good idea, they like to move quickly. Start researching locations and send me a few options by the end of the week. Don't make me regret this, Briar."

I beamed, and for a moment, I thought about hugging him

but thought better of it and simply nodded. "Thank you, Wyatt. I won't let you down."

He grunted and nodded. "Good. Now get going. You've got plenty of work to do."

I turned and fled the swirling wind circle as soon as Wyatt dropped it. With a smile on my face, I went back to the academy, eager to tell Callan that his brother continued to surprise us.

Chapter Fifty-Two

"I'm going to try one more time," I said, raising my hands. Callan and I were in the Evergreen Conservatory a few days after my meeting with Wyatt. For the past thirty minutes, I had been trying to create a version of the verdant shield that wouldn't evaporate.

"*Terram protege,*" I said, focusing as hard as I could on all the plants in the area. A tiny shimmering dome formed around us. But a few moments later, it dissolved, as I had come to expect. Every attempt had the same result.

"I can't seem to make it stick. If I can't do it here, how am I going to manage to cast one that goes around the entire academy?"

Callan looked contemplative. "That dome was larger than the last one. Maybe the practice is working. Plus, you'll be inside the charging circle, and you'll have the Dandelion of Desire to boost your powers."

I sighed but nodded. "I hope you're right. I'll keep practicing. I have my first field study with Wyatt tomorrow. Should I see if he has any ideas?"

"Couldn't hurt," Callan said.

He used his powers to dust the soil and remove any sign of our being there, then we walked to our tree house. "Can you ask him about Professor East? I'd like to know when we can talk to him. He might know more about the shield than most, having been the director here."

"I'll ask. Do you think I should tell Wyatt the last part of our spring equinox plans? How I'm getting into the charging circle?" I was curious to hear his response.

I knew Callan still didn't fully trust Wyatt, but I had seen the way Wyatt looked at his brother, with affection and protective instincts. I didn't think he could do anything to harm Callan, and by extension, he wouldn't do anything to harm me. Wyatt might even truly be trying to help by saving me from whatever Feathergrass might have had in store for me by overseeing my new field studies assignment.

And it was possible that Wyatt could prove to be an asset to the Root and Vine Society. Having a DBI agent in the area *could* be helpful with what we had planned for the spring equinox.

Callan contemplated it for a moment. "What are your instincts telling you?"

"I think he should know. He and the DBI kept us in the dark this year, with the shield and Alex and all of that, but if you see it from their perspective, why would they tell college students their plans? Wyatt is the only one who has shared anything with us. Maybe if he's present when we reset the shield, he could help us somehow."

"That's true. As long as he doesn't have another angle."

"Callan." I rested a hand on top of his. "Can we assume he doesn't?"

He studied me for a moment then nodded. "I guess so."

"I also think perhaps we should return the quill to him so he can stealthily return it to its rightful place. It's not like we need it anymore, and no one can use it without having all the affinity powers."

Callan twined our hands together. "That's a good idea. And if it seems right to tell him about the charging plans in one of your meetings, I'll leave that up to you. So," Callan said slowly, and I could sense the conversation was about to change direction. "College acceptance letters should start arriving soon. I'm hoping to hear from my top-choice medical program."

I squeezed his hand. "There's not a school on this earth that wouldn't let you in, not with the research profile you submitted. You have to be leagues ahead of the other candidates."

"Well, if not, maybe I should become a senator after all. My mom would be happy for about ten minutes, until I started voting against all of her policies."

I tensed. I knew he was joking, but the idea upset me. "No way, Dr. Rhodes. Leave that job to someone who wants it."

"Did I tell you that most of the ivy leagues have special tracks for magical botanists?"

My heart rate sped up. "They do?"

"We do some of our classes with the rest of the students and other, more accelerated studies with other botanists."

"That sounds... incredible," I said.

"We'll find out soon enough. Have you made any decisions about art school now that you've been accepted?" He seemed gently hesitant.

I sighed. "I don't know. It's the strangest thing. For so long, I wanted nothing more than to follow in my mom's footsteps. But now I'm not sure that's the best path for me. The campus she went to is beautiful, but there are hardly any plants there. How would I use my powers?"

"There's nothing wrong with changing your mind. But I support whatever you want to do."

"It seems a silly thing to be concerned about right now," I said.

"Maybe it's exactly the thing to be focusing on. If we succeed on the spring equinox, your future is going to be a question everyone has for you." Callan took my hand. "Some of the schools I applied to have top-tier art programs."

"Are there secret artist tracks for botanists?" I asked, only slightly joking. The idea had piqued my interest more than I was willing to admit.

Callan's mouth quirked. "If there aren't yet, there could be."

I pulled back. He was serious. "Are you asking me to go to college with you, Callan Rhodes?"

"If we can get everything sorted here and I don't have to become a senator and you don't have to go into hiding from my power-hungry parents, then... yeah. I want to go to college with you, local."

"I mean, *technically* we're already in college together." I waved around at Evergreen Academy's campus.

He bumped my leg with his. "You know what I mean."

I stopped joking then and squeezed his hands, looking him directly in the eyes. "There is nothing I would like more than to continue going to college with you."

We sat in silence for a few moments as I considered the new possibility. I ran my fingers along the swirling leaves-and-vines tattoos on his forearms. His skin was warm beneath my hand.

"When did you get these?" I asked.

"When I was sixteen. Right after Wyatt left for Evergreen Academy and I was still home with my parents. They're made from plant-derived ink and were done by a magical botanist."

"Do they have a special meaning?"

"They're a reminder."

"Of?"

Callan hesitated then spoke in a deep, quiet voice. "That I'm not powerless."

I swallowed at the intensity in his voice and remembered the binds of wind that had swept me between two trees and held me in place at the tree conservatory. I remembered the way we had sparred during Capture the Roses. He could dispel strong vines with the flick of his wrist and lift logs on a gust of wind. He was the definition of powerful.

When I moved my stool closer to Callan's, he slipped his arms over my shoulders, and I rested the back of my head against his chest.

"The tattoos must have worked. You seemed like the most powerful person I knew when I first met you."

He let out a little laugh and squeezed me closer. "You've always seen the best in me. Maybe I did seem confident when we first met, but in reality, I was... curious."

"Curious?" I turned my head upward to try to get a peek at his face.

"I could sense something about you very early on. Not your power exactly. That was locked away. But... *something*. And you were the picture of ease. Posing in front of the academy and about to put your hand in a charging ring like a founders' descendant."

"I had no idea I caught your eye so much at that first encounter," I teased, turning fully to face him.

"You caught more than my eye. And you have every day since." His voice dropped an octave, and my breath caught at his sudden seriousness. "I didn't know it then, but the day I met you was a day that would change my life forever. You brought a lightness into my world that I could never have imagined." He touched a finger to my chin and tilted my head upward. "What I'm trying to say is... I love you, Briar Rose."

I sucked in a breath. I had loved Callan for so long I couldn't even pinpoint when it had started. "You do?"

"It's been true for a while, local." He tucked my hair behind my ear.

"How long is a while?"

He thought about it for a moment. "Remember the first Floral Fete, where you displayed your painting, ate those laced cookies, and became extra... talkative?"

"Yes," I said, cringing at the memory, though not even it could dampen the moment.

"I think it started then. The idea of someone poisoning you, even if it was just with truth serum..." He scrubbed a hand through his hair.

"*Just* truth serum. That was one of the most embarrassing moments of my life, thank you very much."

But I stopped teasing and leaned in, and he followed my lead. I touched a hand to his cheek. "I love you back, Callan Rhodes. And in case no one has told you, you *are* powerful and kind and generous and clever, and—"

I didn't get to finish before a whip of wind rushed up and shuttered the wooden windows on the tree house. Then Callan leaned forward, slid his arms around my waist, and kissed me.

Chapter Fifty-Three

"You found this rather quickly," Wyatt said when we met at the plot of land adjacent to Siskiyous Community College and the Wildflower Trail.

"This patch of thin forest hasn't been used in decades. I have proposals in with the college and the city. If it gets approved at the next city council meeting, you're looking at the site of Weed's new botanical garden."

It was strange to be in the woods, spending time with Wyatt without Callan, even if it was under the guise of field studies. Callan would have come with me in a heartbeat if I had asked, but between keeping up appearances for his field study with the politicians in Sacramento, his secret project of creating new medicines, and our normal school duties, he was busy.

"It looks good. A parking area can go right there, off the road. We can put a sign over here, then they can walk between these two oak trees to enter the gardens."

I smiled, surprised at how invested Wyatt seemed to be. He had much more important things to take on, so it was endearing that he was committed to the garden. "Have you secured the funds from the DBI?"

Wyatt nodded. "It's all approved. Just get me the agreement with the city for purchasing the land, and you'll be able to break ground."

"I hope I can make your deadline of midsummer. That's only a few months away."

Wyatt tilted his head. "You've never seen magical botanists plant a garden, have you?"

I frowned. "Not exactly. They've done some service planting in town, but they had to keep it reined in for the sake of the locals."

"Well, then, you're in for a show. Once we get the walls up and some fertile soil in the ground, this place will materialize in no time."

"I hope so," I said, trying to envision what the space would look like when it was complete. It would be a garden I could walk through with my aunt and Bryce, and with Maci. It would be a way to share myself with them without revealing everything. Perhaps it could be a place for my aunt to feel in touch with her magic. I couldn't wait.

"Do you have any news about Professor East?" I asked.

Wyatt nodded. "He's making the rounds through the conservatories, trying to change the tides. He's in Florida now, working to make changes to the state law about human access to the public lands before it's too late."

"Thank the leaves," I said, a spark of hope igniting in my chest.

"The DBI has agents working on similar influence campaigns. Hopefully, we can move the needle. But Professor East wanted me to remind you that Evergreen Academy is the heart of the society of magical botanists. Whatever change we can enact there will reverberate throughout the entire community."

"Professor East said that?" I asked, heartened by the idea that he knew we were working on something and that he thought it was meaningful.

"He did."

The clearing in the forest became quiet except for the sounds of birds singing and jumping from branch to branch. "Did he ask what our plan was?"

"Yes. And I shared what I knew of it."

I nodded. "There's an update."

Wyatt studied me, waiting for me to say more.

"We have a way for me to access the charging circle. And I'll be able to use the Dandelion of Desire to boost my powers."

Wyatt cocked his head again. "How'd you manage that?"

"I won a very unconventional game of Capture the Roses."

Wyatt smiled, and I couldn't help noticing how similar it was to his brother's smile. "Nicely done. And how is making the new Floracantus coming along?"

"I've been practicing daily. I get close, but the shields dissolve after a few minutes. It's like they're not sticking to the soil properly. I was hoping you or Professor East might have ideas about what's going on."

Wyatt looked off into the distance as if thinking through a complicated math problem. "The soil seems to be the key. When Eli helped bolster the shield, he did it by infusing more nutrients into the soil, correct? What has your process been for connecting with the soil when you set up the mini shields?"

"Let me show you."

I went through the steps of using the Floracantus I had created to develop a shield. But after a few minutes, the shimmering dome that only I, the caster, could see, had dissolved.

"The Floracantus's hold on the soil is too shallow," Wyatt said after quietly watching my whole routine.

"How can you tell?"

"Tree affinities are particularly good at understanding soil attachments. And I've had extra training on it with the DBI, since tree communication networks are valuable sources of intelligence. I was sifting through the soil as you were working."

I nodded, my curiosity piqued. "And you could tell the attachment was shallow?"

"It was shallow, but something else was going on. The soil seems to react to you more quickly than most. It's almost as if you're scattering it without meaning to." He crouched and rested on his heels as he contemplated something. "Can you try a different Floracantus? One working with a tree's roots? I want to watch for something."

I wasn't sure where he was going, but I didn't protest. I wanted any scrap of information that could help me make the shield as powerful as it needed to be. I said a Floracantus to increase the water uptake in the roots of a nearby Cypress tree.

"Interesting," Wyatt said once I had completed the process.

"What is it?"

"Have you heard that some botanists have heightened abilities that are slightly outside the realm of plant magic? Like Callan's power sensing abilities. That skill is connected to his wind manipulating powers. All lead tree affinities have some level of wind manipulation, but his are much stronger than most."

I thought about Kai and his ability to waterbend that I had witnessed in Florida. "Yes, I guess I have."

"Sometimes, they're referred to as extra-affinity powers, since they're outside the normal affinity groups. A few pop up every generation, but they seem to be getting more common lately. The DBI has been trying to track the frequency, but botanists often keep these extra powers hidden or don't realize they have skills beyond what's normal. One of those abilities has to do with an increased ability to work with soil. Like the others, it's rare, but based on what I just saw there, I think you have it."

I mulled over his words, remembering when I had found the mushrooms in the soil based on the soil's pH during the fall equinox scavenger hunt. Kaito had seemed surprised that I could sense the soil, but I hadn't thought much of it at the time. And not long ago, Yasmin had mentioned that I was good at manipulating the soil when we were learning how to activate Rosie. Could Wyatt be right?

"If I do have this soil ability, what does it mean? Can I use it to connect more deeply with the soil?"

Wyatt nodded. "Yes. I believe you already have been, but since you haven't had training on it, your skills aren't refined. Thankfully, I once worked with a DBI agent with this skill, so I know something about how he did it." He touched a hand to the ground. "I guess I've got something to teach you in field studies after all."

∽

Wyatt and I continued to meet daily, finding new spots along the Wildflower Trail to practice connecting with the soil. Each session, I uncovered layers of the soil I hadn't paid much attention to before.

Different soil had different profiles and could vary widely based on its inorganic composition, the nutrients in the area, and the organic material that was mixed in. As I learned the nuances of the earth under my fingers, I was able to latch the shield Floracantus more deeply into it. Each day, the shield was lasting longer and longer, and after a week, Wyatt and I went to test my latest shield after leaving it overnight around the Evergreen Conservatory.

"It's still here," Wyatt said, a grin spreading across his face. "It didn't dissolve overnight." He held up a hand, and I high-fived it.

"Think it's permanent, or will it fall eventually?" I asked.

I could sense Wyatt using his tree powers to sift through the soil. "I think you attached it to every level and component, like we were aiming for. Unless you choose to uproot it, that shield's not going anywhere."

I smiled in pure relief then tilted my head up to the sky, letting the warm spring sun bathe my face in photons. "So, you think I'm ready?"

Wyatt nodded. "I think you're ready."

"Will you be on campus for the spring equinox, just in case I need you to check my soil prep?"

"I think you're better at soil prep than me now, but I would like to be on campus to support in other ways if needed. I'll sneak in again, like I did for the Floral Fete. If my mom is there on the spring equinox, as I suspect she might be, I don't want her to see me coming."

"About that. Callan heard through his scouting vines that security may be tighter on the equinox than it was during the Floral Fete. But I think I have a way for you and some of our other allies to get in unnoticed."

Wyatt arched an eyebrow. "I'm telling you you're cut out for the DBI."

I laughed. "Keep dreaming, Rhodes." Then I told him about the petal portals.

Chapter Fifty-Four

"I was worried about this," Heath said. The floral affinity botanist was propped on a velvet green cushion in the secret tree conservatory room in the attic of Evergreen Academy.

While I had been busy working on creating and perfecting the Floracantus that would create the new verdant shield, other members of the Root and Vine Society had been doing their own parts in preparing for our mission.

One of the goals was to make more petal portals so that anyone involved in our plan could have a means of getting in and out of the academy quickly and undetected if needed.

"Duplicating the binding Floracantus to work between the pendants and the petal portals isn't easy. The founders were uniquely connected to the academy. As Briar learned with breaking the curse on her magic, duplicating or undoing founders' magic can be tricky. I'm not sure if I can pull it off," Heath admitted. "Are you having any luck, Briar?"

I tried one more time, but the Shasta lily wasn't holding the magic in the way I felt it was with the original pendants. I sighed. "No."

"Are you sure we need to make more of these?" Meadow asked. "Couldn't we lend Wyatt one of the nine pendants we already have?"

"I want everyone in the Root and Vine Society to have their pendants on them in case something goes sideways and they need to sneak out of the academy," I said. "Plus, I'd like Yasmin, Aurielle, and Coral to have them for the same reason. It wouldn't hurt to have a few extras on top of that for unexpected circumstances. Any advantage we have on the equinox, I want to take."

Meadow nodded. "Good point. But if you and Heath can't get the Shasta lilies to hold the Floracantus, is there anyone who can?"

"Too bad we can't sneak in and use the Dandelion of Desire," Aurielle said. "Maybe a little extra power would help you."

I nodded slowly, an idea forming. "The Dandelion of Desire isn't the only thing that can give magical botanists a boost."

"What do you mean?" Yasmin asked.

"Have you all heard of green zones?"

Meadow's face lit up. "Sure! My mom told stories about them. But they're classified. I've never known where any of them are."

"What if I told you there's one not too far from here?"

"Spill!" Coral demanded.

"You all know my field study last year was classified. Its location happened to be in a green zone, also classified. But I think circumstances warrant letting a few more people in on the secret. The zone is on Mount Shasta, and I know exactly where the epicenter is."

AFTER NIGHTFALL, WE GATHERED AT THE CABIN WHERE Petra and I used to conduct my field studies.

"Can you all feel it?" I asked.

"I felt it when we were going up the trail. It's the strangest sensation. It's like someone added a line of electricity directly into my magic," Meadow said, moss encircling her hands at lightning speed.

Yasmin, Aurielle, and Coral took seats on the other side of the table, and Heath sat between me and Meadow. My friends and Meadow were there for moral support more than anything. Plus, they were all curious to experience the green zone. The task was for Heath and me—the lead floral affinities of the group.

With the glass heating over a camp stove, each of my friends practiced reciting familiar Floracantus with their heightened powers while we waited for the glass to liquify. Yasmin was trying one of the Floracantus from da Vinci's journal, changing the shade of a button fern she had brought with her.

It was exciting seeing the new Floracantus I had shared at the Floral Fete being used around campus. While there were only forty new Floracantus in the book, my classmates seemed to have plenty of fun testing them out. A few representatives from various conservatories had made or scheduled trips to the academy to view the book for themselves. Everyone wanted a glimpse of the previously undiscovered book, which was exactly how I had intended the work to be received.

"Shall we give it a try?" I asked Heath once the glass was pooling in the mortar bowl. I spread the Shasta lily flowers between us.

Heath reached for one of the flowers and poured the softened glass into the mold. He set the flower petals inside it then said the Floracantus we had tried on campus. "Ahh," he said, smiling as the glass began to cool. "That feels right."

Next to him, I tried the process, and instantly, I knew what he meant. The binding Floracantus was holding, and it felt exactly like the ones on the old pendants. "Agreed. I think this is working."

We spent the next half hour pouring a dozen pendants, our friends continuing to experiment with their magic while Heath and I worked.

"I wonder how Hollis and Rhodes are doing with putting

scouting vines near each petal portal," Meadow said, juggling moss balls in the air.

"Callan had a nice collection of the vines growing, so they should have plenty. The question is 'Are we going to need them?'" I said.

"I hope not, because that would mean someone outside the Root and Vine Society knows about the portals," Yasmin replied.

I prodded one of the new pendants to see if it was cool. "I think these are ready to go. How about yours, Heath?"

"Mine too. Ready to head back? I have a date with my notebook and some night blooming flowers tonight."

"You florals, always so romantic," Meadow cooed.

After cleaning up the cabin, we hiked down the mountain. We were mostly quiet as we walked, and I wasn't sure if it was because of the late hour or everyone else's mind was as full as mine as I thought through our plan. The spring equinox was a mere week away.

Once we were in the car and driving back to the academy, I broke the silence. "Who wants to store the pendants until the equinox?"

"I feel like you already have enough of a target on your back after infuriating Feathergrass with the false *Vanished Compendium* at the Floral Fete," Yasmin said.

"Good call. And he knows the four of us are friends, so Coral's and my room could be subject to his 'random' searches as well," Aurielle said, making air quotes.

"Sorry, y'all. Getting caught with my own portal pendant already scares me enough," Heath said.

Meadow stuck out her hand. "I'm pretty sure Feathergrass thinks my mom and I are firmly in his camp of thinking. He hasn't hassled me at all this term except for not taking my studies seriously enough. The pendants should be safe with me. I'll camouflage them with moss."

Heath and I passed our freshly minted pendants to Meadow.

"There's one more thing I wanted to share," Meadow said. "I've been reading the founders' history book I took from Professor East's office, and I found something that might be important."

"What is it?" I didn't want to turn down any sliver that might help make our mission successful. Despite my practice sessions with Wyatt, I was still nervous about how things were going to go.

"According to the book, when the founders put the verdant shield into place, they each contributed a seed to the soil. I think it served as a sort of conduit to their magic."

"You think I need to bring a seed when I implement the new Floracantus?"

"I think you need to bring nine seeds," Meadow said.

Of course. One for each affinity group.

"Again, I don't know if you'll need it, since you're making a new Floracantus, but I thought you should know."

"Thanks, Meadow. I want to cover all my bases here, so I'll make sure to have nine seeds with me at the charging circle." I added it to my mental to-do list.

We had the petal portal pendants. I had a working Floracantus. We had won Capture the Roses, which meant I would have access to the charging circle and the Dandelion of Desire to boost my chances of success.

All we needed now were nine seeds and an uninterrupted visit to the epicenter of the verdant shield.

Chapter Fifty-Five

Six days before the spring equinox, the members of the Root and Vine Society gathered in Vera's Café. Meeting on campus, even in one of our hidden areas, felt like a risk so close to our operation.

When I asked Aunt Vera about using the café after it closed for the evening, she had said yes without hesitation. Though she claimed to not be very interested in her newfound powers, I thought she was excited about the prospect of a handful of magical botanists gathering in her shop. I had entered the closed shop to find platters of her lavender scones and large pitchers of the lemonade that she sold by the truckload in the summer on each table.

Shortly after the café's closure, my friends began to arrive. Yasmin, Coral, and Aurielle had shown up first, then Kaito walked in soon after with Ravenna, Nalin, and Laurus. Hollis and Meadow were fashionably late but only by a few minutes.

"No Rhodes today?" Meadow asked, looking around the room.

I cast my eyes toward the door. "He should be here. I'll tell everyone to have a lavender scone, and we'll give him a little longer."

Five minutes later, the bell hanging from the door of the café chimed, and I rose, a smile touching my lips. Callan walked in, and Wyatt strode in after him.

"Wasn't expecting to see you here," I said to Wyatt though not in an unfriendly way. I was glad to have him present for the final planning session. The three of us gathered near the door, out of the hearing range of the others, who were busy enjoying Aunt Vera's treats.

"He's here to help, but he also comes bearing a message," Callan said. His face was tight, and a muscle in his neck twitched. "From Alex."

I narrowed my eyes. "What kind of message?"

Wyatt spoke. "First, he sends an apology. He claims he got carried away on his first mission, and he never intended to get so close to you or Maci."

I nodded, but I was thinking Alex had a lot more to apologize for than that. Not the least of which was activating my aunt's magic without her permission. But that had happened, and we needed to move on. "And what's the rest of the message?"

"Alex claims that when he was monitoring the school to see who was poisoning the verdant shield, he found patches of jewelweed growing just inside the wall on the south side of campus. According to him, there is a rather large patch."

I nodded, a memory surfacing. "That's the plant Professor East used on me to counteract the poison on my skin when I did my first defensives affinity test. But why is that important?"

"They can do more than counter poison. Jewelweed seeds are explosive. If we have an herbs affinity botanist cause them to ripen, then a tree affinity create a breeze to trigger them, the seeds will explode. With a little modification from the herbs, we could amplify this effect to sound like there are firecrackers going off near the wall."

"Okay..." I said, still not understanding where he was going.

"While Alex doesn't know any details, he is aware that we are planning something and that we could use a distraction while we do it. That much noise near the wall would cause a big one."

I studied Wyatt's face. It was a good idea, but our group would have come up with a distraction if Alex hadn't shared one. "Is that all?"

"There's one more thing," Wyatt said. "Feathergrass is allergic to jewelweed. If we can draw him to the area and one of the jewelweed seeds hits his skin, he'll probably have some swelling and itching and need to go to the apothecary."

My eyes widened. That was useful knowledge, indeed. We knew he had some food allergies that caused sneezing, but if the jewelweed allergy was much stronger... "Do you think it will keep him in the apothecary for long?"

"Someone will have to track down Professor Sage during the equinox festivities. He'll have to brew up a concoction, since jewelweed allergies are rare, then apply it and watch for any lingering effects. I think we could keep Feathergrass occupied for thirty minutes that way," Callan said.

"Well, it's as good an idea as any," I said. "Thanks for the information. Okay, I think it's time to get this meeting started."

I walked toward the pastry counter and turned to face everyone. My heart was full as I looked around the room, seeing every member of the Root and Vine Society, my three best friends at Evergreen Academy, and even a member of the DBI. Each of them had a role to play in our next endeavor, and it was nearly time to kick things off.

Everyone quieted and turned their attention to Callan and me. He had come to stand by my side. Wyatt found a place in the back of the room, and some of my friends gave him curious looks.

"Welcome to Vera's Café, everyone. I hope you've been enjoying the lavender scones," I began, trying to calm the nerves in my stomach. "First, I wanted to start off with some good news. As you all know, I've been practicing making a new Floracantus similar to the one that created the verdant shield. It's been challenging, to say the least, but I had a breakthrough last week when working with Wyatt. It turns out the key was in the soil preparation."

A few people clapped and whistled.

"Thanks. I'll continue to practice over the next few days, but if I can continue to replicate the process, I hope that I'll be able to do the same at the academy. So, next, we can talk about—"

The bell on the door chimed again, and someone familiar entered the café.

The rest of the group turned their heads, following my stare.

"Professor East!" I shouted, a smile taking over my face. I was speechless for a moment, wondering how he knew where to find us. Then my eyes shot to Wyatt. He had promised to deliver Professor East to us when the time was right as his end of the bargain. Apparently, that time had come.

All the members of the Root and Vine Society rose, taking turns to greet our former instructor. He had only been absent from the school for a few months, but it felt much longer. When I saw him, some of the tightness in my chest released.

All thoughts of the updates we had to provide and the questions that were still to be answered melted away. Professor East was back. Everything was going to be okay.

Chapter Fifty-Six

"Hello, botanists," Professor East said once the group had finally settled back into their seats.

Wyatt stood sentinel by the door, listening but keeping an eye on the street as if he were Professor East's personal bodyguard.

"I'm sorry to have had to stay away all this time. I figured it was better for those at the academy to think I had gone away quietly and focus my efforts elsewhere. I knew you all would do our school and society proud, and it appears I was right."

"Have you come to join the fight?" Kaito asked, perched on the edge of his seat.

"Of course. Though I'm sure you're using the word 'fight' in a metaphorical sense," Professor East said.

I bit back a smile. "Has Wyatt told you our plan, then?"

"Most of it. I've heard there have been some recent developments."

"Then let's get you up to speed," I said, taking the lead. "While you've been away, I learned how to create new Floracantus."

Professor East nodded as if he weren't surprised. "Very good, Ms. Whelan."

"We've also studied the enchantment that was used when the verdant shield was put in place. Our plan is for me to override it and replace it with a new version of the Floracantus. One that founders' descendants alone no longer control. We plan to implement it during the charging window on the spring equinox."

"We're going to sneak extra people onto campus to help protect the area while Briar is charging," Meadow said. "We created a few more pendants for the petal portals last night. I assume those portals are no secret to you?"

Professor East nodded, a smile gracing his lips. "I've been known to use them a time or two."

Callan spoke up next. "Hollis and I scouted out the charging circle last night. Feathergrass has surrounded the area with sandhill rosemary. It was clever, actually. Those grasses use allelopathy to inhibit the growth of other plants. They have been magically enhanced, and there's a ten-foot cleared area around the charging circle where no other plants can grow. We couldn't put down scouting vines or anything that might lead to our advantage. We know Briar can get through because she won Capture the Roses, but we would like to have a few others there to support her if she needs it. Ravenna, do you think you could undo his Floracantus to make the sandhill rosemary less potent?"

Ravenna's brow furrowed. "Feathergrass is famous for that sort of Floracantus. I don't think I'll be strong enough to overpower it. Maybe with Briar's help?" The grasses affinity botanist turned to me.

"I can try, but I have a feeling Feathergrass has set up sensors, so he'll know if we do it. I think we may be better off leaving his charms in place so that he has no reason to suspect his defenses are down."

"Lull him into a false sense of security," Hollis said. "I like it."

Callan's face was tight, his arms crossed, and I could tell he was contemplating the situation. "It will mean Briar is going into the charging circle alone. If anyone else goes through and his defenses are still up, he'll know."

I could tell by the tone of his voice he wasn't happy about that. He had wanted to go with me to the charging circle if possible. He didn't like any idea that potentially put me in harm's way, but it seemed we had no other choice.

Professor East looked approvingly around the room. "You all have done good work here. The things to remember as we go into the spring equinox are to expect the unexpected, be prepared to adapt, and always have the plants on your side."

"Good advice," Callan said, nodding to Professor East. "Now, let's talk about how we're going to get you reinstated."

Chapter Fifty-Seven

Two days later, as I emerged from lunch in the teahouse, I felt a tickle on my wrist. I looked down and caught the leaf message that was gently nudging my forearm.

Tree house after class?

I wrote a quick note of confirmation in return and sent it off in the leaves. Had something happened? We were breaths away from the spring equinox, and we had dozens of small and large pieces that needed to come together perfectly. *If even one of them falls through...*

No. I shook my head at my racing thoughts. There was no need to panic prematurely. I took a deep breath and returned to the teahouse to brew a chamomile-and-ashwagandha blend.

While the warm drink soothed my stomach and gave me something to do with my hands, I was still anxious during my afternoon classes, and Coral waved a fern in front of my face when it was my turn to diagnose and heal one of the sick plants on our lab table.

"Earth to Briar. Everything okay?" she asked.

Nodding, I tried to focus on the plant in front of me, which was a wild sweet potato. I studied the fuzzy white substance that covered the underside of its leaves. I skimmed a textbook to search for the name. "White rust," I said.

My friends scribbled the name in their notebooks.

"Clearance methods..." I tried a few different techniques with my magic until I landed on one that worked best. "Internal oil production then sweep."

We finished our pathogen analysis, then I said goodbye to my friends. When I reached the tree house, Callan was also just arriving.

"What's going on?" I asked, searching his face for any clues about why we were meeting.

"Everything's on track. I thought maybe you could use a little time to relax before the big day tomorrow. And there's something I've been wanting to show you."

My nervous system settled at his words, and I let out a soft breath. "Good, because I thought you were going to say our entire plan had fallen apart."

"If that happens, I won't wait until after class to tell you."

I prepared to climb into the tree house, but Callan took my hand and led me deeper into the forest. "We're going somewhere new today."

"Oh?" I asked, intrigued. The Evergreen Academy grounds were huge, and there were plenty of places I had yet to explore.

"Nothing secretive like the Evergreen Conservatory or a new petal portal, in case that's where your mind was going." A hint of humor filled Callan's voice.

"You mean this academy doesn't have *more* secrets to reveal to me?" I teased back.

"I don't know about the academy, but nature does."

We reached an area full of lodgepole pine trees, and Callan stopped. He used his wind powers to make a cushion of pine needles, then he lay on his back, linking his arms behind his neck.

"Um, everything okay down there?" I asked, confused.

"Just come lie down. You'll see." A touch of wind gave me a little nudge, and I lay on my back beside him.

"Look up at the canopy," Callan directed.

I did, and I observed the trees and the cracks of sky between them, wondering what I was supposed to be noticing.

"See how none of the crowns touch? It's called crown shyness. Sometimes, I like to come and look for interesting shapes. It reminds me of the pattern on a giraffe's body, with all the patches."

I let my eyes relax and take in what he was talking about. Once I did, I smiled. "Crown shyness, huh? Like the trees don't want to touch each other? Is this a tree affinity thing?"

"No magic here, local. Just nature. A few tree species do it."

"They look like puzzle pieces right before you fit them together," I said.

"It's commonly caused by wind abrasion, though there can be other factors."

"Leaves, I like it when you talk botany to me."

A leaf flew up and playfully touched my cheek.

"Usually, I leave them alone and just watch, but I thought we could have a little fun today." Callan reached out with his wind powers, and the tree canopies began to sway.

I grinned when one of the gaps between them formed the shape of a B.

"You want to try?" Callan asked.

"My wind powers aren't nearly as strong as yours, but I'll give it a go." I focused on connecting with the trees around us to have control over their canopy movements then used a little wind to sway them so that the gap between two of them formed a large C. "Not as clear as yours," I said.

Callan focused on the canopy again, and after several moments, the lines of sky between the treetops had formed a large heart.

I smiled then rolled over to my side to rest my head on my

hand, looking at Callan. "I'll admit this is a pretty great distraction from thoughts of tomorrow."

"Mission accomplished," Callan said, rolling over and facing me as well. He played with a tendril of hair falling across the side of my face. "Remember that you've prepared for this. The whole crew is going to be there, and we'll be backing you every step of the way."

"I know." I took his hand in mine, playfully scrunching our fingers together. "I'm nervous, but I know it has to be done."

Callan squeezed my hand.

My heart leaped at the quiet moment with him, and when he lay back, I moved to rest my head on his chest and angled my face toward the trees again. We studied the crown shyness phenomenon in silence for another half hour until Callan gently helped me to my feet, and we treewalked back to the academy.

The vernal equinox was coming the next day—whether we were ready or not—but this was a memory I would hold on to.

Chapter Fifty-Eight

On the morning of the spring equinox, the students of Evergreen Academy gathered for a few hours of planting at the new botanical garden. I caught sight of Oren working with some of the tree affinity students and waved.

The forester who had helped me save Frank and unblock the quill returned the wave and walked my way. The botanical garden project had pulled him into our community, and he seemed happy to be spending time with other botanists while focusing on their shared passion—trees.

"Hey, Oren. How are the trees doing?"

"Coming along nicely. They'll be providing good shade soon."

"Have you had any luck with the riddle?" I asked quietly.

"Not yet. The directions from yours gave me some ideas, but I'm sure each Renaissance botanist crafted theirs a little differently. It's only a matter of time before I figure it out. I've also been trying to determine what our family plant could be, like your Rosie. I'm sure it's a tree, possibly even the one my tree house is built in. The family lore always said it grew from a cutting."

"Sounds promising," I replied.

Meeting other Renaissance-descended botanists like Petra and

Oren made me feel less like an enigma. Even though they didn't have all the affinity powers, they shared the connection to the book and the Floracantus-making recipes inside.

I said goodbye to Oren and tried to lose myself in transplanting some mild but still magnificent defensive plants from the academy into a portion of the garden, but my mind was racing.

Tonight was the night. For better or worse, we would make our attempt at resetting the verdant shield. Mentally, I went through my checklist to ensure things were in place.

Meadow had the petal portal pendants for sneaking people onto campus. Callan and Hollis had plans for distraction and offense while I was at the charging circle. I hated to admit it, but Alex's intel about the jewelweed patch was likely going to be useful.

When our work at the botanical garden wrapped up, we headed back to the academy. I went to my room to change and donned a knee-length lavender dress with a tulle skirt and cap sleeves. I used my floral affinity to weave tiny purple pansy petals around the waist and along the neckline then added a few to my hair.

The dainty dress was comfortable and airy, elegant enough for the spring festivities and easy to move around in for the mission I would be conducting later in the evening. I slipped the seeds I would need into the dress's pocket, swiped some gold sparkles across my eyelids, and squared my shoulders.

My mind was so focused on the upcoming mission as I descended the stairs and left the school building that I almost missed the archways of wisteria leading all the way from the flower gardens to the meadow by the pond. Not until one of the flowers stretched close to my face and tickled my cheek did I focus on the landscape around me. Butterflies flitted from bloom to bloom as if racing to crisscross the expanse of the path.

Coral whistled. "The florals must have been working nonstop since this morning."

"They must have," I agreed, breathing in the calming scent of the wisteria and focusing on the world around me. The academy had been transformed into a spring floral fever dream, even more so than at the Floral Fete or any event I had attended in the past.

The trees and florals were obviously working together, because flowers literally floated in the air. A few of the flowers landed in each of the guests' hair, marking us all as members of the party.

When Heath greeted us with martini glasses with edible flowers floating on the surface of the drink, I raised my glass in appreciation. "Incredible work."

"The vernal equinox committee has been planning this for weeks. They wanted to do something extra special this year," he replied.

"I'd say they were successful. I think this may be the most beautiful spring equinox the academy has ever seen," Yasmin said.

"How can the school look this beautiful when things are going so wrong?" Aurielle asked.

"I think that's the point the students were trying to make," Heath answered. "Not everyone fights in the same way. Some of us continue to create the beautiful things in the midst of all the chaos so that once the struggle is over, there is something worth coming back to."

I inhaled sharply, knowing deep in my gut that, even though the Root and Vine Society was doing the heavy lifting in the plan, the work of keeping the academy a place we all wanted to be and showing that it was worth fighting for was just as important.

At the end of the night, if everything went well, the environment that the floral students had created was the type of school I wanted to come back to. And I was willing to fight for it.

Chapter Fifty-Nine

Heath's words and reminders about what we were fighting for energized me, adding a zip of motivation to the nerves that were already pulsing through my veins. As we continued to walk under the wisteria-covered trellises toward the pond, I looked around, searching for only one person.

Despite any nerves I was feeling about the night, my heart soared when I caught sight of Callan. He wore a perfectly tailored pair of pants, a vest, and a white dress shirt with the sleeves rolled up so that I could catch the rich lines of the browns, blacks, blues, and greens in his tattoos. His hair was tousled just right, a tendril on the top of it catching a bit of a breeze.

I froze, wanting to take in how he looked in the moment, a coy smile pulling at the corner of his mouth at something Hollis had said.

Coral elbowed me. "Spores. Hollis cleans up good."

"We already knew that," Yasmin muttered. "Callan, too, of course. What is it with founders' descendants men? Is there something in their DNA that makes them look good in a suit?"

"While you all are ogling, I'm getting some food," Aurielle

said. "We're going to need our energy if we want to pull this off tonight. And we still have to monitor our research presentations."

As my friends began to make for the appetizer table, Callan turned, and the smile that was only partially there with Hollis stretched across his face. We were striding toward each other when I spotted someone familiar in the background, speaking with Feathergrass.

"Your mom is here," I said, nodding in her direction and keeping my distance from him.

"I thought she might be."

"Should we pretend we don't know each other?" I asked, unease settling on me. That was how it had been the previous times she came to the academy.

Callan stepped forward, put his hands around my waist, and gently tugged me toward him. "No. I meant what I said when Wyatt showed up. We're stronger together. I'm done being afraid of what they might do."

Heat rose in my cheeks at the feeling in his voice. "So we don't have to sneak around if I want to put my hands on you?"

Callan entwined my hand firmly in his. "I don't plan on letting you go all night."

"Until the charging hour," I said, though I was reluctant to break the moment. The idea of holding hands with Callan all evening almost made me want to scrap the entire plan—almost.

Callan squeezed my hand. "Even then, I won't be far."

When we headed toward the dinner table, Wendy Rhodes intercepted us. She eyed our clasped hands meaningfully. "Well, I was under the impression you two were barely friends, and now look at this. Quite the development." As she assessed us, I got the distinct feeling she was plotting how to use our relationship to her advantage.

"Happy equinox, Mother," Callan said, his voice neutral. "Is Dad here?"

"He had business to attend to at the capital. Speaking of

which, how is your field study assignment going? They said you haven't been to Sacramento recently."

"You didn't hear? I transferred my field study."

I straightened, turning to Callan in surprise. I quickly hid the expression, though. The discussion was between him and his mom.

"What?" Wendy cast her eyes around before stepping closer and pitching her voice low. "Callan, that is unacceptable. If you want to be a senator—"

"That's the thing. I *don't* want to be a senator. I never have. I want to be a doctor and a medical researcher. I have since I was a kid. You know this, but you choose to ignore it. So now I'm ignoring your wishes and pursuing the research *I* want to pursue."

I tried to keep my face relaxed, but I was cheering inside. *Leaves*, Callan was attractive when he was standing up for himself.

"I suppose you had something to do with this?" Wendy asked, turning her attention toward me. "Are you still under the belief that botanists should follow their... What was the term you used? Oh yes. *Passions*."

"Absolutely," I said, not hesitating for a moment. "You're lucky that your son's passions are ones that are going to directly save lives and make our world a better place."

Wendy narrowed her eyes. "I thought I explained this already. The world needs a firmer hand from magical botanists. Plants are being destroyed at an unprecedented rate. If we don't get more botanists in positions of power—"

"Mom," Callan said, taking a step forward so that he was positioned between me and Wendy. "This ends now. I'm going to medical school. Briar is going to do whatever she wants. We're adults, and you don't have a say in it."

Wendy's face became very still, and she looked at Callan then me then our intertwined hands and back at Callan again. "Youth. Always thinking you have it right."

"Following our dreams and believing we can make the world a

better place through our actions isn't a delusion of youth," I said, meeting her eyes. "It's our superpower."

Wendy pursed her lips and held my gaze for several moments. When she finally spoke, she said, "I hope I'll never have to say I told you so." With that, she turned and went back to the head table with Feathergrass.

"There. Let's hope that bombshell will keep her distracted while we get down to business," Callan said.

"Are you okay? Did you really transfer your field studies assignment? Are you working on the medicine research fully now? Did Feathergrass approve it?" I asked.

"Yes to all except for Feathergrass's approval, and I feel better than I have in a long time."

"For what it's worth, I'm proud of you."

He touched a hand to my face and ran a finger along my bottom lip. "That's worth a lot, Briar. It's worth everything."

Hollis cleared his throat. "Hate to break up this little love session, but how about you two try not to draw the attention of the whole academy tonight?"

I looked around and noticed that most of the students were getting seated for dinner. "What?" I turned to Hollis. "Eyes aren't on the fern founders' descendant for five minutes, and you have to intervene?"

Hollis grinned at me then said to Callan, "She's a keeper."

"I know. Let's get seated." Callan took my hand, and we went to the table, taking a spot by some of the tree affinities.

My friends were sitting directly across from us, with Hollis and the other ferns, and Meadow was pretending she was too cool for any of us, as planned. Aside from Callan's little display of affection that I hadn't seen coming, the plan was to keep everything about our actions as normal as possible.

Before the meal was served, Feathergrass rose for what was Professor East's traditional speech. "Happy equinox, botanists. With the changing of the seasons, I hope you can all reflect on your accomplishments this term. Consider whether you're working as hard in your studies as you should be. Judge whether you're giving your all to your field studies assignments. And most of all, consider how you can pursue excellence in magical botany so that you may climb the highest ladders of our society and change the way humanity interacts with plants. If you are ever unsure if you're being ambitious enough in your plans, please do not hesitate to make an appointment with me."

Feathergrass stood for a few more moments as we gave a weak round of applause, then he took his seat.

"Lamest equinox speech ever," Coral whispered.

"Let's hope it's the last one he ever gives," Hollis said.

We brought our glasses together in a toast at our section of the table.

"Cheers to that," I said.

Chapter Sixty

The vernal equinox dinner and dessert passed uneventfully, if you could count an outdoor garden party with flowers floating in the air and blooming in front of our eyes on the tables as uneventful.

By the time the window for recharging neared, I was ready to confirm that everything was in place.

"Okay," I said, taking a deep breath as members of the Root and Vine Society gathered in the forest. Laurus and Kaito had made sure the food that had been served would give the guests an extra sprinkle of endorphins, and we could hear the rest of the school making merry by the pond. It was now or never. "It's almost time for me to meet the others at the wall. Does anyone have anything new to report?"

Meadow nodded. "My mom's coming. She wants to be here to show that this has support from more than just students. She'll meet us at the wall."

I raised my eyebrows but nodded.

"The jewelweed pods are all primed to explode... loudly," Laurus said, excitement gleaming in his eyes. "I spent a lot of time on the cellular adjustments, and when I did a small test, it worked like a charm."

"Nice work," I said, hoping the distraction we had planned for Feathergrass would function as designed. With Laurus on the job, it seemed a safe bet.

"I got the intel from Professor East's office during dinner," Kaito said. "Feathergrass seems to know about two of the petal portals, but thanks to Aurielle and the cartography class, we can use one he doesn't know about. Enter by the orchards, and you should be clear."

"I placed scouting vines near all the portals as a precaution," Callan said. "I'll keep tabs on the one by the orchard to make sure you're all clear, and I'll send a leaf message if I get word of any problems." He scribbled something and sent a leaf floating on the breeze, presumably alerting our waiting coalition members of where to meet me.

"And I'll make sure the Wisteria Windchimes are near the board members to keep them calm and not suspicious," Heath said. "At least until the jewelweed starts exploding."

"Good thinking. And with Callan and Hollis around the festivities, they may not suspect anything is going on. They're used to Meadow running off," Nalin said.

Meadow pulled a face but didn't deny it. "Glad my frequent wanderings are coming in handy tonight."

"I've got the *Recipes for Deception* book in my bag, just in case," Laurus said, and I couldn't help but smile. Everyone had come together with their own contributions, and we just had to pull it off.

"Everyone have their petal portal pendants on them in case you need a quick exit?" Kaito asked.

Nods rippled around the group.

I patted my pocket, feeling for the nine seeds Meadow had encouraged me to get. They formed a damp lump against the fabric.

"Are we ready to do this?" Meadow asked. The stack of the petal portal pendants we had made were around her neck. She must have sneaked away to get them after dinner.

At her question, the members of the Root and Vine Society gathered in a circle. Heath blew a handful of daisies into the air, Kaito tossed in some shamrock clovers for luck, and Callan caught them on a tendril of air so that they floated softly around us in slow motion.

"Good luck, everyone," I said.

"Luck and legumes," Kaito replied, and everyone echoed the words.

It was fitting to learn a new magical botanist-ism at that moment. "Luck and legumes," I repeated.

"Let's go show those board members who's the botany boss," Meadow said.

The group nodded, Yasmin caught my eye and gave me a smile and nod of encouragement, then we split, each of us off to our individual tasks.

As the rest of the group dispersed, Callan took my wrist and pulled me close. He brushed his lips against my forehead in a soft kiss, and I savored the tenderness of it. "You've got this, local."

"Of course I do. I had a good tutor."

He smiled, and some of my anxiety ceased. "I'll see you at the charging circle in thirty minutes," Callan said.

"I'll be there."

Chapter Sixty-One

My heart squeezed when I saw the collection of magical botanists waiting outside the wall when we climbed over. Meadow's mom was there, Kai and Nevah were standing with hands intertwined, and Wyatt and Professor East were just arriving.

In addition to the Root and Vine Society, we had assembled a powerful coalition. And it was time for us to put our strengths together and challenge the structures that had been in place for decades.

After saying hello to Meadow's mom, I greeted Kai and Nevah. "Long time no see."

"What's a little cross-country trip to take down a grass affinity with world domination plans?" Nevah quipped.

She and Meadow bumped hands, clearly familiar with each other.

We were exchanging greetings as normally as possible, but there was tension in the air.

"Are we ready to go in?" Wyatt asked.

I tensed as headlights crossed us, and we each turned to the approaching car. When it parked and a figure emerged, I smiled. "Eli! What are you doing here?"

"Rhodes extended an invite," he said. "Figured as the only one here with experience using an unsanctioned Floracantus and falling ill from it, I could be here to lend a healing hand if needed."

"Thank you," I whispered, unable to say more because of the thickness in my throat. Every single person was there to support our mission, which included supporting me, and I would never forget it.

Eli gave a firm nod in response and positioned a small bag over his shoulder.

"It's showtime," Wyatt said, skipping any preamble as he glanced up at the dark starlit sky.

"Put these on." Meadow passed the Shasta lily pendants around.

No one asked questions as they pulled the pendants over their heads and tucked them into their shirts.

"Meadow will lead in, and I'll bring up the rear," I said to the group. "From there, I'll head straight to the charging circle. Charging doesn't normally occur until closer to midnight, so I'm getting in at the earliest opening to avoid attention. The rest of you are welcome to do whatever you'd like, whether it's providing security or distractions."

"I'm with you," Eli said, nodding to me.

"Same," Wyatt said firmly.

Professor East whisked stone steps into place with some wind, forming a staircase against the wall. Meadow climbed it and disappeared over the other side. Then one by one, we each followed her.

When my feet landed on the academy side, I took a deep breath. This was it. All the necessary players were on campus. The charging window for the verdant shield started in fifteen minutes. Everything we had been planning for the past month was coming down to whatever happened next.

"Callan and Hollis should be setting off the jewelweed right about now," I whispered to the group as we approached the glass academy building, stepping carefully as we rounded the corner to the charging circle in the dark.

"We're off to keep the festivities... extra festive. We'll make sure the visiting board members stay busy," Nevah said before peeling off toward the pond with Kai.

Professor East seemed to have vanished, likely off on an important mission of his own.

"Good luck, B," Meadow said, then she skipped off after them with her mom.

As they began to walk away, a series of loud booms exploded in the distance.

A smile touched my mouth in spite of the nerves. "The jewelweed must be working," I said. "Which means Callan should be heading this way any time."

Wyatt pointed toward the tree line. "Here they come."

Callan and Hollis approached our group, and Hollis was grinning, his eyes slightly wild. "Did you hear that?"

"You always were a bit of a pyromaniac." Wyatt snorted.

"This is our window," Callan said, not wasting any time. "Briar, the circle should be coded to your DNA to get through to access the Dandelion of Desire tonight."

I snuck a look toward the circle, nerves churning in my stomach, but it was simply a stone circle in the dark. I tried to let the plainness of the setting calm me. Everyone else had done their part. Now I needed to do mine.

"Ready?" Callan asked.

Nodding, I stepped into the warded area. I let out a breath when I made it safely through. From there, I went straight to the soil and touched my hands to it. Using the skills I had been practicing with Wyatt, I connected with each layer and component of the earth, prepping it for new magic.

I could feel the original verdant shield Floracantus tied to it, and I did my best to loosen it without removing it completely. I needed to wait just a little longer for that.

Soil prepped, I turned toward the Dandelion of Desire, removed the phytoglass cover, and picked it up from the pedestal where it rested.

I ran through the steps I would need to do in my head then reached into my dress's pocket and pulled out the nine seeds that had rested there all evening. I closed my eyes, and pretending I was doing nothing more than blowing out the candles on a birthday cake, I blew on the Dandelion of Desire.

When I opened my eyes, the seeds were releasing in slow motion, scattering around the charging circle like drops of dry rain.

Instantly, I felt a buzz along my skin, almost like a tickle. I shook the dandelion seeds off my body and adjusted to the extra power running through me. My magic felt even stronger than it had in the green zone. It was now or never.

"The charging window is open," Callan said. He locked eyes with me and nodded. "Go ahead."

I turned toward the circle of stones, knelt, and touched one hand to the soil. Dropping each seed in one by one, I connected with the plant material within each. I ran through every step I had practiced with Wyatt, and once I felt fully connected, I opened my mouth. "*Terram protege.*"

Immediately, the supercharged magic began to flow out of me. I pressed my palm to the soil, working hard to maintain my hold as my new Floracantus battled to push out the old one. It took longer than any practice session had, and I began to sweat as I maintained my concentration.

Then there was a ripple across the ground, as if we were experiencing an earthquake. Distantly, I heard Callan and Hollis gasp, and I forced myself to shut that out and focus entirely on maintaining the connection. If my senses were correct, the old verdant shield had just dissolved.

Finally, a bubble of clear shimmering air formed around me. It spread around the charging circle then enveloped Callan and Hollis, and soon, it was to the tree line and extended completely out of sight.

I held and held, using every drop of magic within me, until I began to feel resistance. Then at last, I pulled my hand back and toppled into a half-seated position, exhausted.

With effort, I swept my gaze to the charging circle. Each of the stones that composed it had split open and partially disintegrated, replaced with nine blooming plants, one for each affinity.

I laid my pulsing head against the earth as my body went numb. My vision narrowed, and everything faded to darkness.

Chapter Sixty-Two

I awoke to the feeling of my head being cradled, and when I opened my eyes, Eli was examining my face. I was disoriented, and I tried to look around. *Where am I? What is Eli doing here?*

Then a warm hand slipped into mine, and Callan's face appeared in my vision. "Briar," he said, his voice so tender that I wanted to ask what was wrong.

"She's awake," Eli said. I felt a touch on my wrist. "And her pulse is coming back to normal." Eli directed his next words to me. "I'm going to sit you up."

He assisted me into a seated position then pressed a wafer into my hand. "Eat this."

I didn't protest—the wafers had helped me in the past—and chewed the soft cracker-like substance. Within seconds, my head began to clear, and the evening's events came rushing back. "Did it work?" I asked.

Callan smiled, still holding my hand. "By all appearances, yes. How do you feel?"

"A little groggy, but the wafer is doing its job."

"I think you'll recover quickly," Eli said, still checking my vitals. "When Callan and I had incidents with the shield, we were actively going against the restrictions in place. You blew those old restrictions out of the soil. I think your reaction was your body's response to using so much power at once. But color is returning to your face, so I don't think the effects will be long-lasting."

"That's good news," I said, beginning to stand.

Callan used both hands to help pull me up. I smoothed the tulle fabric of my skirt.

"You sure you don't want to go lie down?" Callan asked.

"And miss out on the rest of the fun tonight?" I teased. "Never." Since my main piece of the mission was done and my energy was coming back, I was strangely exhilarated.

Callan shook his head, smiling ruefully. "Eli, do you think she's clear to walk?"

Eli gave me another wafer, forced me to drink a few swigs of a special tea blend from a travel thermos he had packed, then nodded. "I think she's good to go. Nice work tonight, Briar. That was impressive."

"Thanks. Was there an earthquake?" I couldn't tell if I had dreamed that bit or not.

"I think that was a ripple effect of the old shield being removed. We'll have to take that and the nine blooming plants replacing the stones as confirmation that it worked," Callan replied.

"Do we know how the distraction went with Feathergrass? Did he have contact with the jewelweed?"

"Not sure," Callan said. "But it's time we found out."

We ran past the academy building just in time to see Feathergrass running out of it. Professor Sage was calling after him. "I need to put some more salve on that jewelweed rash!"

"You!" Feathergrass yelled, pointing as he spotted me. "What is going on?"

"Having a little trouble with an allergy?" Hollis called, drawing Feathergrass's attention away from me.

I took the opportunity to join my friends in the meadow by the pond, where festivities had come to a halt. Botanists were gathered in the well-lit area, looking around as if preparing for an attack. A few students crouched under the cocktail tables.

"It's all right!" Callan called, and all heads turned to him. He was standing under the massive jacaranda tree, and I could practically feel the power rippling through him. The leaves of the tree stood upright, then dozens of them tore away and floated around Callan, demanding attention. "It wasn't an earthquake."

"Then what happened?" several voices called.

"The shield has been reset," Callan said.

"What are you talking about? You did the recharging without me?" Feathergrass asked, stepping forward as if getting ready to take charge of the situation. He was rubbing one of his forearms, which must have been where the jewelweed had made contact with his skin.

"Not recharged. *Reset.* With a new Floracantus." Callan paused to let the words sink in. The space around us went silent. "By a magical botanist with all the affinity powers."

For the first time since I had known her, Wendy Rhodes looked stricken. She put a hand to her mouth, and her eyes flitted between her two sons.

Feathergrass was staring in the direction of the charging circle, his mouth slightly open with disbelief.

"That's impossible," Wendy said. "No one but founders' descendants could do that. Briar tried to recharge it last year. It rejected her."

"You're not hearing me," Callan said. "Briar created a *new* Floracantus. She has the ability to create them from her Renaissance botanist ancestry. We thought that ability was long lost, but we were wrong. And with the new Floracantus she used, the shield is in place as long as all the plant groups exist here on campus."

Feathergrass recovered more quickly than Wendy. "But there are so few defensives. And the fern population is shrinking. What if there are no students attending from those affinities? What happens to the shield?"

"It's not about the students. It's about the plants. As it always should have been. As long as all nine plant groups grow in this soil, the shield is in place. And if anyone ever tries to sabotage that," he added, glaring at his mother, "they'll be cut off from their powers here."

Murmurs rippled through the group of collected botanists.

"Magical botanists have always been stronger together," Callan continued. "Not separated into founders' descendants or affinity groups. Do plants live in isolation in nature? Hardly ever. Sure, they compete for resources. But they all have their niche. This world wouldn't be what it is without *all* of them."

Callan nodded to me, and I stepped forward.

"Go ahead," he whispered.

"Outside these grounds," I called, "we can't treat humans like the enemy. Our population of magical botanists is shrinking. The answer to that isn't to further separate humans from plants, to kick them out of natural spaces. Instead, like with the botanical garden we're creating in Weed, we need to invite them into nature even more."

When I saw a few nods of encouragement from the crowd, I continued. "Humans need good food. They need medicine, clothing, building materials. They need temperate climates and beautiful, natural spaces to relax in. They need clean water and air. None of that would be possible without plants. So instead of trying to shield the plants from them, we need to remind them of the role plants play in their lives. Education. Experiences. These are the things that take root. This is what botanists should be dedicating our lives to."

I looked pointedly at Feathergrass. "If some of us here get patents and hold positions of influence, there's nothing wrong with that. But that path isn't for everyone, and there is space in this world for all of us. Each of our unique gifts and dreams is going to make our world a better place."

A chorus of "Hear! Hear!" came from the crowd.

"Evergreen Academy was built on a noble idea," I continued, not trying to cover the emotion in my voice. "That idea was for magical botanists to come together to study, so that we could take what we learn, go out into the world, and bloom in whatever way we were meant to. And that is what Evergreen Academy will continue to be as long as the students here have anything to say about it."

Cheers rang out even more loudly, and flowers rose into the air on invisible spokes of wind once more. A shadow moved at the tree line, and I knew it was time to hand over my platform.

"Now, I would like to introduce someone we've all been missing. Botanists, please give a warm welcome back to Professor East!"

When I said the name, Feathergrass's eyes widened, and for the first time, he looked truly nervous. Wendy Rhodes was squeezing her hands against the back of the chair in front of her.

Professor East stepped out of the woods and came to stand in front of the students and faculty of Evergreen Academy.

Chapter Sixty-Three

The arrival of Professor East was like a summer rain to a thirsty flower bed, seeping into the cracks and providing instant relief to the soil and roots within. Students who had been huddled around the tables, still concerned after the minor earthquake, straightened and stepped forward, murmuring excitedly.

"It's wonderful to see you all," Professor East said, sweeping his eyes around the field and acknowledging everyone present. "It looks like this has been quite an eventful equinox."

"Are you going to fight me, East?" Feathergrass asked, drawing everyone's attention back to himself.

Professor East simply picked up a glass bottle from the nearby table and raised it in the air. The cork was out of it, and empty bottles littered the table. Nearly every botanist in the clearing seemed to have had a glass.

"Not all disagreements need to be settled by violence," Professor East said loudly enough for everyone to hear. "I placed a special elixir in each of your glasses after dinner. An elixir of ingredients all grown here on the academy's grounds. It will determine whether your intentions toward the academy are in line with the original goals here. I think we should let the plants decide whether you stay or go."

Callan and I exchanged glances. We hadn't known about that part of the plan, but we should have guessed Professor East would put his legendary harvester affinity to use. I briefly wondered how he had managed to do it unnoticed.

"No such elixir exists," Feathergrass said.

"Come on, Feathergrass. You don't think I could have grown some plants with special abilities in all the time I've been here?"

Feathergrass stiffened, and Wendy looked between the two men. "Why should we trust your elixir? You could have adjusted it to do any number of things."

"Ah, that. Well, I guess you're just going to have to take my word for it. The elixir has an interesting mechanism of action. At midnight, if it deems you disloyal to the academy, you will have fifteen minutes to leave before the roots of the walking palm escort you off the campus grounds."

Wendy paled.

Professor East looked at his watch. "Any second now." He poured himself a glass from the open bottle and took a drink, making it clear that he was including himself in the test.

A deep rumbling came from the ground, but it was different from the earthquake-like motion that had occurred when I reset the shield. The leaves at the tree line rustled, then the giant, stilted roots of the three walking palms began to creep forward.

I'd known the interesting trees with above-ground roots existed at Evergreen Academy, but I had never seen them move before. It must have taken an incredible amount of magic to trigger the trees to move so much. From the gasps and murmurs coming from the rest of the partygoers, I assumed it was a first-time event for them too.

I glanced at Callan again and saw a gleam in his eye as he nodded at Professor Bowellia. The tree affinity instructor must have helped Professor East set everything up.

The palms moved toward Feathergrass and Wendy, their massive stilt-like roots creeping in mesmerizing motion, until they cut the two board members off from the rest of the group and formed a cage around them.

Feathergrass used his grass affinity powers to make bamboo shoots rapidly sprout from the earth in an attempt to push back the walking palms. But the bamboo was easily broken, and the walking palms trampled the sprouts with their roots in slow, methodical fashion.

Nearby, the few other members of the board who were visiting stiffened. Primrose Marsh put her hand to her mouth.

"All right," Wendy said firmly. "That's enough. We'll go."

The walking palms retreated, their roots moving backward, but still stood by.

"Do both of you hereby submit your resignations from the Board of Regents, by reason of deliberate harm to the school in the poisoning of the verdant shield last year?" Professor East asked.

Gasps came from the gathered crowd.

"I'm sure the council members at each of the botanical conservatories will be disappointed to hear this news," Meadow's mom said, stepping forward and crossing her arms.

The pair of former board members looked like they didn't want to agree, but when the walking palms crept closer once more, Wendy gave a stiff nod.

"Excellent," Professor East said. "Then please see yourselves out."

Wendy cast one look back at her two sons then straightened her shoulders and began to walk toward the academy's gates.

As I watched her go, a knot of concern formed in my stomach as I wondered how the two Rhodes brothers were feeling. Would they always be in opposition to their mother, or would she come around to understanding why they disagreed with her? And where did their dad stand on all this? I was glad that Wyatt and Callan seemed to have each other, at least.

At Wendy's departure, the group emitted a collective exhalation. My shoulders relaxed, hopeful this might end quickly.

But Feathergrass didn't move.

"Your interests are not in line with those of the students and the academy, Frederick," Professor East said. He nodded toward Wendy's retreating figure, the instruction clear.

"You're going to let students dictate how you run this place?" Feathergrass scoffed. "I thought you had more cactus spine than that."

"My students happen to be right. But even if they weren't, dramatic changes to the school or to the society shouldn't be implemented on the whims of a handful of people. Founders' descendants don't define our students here at the school, and affinity powers don't define botanists in the wider community. We are all magical botanists, and we all have a purpose in this world."

"Then why don't we settle this right now with a battle of the plants. The strongest botanist will be the director of Evergreen Academy," Feathergrass said. One of the walking palms edged closer to him, but he sidestepped it.

"Strength is only one aspect of leadership, Frederick," Professor East said. "We do not teach our students to fight at this school. That is not the purpose of our relationship with plants."

"And that is precisely the problem. Our botanists need to be more aggressive if we want to have the upper hand against humans," Feathergrass said.

A few gasps came from the assembled students. We had known those were his intentions, but he had never said it so bluntly.

When Professor East didn't respond, Feathergrass put up his hands and said a Floracantus, and sandhill rosemary sprang from the ground around him. Immediately, the enhanced allelopathy from the grasses began to choke out other plants in a circle around him, spreading outward. The roots of any plants the rosemary met shriveled and died on the spot. Feathergrass was clearing a path. I remembered Ravenna saying he was famous for that move.

Well, I *wasn't* famous for it. I had never interacted with sandhill rosemary, but there was a first time for everything. Everyone kept telling me how powerful I was, and I was going to put that to the test.

I reached out and connected with the grasses, tugging on their tissues. At my whispered words, their progression slowed. Soon, they were reversing course, shrinking inward until they surrounded Feathergrass.

His eyes wide, he cast his gaze around the group until it landed on me. "You don't want to cross me, Briar. You could be a powerful ally to the grasses."

"I might be a powerful ally to the grasses." I nodded toward where some of the grass affinity students were gathered, watching what Feathergrass was doing in obvious shock. "But I will never be an ally to you."

I pushed the sandhill rosemary closer around his ankles, and frustration flickered across his face as he struggled to combat my magic.

His eyes narrowed, and he raised a hand.

Before I could react, vines snaked from the forest and wrapped around Feathergrass's hands, twisting them behind his back in living handcuffs. I recognized that move and cast a glance at Callan, who was concentrating on the former board member.

"That was a quick reaction," I whispered.

"I could sense what Floracantus he was about to use, and it wasn't a nice one."

Right. His power-sensing abilities, the ones theorized to be connected to his wind-manipulating powers.

Feathergrass turned to Callan, obviously realizing where the vines had come from. "Not siding with your own mother? What a disappointment you must be."

Anger welled up inside me then, and my fingers dug into my palms. I rarely experienced the face-flushing emotion that was coursing through me.

"The only disappointment is you, Feathergrass," I called. "Claiming to be a leader in our society while simultaneously undermining everything we stand for." As I said the words, the soil around Feathergrass began to loosen, dropping him lower into the ground centimeter by centimeter.

He tried to free himself from his handcuffs, but Callan's spell was strong, and I was fast. I connected with the vines that Callan had already moved into place and slid them around the rest of his body, wrapping Feathergrass up like a cocooned butterfly. I stopped the vines just below his neck. "Looks like you're out of your depth."

Feathergrass grimaced, looking at the crowd, clearly embarrassed that there was an audience for what was happening to him. Twisting within the vines, he turned to Professor East once more. "Letting the students do the dirty work for you? I expected better."

"Weren't you the one advocating for more powerful use of force from botanists just a few moments ago?" Professor East asked, his voice calm, as if he were giving a lecture on pollinator and plant relationships. "Since you insist on not leaving peacefully, I feel compelled to warn you that you are surrounded by botanists with extra-affinity powers."

Chapter Sixty-Four

I cocked my head to the side, wondering what Professor East was implying. Whispers reverberated through the gathered botanists.

"Which extra-affinity powers?" Feathergrass asked, still squirming slightly within the bounds of the vines that held him in place.

"A wind manipulator." Professor East nodded toward Callan.

"A soil manipulator." He nodded at me.

"A water bender."

At those words, Kai stepped forward, a ball of water forming in his hands. Murmurs rippled through the crowd.

"And a light bender," Professor East said.

Confusion rippled through me. *A light bender?* I hadn't heard of that extra-affinity power yet.

Feathergrass's eyes were wide as he cast his gaze between Callan, Kai, and me. He asked the question that was running through my head. "Who is the light bender?"

With a soft glimmer, Professor East disappeared from where he stood then emerged a few moments later standing right next to Feathergrass.

My mind was swirling, barely able to believe my eyes. Professor East was a light bender? He could make himself *invisible*? I was reminded of how Kai had made us invisible in the water at the aquatics conservatory.

"I believe you've wondered, quite vocally at times, how I got this job over you, Feathergrass," Professor East said to the startled man. "But not everyone chooses to show off all their powers. This one was known to very few until recently, but I think the time has come to remind you—and other members of the Board of Regents —that it isn't just founders' descendants who have power. Of the four of us with extra-affinity powers here, only one is a founders' descendant. The board should think carefully about choosing to create class systems within our society—and especially within our schools and conservatories—going forward."

The walking palm inched closer, forcing Feathergrass to shuffle backward a few feet, the vines moving with him.

"This can't be. Extra-affinity powers are rare. For four to be here at the same time…" Feathergrass's voice was slightly shaky, and I heard resignation there for the first time.

"Some magical botanist genes seem to emerge exactly when they're meant to," Professor East said. "Or perhaps it is completely random. Either way, your theories about what makes us powerful are incorrect. I think it's time you left, Feathergrass. The students and faculty here have an equinox they would like to celebrate." Professor East nodded to Callan and me, and we slowly released the vines binding Feathergrass.

Once free, Feathergrass sent the grasses rippling in all directions, whipping up a minor wind around everyone's feet. Shouts of alarm came from the gathered botanists, but the grass affinity students quickly calmed the stalks once more.

Magical botanists stepped forward to surround Feathergrass. I held back a smile as I looked proudly at the people creating the circle, which included every member of the Root and Vine Society.

Every affinity group had come together, and there was no denying that we were stronger that way.

The walking palm seemed to have lost all patience, and it forced Feathergrass between its above-ground roots and shepherded him toward the front gate. Feathergrass didn't put up any further fight. He was outmatched, and he knew it.

"I'll make sure he goes out and stays out," Wyatt said, nodding at Callan before following the walking palm.

The silence of the crowd evaporated immediately. Talk of light bender powers sprang up around us. The grasses got a song rushing through the fields, setting a lively backdrop that signaled the party was back on.

Once Wyatt was out of sight, I turned to Callan. "I know Professor East prefers nonviolence, but it was kind of satisfying tying Feathergrass up with those vines."

A smile tugged at the corner of Callan's mouth. "He didn't leave us with much choice."

"We can vine-lasso pretty well together, Rhodes," I teased.

"Nature-blessed matches, remember?" He took my hand, running a finger over the emerald ring he had created for me on my first day at the academy.

I eyed him curiously. "I thought you didn't believe in those."

"I didn't. Until I met you."

Clasping Callan's hand, I squeezed it. The feeling of our hands touching was its own kind of magic. "Some night, huh?"

He returned the pressure in my palm, his skin warm and reassuring against mine. "It's always some night with you, local."

Chapter Sixty-Five

The morning after the spring equinox, the students and faculty of Evergreen Academy gathered in the teahouse. Sunlight streamed through the tall glass windows, the fragrance of herbal tea and organic coffee filled the air, and the buzz of happy magical botanists enjoying their first meal of the day was so familiar that, for the first time in weeks, I was completely at ease.

"How are you feeling this morning?" Yasmin asked, stirring her chia pudding while studying my face.

"Thanks to Eli and his concoctions, I feel as good as new," I replied.

"It's not every day someone uses months' worth of magic in one night. That was pretty amazing."

"I'm just glad it worked and that the shield seems to be firmly in place." I had been reaching out with my magic to sense the shield multiple times throughout the morning already. Having created it, I could feel it in a way I hadn't been able to before. No one else seemed bothered, though, and I supposed I should have felt honored by their complete faith in my abilities.

Instead of talking about the new verdant shield, most students were discussing the resurgence of extra-affinity powers. I smiled as I listened to the conversations floating around the room over tea and matches of Roots and Xylem. I was just as curious about the history of the powers as the others were.

"Where are Aurielle and Coral?"

Yasmin pointed upstairs. "Still in bed, I assume. Everyone partied *way* too hard last night after Feathergrass got served the walking palm justice. The herbs started serving the strong drinks, and everyone was running around, hiding behind trees and pretending to have light bender powers."

I laughed. "Have you seen Callan this morning?"

"He and Hollis went to check the grounds. They wanted to make sure everything was secured at the petal portal everyone came through and see if there was any damage to the area where the jewelweed bombs were set off."

Nevah and Kai walked into the teahouse then, and they got food and joined us at our table. "What's it like being back at the academy?" I asked after greeting them.

"The food at the aquatics conservatory is tasty, but nothing beats the breakfast spread at Evergreen Academy," Kai said. I noticed the heaping quantity of food on his plate.

"Is it okay that Professor East revealed you have waterbending powers?" I asked him, remembering how Nevah had wanted us to keep quiet about it.

"It's fine. He ran it past me beforehand, just in case he needed to use the information. There have been rumors about my abilities for a while, since I used the ability for a display Nevah and I did when we were students here. Most people didn't catch on, since the power is rare, but a few people who remembered it were suspicious. I'm kind of glad it's all out in the open now and that there are others with extra-affinity powers."

"Well, now that it's officially out, I assume you'll be climbing the ranks at the aquatics conservatory," I said, raising my eyebrows.

Nevah laughed. "That's putting it mildly. A few select people there already knew about it, but I imagine the rest will be lining up for autographs when we get back."

"*Rivers*, I hope not." Kai formed a bubble and blew it toward Nevah so that it popped on her nose.

"When do you head back to Florida?" I asked.

"This afternoon," Nevah said. "We both have time-sensitive research we need to get back to. Plus, we want to be there to show our support for the changes Professor East lobbied for while he was there. The conservatory plans to take a vote on banning humans from the state parks."

"Which way do you think it's going to go?" I asked.

"If I know Professor East, he made a strong case," Nevah said. "And word of what happened here last night is probably already spreading. Primrose Marsh witnessed it all firsthand. Any influence Feathergrass and Wendy Rhodes had must be dwindling by now. Even if they don't end up facing serious punishment for poisoning the verdant shield, Feathergrass's attack with the sandhill rosemary might trigger something. Any affront to noninvasive plants is a major faux pas in our society. He's going to be persona non grata in magical botanist spheres of influence."

I nodded, glad to hear it.

Aurielle and Coral entered the tearoom then, followed shortly by Callan and Hollis. Each of them got breakfast and hot drinks then joined us. Other members of the Root and Vine Society, seeing us gathered, migrated to our table.

"Well, aren't we just a merry band this morning. Secret society members, meeting in broad daylight," Hollis said, squeezing onto the bench seat next to Coral.

Callan stood behind me and sipped his coffee as he absent-mindedly played with my hair. I loved the new casual way about him. There was no tension, no wondering if scouting vines were watching us.

"How's the area where you set off the jewelweed?" Ravenna asked them.

"Looks fine. We cleaned out the remaining pieces so they wouldn't randomly explode. And we got rid of the steps you all put up against the wall at the orchard petal portal. We walked and drove around most of the perimeter, and everything looks back to normal," Hollis said.

"What do you plan to do with the *Vanished Compendium*, B?" Nevah asked. "The real one."

"I've been thinking about that. I want to share it with the rest of the community. Should we put it on display here, like I did with da Vinci's book?"

The decision about what to do with the book had been weighing on me. I had learned how to use the Floracantus instructions da Vinci left behind, and Oren was working on his family riddle, but there were other riddles in the book. Some of those bloodlines might have died out, but surely a few of them had descendants out there.

Would those people want to know about their ancestry? To activate their powers? To learn the art of magical botany and eventually craft their own Floracantus, if others were born with all the affinity powers? I wasn't sure how to approach it all, but I knew that the book belonged to more than just me.

"I imagine the conservatories will want to get it on a traveling exhibit eventually," Nevah said. "It's the find of the century."

"And what about the other book? The one that's been on display here since the Floral Fete?" Kaito asked.

"Well, I think it needs a new name now that everyone is going to know it's not the real *Vanished Compendium*," Meadow joked. "How about *Da Vinci's Lost Book of Floracantus*?"

I knew she was joking, but I smiled. "I like it. Simple. Descriptive. Let's run with it."

At that moment, I glanced toward the doorway to see Professor East entering the teahouse. He moved to the stage area, and the room quieted immediately. His presence had always commanded attention, but since the students knew he could make himself invisible, there was an extra tinge of awe in the air.

"Good morning, magical botanists. Congratulations to those of you who managed to wake up at a reasonable hour this morning. Professor Sage and the kitchen botany rotation students have made sure your breakfasts have extra-restorative ingredients in them. Now, I know there has been a lot of excitement this year. But we still have one more term to go, and there is plenty of learning to be had. So I have never been happier to say classes will resume on Monday as normal!"

Cheers threaded through the room as if he had just announced we'd won the lottery. I guessed for magical botanists, getting to study and work with our plants in the way we wanted *was* the ultimate joy.

"So, what's next for the Root and Vine Society?" Meadow asked.

"Know any more magical academies that need saving?" Kaito quipped.

The response was a mixture of smiles, eye rolls, and laughter—the room was filled with *so much* laughter. I glanced around to see students eating, drinking, jotting things down in notebooks, examining specimens under microscopes, and interacting with the plants in the room.

Callan got my attention by running a finger along the back of my hand. "Challenge you to a game of Roots and Xylem?"

I grinned. "You're on."

Evergreen Academy was back to normal, and it couldn't feel more right.

Newspaper excerpt

Weed Press

By Laila Zannato

Researchers at the enigmatic Evergreen Academy have discovered a plant species long thought to be extinct. The flower, which has been given the common name Thornless Rosie, will be put on public display at the grand opening of the brand-new Weed Botanical Garden, which will be dedicated in memory of Tessa Belrose, a beloved member of the Weed community. The botanical garden will be run by Tessa's twin sister, Vera Belrose, owner of Vera's Cafe, in conjunction with the Evergreen Academy. To see the new botanical gardens and get a picture with Rosie, visit the grand opening on June 12 between 10 a.m. and 5 p.m.

Midsummer

"You picked an epic day for a grand opening, local. The botanical gardens look spectacular, and the weather couldn't be more perfect," Callan said, gazing around the space, which was rapidly filling with people.

"Technically, the midsummer date was Wyatt's deadline, not mine. It is pretty great, isn't it?" It was hard to believe, after the adrenaline-fueled spring equinox, that the summer solstice was going to be nothing but the pure magic it had always been intended to be.

We were there for the ribbon cutting at the new botanical garden, and Callan, unsurprisingly, had dressed for the occasion. His short-sleeved dress shirt showed off the tattoos that I loved, and his hair was styled like a runway model's, with an effortless tousle to it. I briefly wondered if he used his wind manipulating powers to get his hair to swoop that way. I hoped that one day I would find out.

"Is your aunt here yet?"

"She and Bryce are inside, getting a preview of the gardens." I lowered my voice. "I can't imagine how the flowers in there are reacting to her right now. I hope she doesn't blow all our covers."

A car pulled up, and when Oren stepped out, a grin spread across my face. It was comforting to know that the tree affinity botanist would continue living in Weed, tending to the trees along the Wildflower Trail and taking a lead role at the botanical garden. "Hello, Oren. Thanks for coming."

"I couldn't miss this," he said. "Had to see how my saplings are doing. Plus, I wanted to talk to you. I think I may have cracked the riddle."

I gasped. "You did?"

"Obviously, I can't test it out, but I felt a little something that tells me I'm on the right track. I'm going to reach out to some of my extended family and spread the word in case anyone is ever born with all the affinity powers. Would you two like to come over for tea again sometime?"

"Absolutely," I said.

"It's a plan. I'd better get inside and make sure my trees are in top shape for the guests."

Oren and Callan shook hands, then Oren proceeded into the botanical garden.

"That's exciting," Callan said, turning to me. "You two will be able to compare notes soon."

"Finally. I'm so curious how Cesalpin's technique compares to da Vinci's, even if we can't test it out yet. They both left interesting legacies through those riddles."

Callan walked over to the sign at the entrance to the botanical gardens. Below the name and some other information about the gardens were the inscribed words:

In loving memory of Tessa Belrose

"A place this beautiful dedicated to your mom... It's perfect." Callan turned and brushed a piece of my hair out of my face with such tenderness that I wanted to take his fingers and hold them there forever.

I swallowed a lump in my throat. "There are going to be monthly painting classes held in the gardens, weather permitting. She would have loved it. Speaking of legacies... I thought that my going to art school was the way to carry on her legacy, but maybe this is her legacy instead."

"Her legacy is *you*," Callan said tenderly.

I nodded, touching my hand to the words on the sign. "She'd be happy we're going to college together." I had received my acceptance letter, and we were already making plans for the fall.

Callan was studying medicine, of course, and I would be studying art history—the history of botanical art, to be exact. I had a feeling da Vinci and his contemporaries had a few more secrets up their sleeves. As a bonus, the university had a massive botanical garden nearby, and we would be able to conduct research and use our magic there.

A truck pulled up, and I recognized a few members of the city council, who were there for the ribbon cutting.

"It's time for the big show," I said.

When the council members and press crew—which consisted of a college student majoring in journalism—approached me, Callan stepped out of the way, leaving the spotlight to me.

I watched him walk over to another truck, where Wyatt was pulling up. The two seemed to greet each other warmly enough. I smiled and turned back to the camera.

"Ready to do this?" the mayor asked, helping me clasp a pair of cardboard scissors as large as my body.

"Absolutely," I replied.

We symbolically cut the scissors through the bright-red ribbon across the entrance gate, the gathered crowd cheered, and the Weed Botanical Gardens were officially open to the public.

"Can I steal her?" Callan asked after patiently waiting for over two hours for me to meet with various visitors and walk through areas of the botanical garden with them.

The turnout had been a smashing success. Maci had come along with a few of our friends from high school and SCC. Everyone from Vera's Café was in attendance. Then others, so many others, who I didn't know or didn't know well, had come. It brought a smile to my face each time I saw someone point out a plant to a family member in delight. I hoped the space would be an oasis for them, like Evergreen Academy had been for me.

I took Callan's outstretched hand and followed him into the rose garden. "Is everything okay?"

"I know you're the guest of honor here, but there's something I want to show you, and today is the only day I can."

I narrowed my eyes. "What is it?"

"Think you can sneak away for a bit?"

"Sure. Let me just say goodbye to Aunt Vera and Maci. I think things are wrapping up here anyway."

After I said my goodbyes, we climbed into Callan's truck. My curiosity was overflowing as we cruised toward the academy. We reached campus and parked, and when I stepped out to encounter a purple bloom floating through the air, I let out a scream of delight.

"The jacaranda tree!"

Callan grinned, and the smile met his eyes, lighting up his whole face. "You didn't get to see it last midsummer, so I didn't want you to miss another chance."

He took my hand, and we walked around the academy building toward the pond. I gasped when I caught sight of the jacaranda tree, its violet flowers brilliant and beautiful on the one day of the year it magically bloomed. Its presence seemed to take over the entire space, its petals dotting the air like confetti.

"It's stunning," I said.

"Yeah, it is," Callan replied, but I noticed he wasn't looking at the tree. His eyes were on me.

We joined the crowd of magical botanists who were celebrating midsummer. The Evergreen Academy midsummer gathering was open to everyone now, not just founders' descendants and people of influence.

Many of the botanists were gathered around where the *Vanished Compendium* and *Da Vinci's Lost Book of Floracantus* were on display. I smiled, hoping the books were connecting us with our past and giving us inspiration for the future.

Wyatt approached as we sipped our watermelon sun tea by the pond that came to the tree's edge. "Great job today, Briar. The DBI is going to be very happy with the turnout at your grand opening." He raised his glass, and I reached over to clink mine against his.

"Couldn't have done it without you," I said, meaning every word.

"Are you sure you have no interest in the DBI?" He glanced sideways for the glare that question usually brought on from Callan. But Callan seemed completely relaxed, and he waited for my response.

"It's not a no," I said, providing the opening for the first time. "But it's not a yes right now. I'll be going to university to study the history of botanical art. I think my ancestor has a few more secrets for me to uncover, and I'd like the chance to get to know him a little better."

"Solving ancient botanical mysteries from an author of the *Compendium Floracantus*? You're just begging for the DBI to recruit you even harder," Wyatt said, humor in his voice. He turned to his brother. "And you're off to medical school. I always knew you were going to change the world. Nothing will make me happier than seeing you in a white coat someday."

"Don't jinx it," Callan said dryly, but I heard a touch of

emotion in his voice. The validation from his brother meant a lot to him.

"Well, I'm off to mingle. See you two later." Wyatt raised his glass in farewell then left us alone under the jacaranda tree.

Callan took my drink from my hand and set it on one of the garden tables that were tastefully incorporated into the area for the celebration. Then he pulled me close, his hands settling around my waist.

"Have I told you lately how beautiful you are, local?"

My cheeks heated. "Not since noon."

"Inside and out, Briar. I've known it since the moment I first saw you, and you've proven it every day since."

"The first moment you saw me? When I was trespassing, you mean?" I teased, but there was a spark in his expression, and the words died on my lips. My eyes moved to his mouth.

"I really want to kiss you right now," he said softly, drawing me even closer.

"Then do it," I replied with a hint of a challenge.

His hands went to my face, and I closed my eyes as his lips met mine. They were warm, soft, and inviting. My posture relaxed, and I wrapped my arms more firmly around him. We pulled each other nearer, and Callan deepened the kiss.

We had kissed at the academy before, but I marveled at how relaxed and lost in the moment I felt. No one was spying on us with scouting vines. There was no grand scheme to sabotage the academy or to convince me to use my powers to benefit a particular affinity group.

It was just us, a boy and a girl. Two magical botanists. Hearts that had found each other despite how different our worlds had been not very long ago.

We knew there would be challenges ahead, new adventures to face, and unexpected twists in life's path. But we would face them all together.

When I felt something touch my hair, I pulled back, my eyelids fluttering open to see soft petals of the purple flowers above us gently raining down. "Sorry," Callan said, not moving his hands from me. His lips hovered against my forehead and I could hear a smile as he said, "I think that might be my fault."

"Our kisses are never normal, are they?" I marveled at the purple floral show around us.

Callan leaned in again to whisper into my ear. "Normal? What have I told you, local? You weren't born for normal."

I was biting my lip as he lifted my hand in his and twirled me under the raining petals. Then he pulled me into an embrace that smelled of peaches, sandalwood, and home.

Leaf message

Leaf message from Callan Rhodes to Briar Whelan:

I need to reclaim my dignity after that last game of Roots and Xylem. Rematch?

The end

Want more magic?

Want to know what your plant affinity power would be?

Want to join the Society of Magical Botanists reader group on Facebook?

Go to Heather Schneider's Bonus Content page on her website (heatherschneiderauthor.com) for access to all of the above!

Do you want to follow other writing projects Heather is working on?

Sign up for Heather's newsletter to stay up on the latest new releases and reader opportunities.

If you enjoyed the story, please leave a review. Reviews help indie authors find new readers, and help readers find new books to love.

Thank you for reading and being part of Heather Schneider's reader community!

Also by Heather Schneider

Books by Heather Schneider:

- Meet Me in St. Louis (young adult romcom-mystery)
- Chasing Cheer (Magical Emerald Hollow book 1)
- Finding Cheer (Magical Emerald Hollow book 2)
- Evergreen Academy (Society of Magical Botanists book 1)
- Evergreen Conservatory (Society of Magical Botanists book 2)

Acknowledgments

As I wrap up this trilogy, I'm filled with gratitude to everyone who fell in love with this world and helped to share it with others.

Thank you to my fabulous ARC team for this book and the entire Society of Magical Botanists trilogy. This indie author could not get her books out into the world without you! Your passion for this story helped give it wings.

To my awesome beta readers, Danielle McCloskey, Abby Ortiz, and Chelsea Quigley, thank you for the input that made this story so much better.

Thank you to my amazing, supportive family and to my mom for reading pretty much every edition of these books.

Zach, you get a special shoutout for taking all my signed copies to the post office this year. Your courier services are nearly as good as Callan's leaf messaging powers.

To my author friend, Bethanie Finger, thank you for the writing sessions filled with warm drinks and good conversation.

To Julia Couch, thank you for helping me coordinate all the fun things and for your bright spirit and friendship.

Thank you to Mary at Mary's Literary Services for helping me create beautiful graphics for this series, and to Shelby Cross at Indigo Art Studio for creating gorgeous character art to help us all imagine Briar and Callan.

To my cover designer, Krafigs Design, thank you for creating another beautiful cover to tie this series together with a magical bow.

To the editors and proofreaders at Red Adept Publishing,

thank you for the feedback and edits that made this series the best it could be.

Last but not least, thank you to God for giving me a love of writing since childhood and being by my side as I brought this series to life.

About the Author

Heather Schneider is an author of young adult and adult contemporary and cozy fantasy novels, always with a love story.

Heather lives with her husband and their two dogs. When she's not writing, you can find her reading, listening to podcasts, traveling, or spending time with family.

As an indie author, Heather loves engaging with her readers!

Please connect with her on Instagram or Facebook @heatherschneiderauthor and leave a review wherever you review books.

You can visit her website and subscribe to her newsletter at heatherschneiderauthor.com.